BLUE
RUNNING

Published by Moonflower Publishing Ltd.
www.MoonflowerBooks.co.uk

1st Edition

Copyright © 2021 Lori Ann Stephens

ISBN: 978-1-8382374-8-6

Moonflower Publishing Registered Office: 303 The Pillbox, 115
Coventry Road, London E2 6GG

MOONFLOWER

Texas, our Texas! All hail the mighty State!
Texas, our Texas! So wonderful so great!
Boldest and grandest, withstanding ev'ry test;
O Empire wide and glorious, you stand supremely blest.
God bless you Texas! and keep you brave and strong,
That you may grow in power and worth, thro'out the ages long

Texas State Song, 1929

BLESSING

In Blessing, we were all under the eye or the heel of God, and neither was very comfortable. You could get away with a lot in the piney woods of East Texas, but as Daw liked to say, soon your sins will seek you out. And even though my father was an occasional drunk and frequent bastard, I tended to agree with him. Depending upon the secrets in our hearts, here came God's blessing or curse, cutting across the main farm road, stirring up leaves or dropping cardinals like darts, delivering cows into the mouths of tornadoes or painting sunsets as vast and pink as a long-held breath.

Do you remember Blessing like that? God's Country. It was ours to inhabit. We knew every house in the neighborhood, every car. Every blacktop street that stuck to our bike tires in August. All the paved ones that turned into gravel and then, farther on, piddled out into dirt roads that meandered across the country like cattle dogs. We knew how to get back home, where we'd use a stick to pry the gooey pebbles and dirt from our treads. We knew that outsiders were unwanted, and that three churches in a town with two traffic lights was like splitting an election, but at least all the candidates were Republican. Before we were ten, we knew the police station and the liquor store and Mack's Insurance and the First Republic Bank on Main St, and on Elmwood Lane the karate school and the Italian restaurant and the Corner Grocery and the empty store that had been For Rent for ages and ages. And farther down, a church and two schools. Three miles across the flood plain, the Gulf gas station, wallpapered with decades of cigarette smoke and short-order grease, was the most reliable source of news. Everything else was in the next town, too far and too dangerous for a kid to go on a bike.

Texas was beautiful and ugly, kind and cruel, and every child knew it. That's how war is. Even ten years after The Secession, we carried it in our bones as we climbed the steps onto the bus, saluted the Lone Star flag, and sang our allegiance.

This is the story you missed. This was fourteen, the tender year. This was one month from Blessing to freedom, and the price we paid.

ONE

I once had a mother who loved me.

"She just didn't love you enough," Daw liked to say. He'd sniff and smirk like a father does when he's confronted with the mysterious eyes of his fourteen-year-old daughter. Then he'd crush his beer can under his boot. That was the start and the end of any conversation about my mother.

She didn't love you enough. The crush of aluminum. The smell of warm beer.

She left us before the Wall, so I fashioned a memory of her from other things that were too delicate and expensive for me and Daw to have. Her eyes were flecks of gold, her laugh wind chimes. Then, when I was in third grade, I stumbled on an old photograph in Daw's drawer and I didn't have to imagine anymore. Instead of finding a clean pair of socks, I'd dug up a pretty blonde woman in a white robe. I suspected it was my mother right away. She was laughing, and her bare knees peeked out from the robe as she leaned sideways. I wondered if she was naked underneath. I wondered if Daw had taken the snapshot. Had Daw ever been funny enough to make a woman laugh? I traced her cheek with my finger. I'd never laughed that hard or looked that pretty. It seemed impossible that I could be related to her. But on the back of the photo was my mother's name: Marla. I slid my finger over her smooth hair, then tucked the photograph back into Daw's dresser. Even at eight I knew she was Daw's secret, not mine.

I didn't hate her for leaving us, but I did wish Marla had hung around long enough to tell me how to *be*. I'd spent my entire life in Blessing, but I never felt like a Blessing girl. My hair was never long-long, never seemed to grow past my shoulders no matter how long I let it grow. I didn't have sleep-over friends, and I wasn't good at skeet shooting or cheerleading. I didn't know how to laugh that way girls did, and make the boys want to inch closer and rub their shoulders. I didn't want boys to rub me anywhere.

When we were younger, kids who were lucky enough to have birthday parties invited everyone in class. That was the only polite thing to do. I'd been to some of these gatherings, seen the insides of a few houses. Those smells in other houses – clean laundry, warm pecan pies, vanilla candles, musky-sweet cat fur – were secrets I took home with me, all of them a comfort that life could be better. Eventually though, we got old enough to throw politeness to the wind and only invited our real friends to birthdays.

I was short and flat-chested and my dad was a drunk. I hadn't been to a party in three years.

Then, the year I turned fourteen, Maggie Wisdom moved to Blessing. She wasn't like the rest of us. Her clothes were too fancy and her heels were too high. She talked too fast and she didn't wear boots. I was the only one who sat beside her on her first day of school and found out she was from Austin, which explained practically everything. On the bus home, I found out her daddy was rich. They were the ones who'd built the mansion at the top of the hill.

I had her for the whole summer. For three months, people stopped talking about Blue's drunk daddy and Blue's ugly clothes because they were talking about Maggie, who'd somehow charmed

8

the whole of Blessing with her money and her camera-flash teeth and her talent for singing like an angel and skeet shooting like the devil. For the first time, I was almost normal.

Then high school started, and the Pretty Ones patted a stool at lunch and Maggie sat down at the far end of the cafeteria. She fit right in with them. Maggie stopped sitting with me and things went back to the way they used to be.

It was almost as if Maggie and I hadn't ever gone on bike rides that lasted all day, hadn't freed the squirrel from the mouse trap, hadn't drawn tattoos on each other's wrists with permanent marker. Almost as if I'd imagined she was my best friend.

That September, during the first weeks of high school, I found myself hopelessly lost in the wrong wing of the school, in real life and in my nightmares. Everyone was so tall and the halls were so wide. Between classes, I trailed behind strangers who laughed and teased and jostled each other, all of us wading our way to the next class. Swept by a strange desperation, I once laughed with a group of older girls in front of me like I belonged to them, until one of them turned around and smirked, "Why are *you* laughing, girl?" I shrugged and ducked away, my cheeks hot with shame.

In the cafeteria one day, I opened my lunch bag and stared at the peanut butter and jelly sandwich. Wrinkly apple. Broken cookies. I missed Maggie's lunches. Trading my broken cookies for her Babybel cheese wheels because her mom didn't buy sugar treats and my Daw didn't buy fancy cheese. I loved to pull that white tab across the red wax, which opened up like a perfect little present each time. But Maggie was with the Pretty Ones now.

The end of the day was no better. The Armory line was clogged up again because somebody's cartridge was missing.

"I've told y'all before," the Armory Secretary yelled. "Have your IDs out and get in a straight line. Y'all won't get home till five if you don't get lined up right. I swear to God."

The freshmen weren't used to the checkout process, so it took us longer than the sophomores to get holstered and out the doors. Most of us carried hand-me-down guns from older brothers and sisters, but I was an only child and Daw was the only deputy, so I got his old police-issue Glock. It was too big for my hands and too damn heavy, but it shot straight.

I climbed onto Bus 5 and hurried to the first window seat. While we waited, I searched for Maggie on the school steps again, where she always waited for her mom to pick her up. A few times, I'd caught a glimpse of her and I smiled. She always smiled back, but a little too politely. But today there were no smiles, no Maggie, as Bus 5 rolled out of the lot and onto the farm road. It carried us away from the matchbox houses near the school, across the long, vast floodplain, where the yellow grass was stiff from drought, past the rusted, empty horse shed and the giant oak where the cows sat in the shade of its sprawling branches like black stones in the distance. We passed the only new housing development in the county, with two fancy houses made of limestone and brick, then turned onto the tar road with its craters and cracks that the bus driver weaved around at a crawl.

The Armory Secretary was right: by the time the bus dumped me off at the stop sign, it was close to five o'clock. I walked down the long gravel path to our mobile home, kicking pebbles into the grass and trying not to look at my home. We lived in a white single-wide with the skirt half torn away, black trash bin overflowing, a scraggly rose bush we'd planted a few years back when Daw was sober and cared about things for a while. The rose bush was the only thing that hadn't died, and it had enough breath to spit out one yellow rose every year. That said, our home wasn't much worse than the others that lined Mountain View Road, where there were no mountains and no views to speak of.

Daw's patrol car wasn't in the driveway, so I climbed the sagging wooden steps, pulled open the screen door, and tossed my backpack on the couch. I went straight to Daw's room and pulled my mother's photo from the back of the drawer so I could talk to Marla, which I'd gotten into the habit of doing. I crossed over to the window where the light was better, stared at her creased eyes and called her to me. She rose like a ghost, laughing at some joke I told, her voice bubbling over in giggles. In about thirty seconds, she'd be in tears. She'd end up with a stitch in her side, bent over and smiling through the pain. Then she would straighten up and cock her head and look straight into the hurt I was hiding. She would know what to tell me. If she were still here, she'd know how to fix everything with me and Maggie. Make us friends again.

Some movement made me look out Daw's window. Too late, I saw the glint of Daw's patrol car parked in the back yard. I'd been so lost in thought I hadn't heard him drive up. My heart skipped up into my throat even before I realized he was standing in the room behind me.

"What are you doing in here?" Daw said.

I tucked Marla's photo in my front pocket and turned around to find he was standing in the doorway watching me.

"Hi, Daw. There you are. How was work?" I moved over to the dresser and stepped backwards, slowly pushing the top drawer back in place.

I could always tell when he'd been drinking – his breath smelled like rusty nails and his left eye drooped. If he was drunk, he'd fall into bed soon and I wouldn't have to cook dinner. I'd just make a peanut butter sandwich for myself. But if he was sober, he'd ask me a thousand questions and find a problem with every single answer.

"You got any laundry to wash?" I leaned over and picked up something heavy from the floor. It was hard to tell in his room full of shadows, but the musty smell told me I'd picked up a pair of jeans, the belt still looped through. I grabbed an old sock and a pair of boxers crumpled on the floor. "I thought I'd get started early because I got homework."

When I passed him, I took a whiff and wrinkled my nose. Rusty nails.

"That's real nice," he said, half burping out the last word. "Hey, Blue. You missed one." He pointed to a sock half-hidden under his bed.

I grabbed it, and Daw followed me to the washing machine.

"Watch your step," I said. The washing machine had leaked last year, and now the floor around it had bloated up and creaked under foot. I kind of hopped over the soft spot. Once or twice a week, we'd say out loud, "We got to fix that board," but nothing ever came of it.

"We got to fix that board," Daw said. He leaned against the wall and watched me toss his clothes into the machine. There were still some clothes in the tub, forgotten from last week and soured, so I turned the dial, tossed in a half-scoop of detergent, and washed the whole lot.

"How was school?" he asked, trailing behind me to the kitchen like a puppy.

"Fine," I lied. He didn't know that Maggie and I hadn't spoken much since classes began. I knew better than to tell him, because I didn't want him to say bad things about Maggie or the Wisdoms, because that's what Daw did. He'd let little things get under his skin like a splinter and fester until he said things people didn't like.

"How was work?" I opened the fridge and pulled out the peanut butter and grape jelly. "I hate cold peanut butter."

"Why you keep it in the fridge then?"

"'Cause the roaches."

"Yeah," he said, then half-swallowed another belch. "We got to fix them. I need a beer."

I leaned into the fridge. Seemed like he'd had two six packs in there that morning, and now there were only two cans left. I considered hiding the beer behind the potatoes, but I wasn't good at hiding things from Daw.

I pulled a can from the top shelf, opened it, and set it on the table. I sat across from him. Part of me wanted Daw to talk like we used to. Part of me wanted him to go back to work. When I was little, he'd come home a few hours after the bus dropped me off, and I'd be waiting for him, kneeling on the couch, looking out through the window, aching to hear about how the world needed saving and he was up for the job. He'd erase the drudgery of school and the cruel teachers and the crueler kids. But then he failed the Ranger exam and started drinking and ranting about California and the Scalers and inflation and why is the house such a pigsty and couldn't I clean up just once in a while around here?

Daw threw back his beer. He caught me watching him and gave me an odd squint, like he didn't recognize me. Or maybe he was about to catch me with that photograph in my pocket.

I walked over to where I'd dropped my backpack and fished out my notebook. I wasn't used to Daw being home so early. His eyes followed me around.

"Why are you looking at me?" I said as I set my notebook on the table.

"I'm not lookin' at you," he said.

He watched as I hunted through the junk drawer and settled on a nubby pencil without an eraser before coming back to the table.

"You're watching," I said.

I'd rather have had the old days, when he'd come home with stories about illegals that passed through, and how he nearly got shot. Sometimes he actually did get shot, though. The first time I stitched him up I was nine. He'd come home with a forehead of meat, bleeding into a rag, and before I realized what was happening, I had a needle in my hand and my heart in my throat.

"Come on, now. Stop crying," he'd said.

"Why can't we go to the doctor?" I'd asked, nearly beside myself.

"Because we can't."

"I can't do it."

"Yes, you can, but you have to stop crying."

"Let's go to the hospital. Please?" I'd begged.

"I don't have the money, Blue. I still owe them that twenty-five grand from seven years ago, and I'll be damned if they're going to charge me another goddamn penny."

"It's going to hurt. I don't want to—"

"Blue!" Daw had snapped, grabbing my free hand. "Just sew my damn head up." He was frustrated, but still gave me a crooked smile, which gave me the courage to stick the needle into the edge of his brow, push it through the skin, and draw up the thread. When I pinched the skin tight, the wound didn't look so scary, and Daw didn't flinch once, even with all the blood. He distracted both of us by complaining about the hospital bills, the insurance crooks, and rich doctors who only cared about paying off their fancy yachts and beach houses in Galveston.

I'd bandaged and stitched up Daw four or five times since then. My hands hardly trembled anymore, and Daw said I was so efficient with the whole process – sterilizing and threading the needle, the peroxide and cotton balls and bandages I kept all in a box – I could open my own hospital.

The scar at the edge of his brow was the worst of all my stitches, but even that jagged line was just a pink etching now.

I felt bad for him. He didn't have any friends either. We were two losers, sitting in a mobile home with rotting floorboards and a roach problem.

An hour later, Daw was passed out on the couch, and I was finished with my homework and stirring mac and cheese. Except the milk had gone bad, so I had to use water.

I wondered what Maggie was having for dinner at her shiny table with the candlesticks and cloth napkins. Her father was probably talking about things mayors talked about, and Mrs.

Wisdom was no doubt calling Maggie to the table for the third time.

I stirred the liquid cheese and wondered what Marla was eating wherever she was, smiling with her head tossed back and her hair shimmering.

TWO

When you're fourteen, sitting alone in the cafeteria is like wearing a ten-pound blanket. Your aloneness is protection from noise and meanness. It's not altogether unpleasant, but dang if it doesn't make you conspicuous.

I sat with my dollar store bag and ignored the other kids. When the autumn term started a few weeks ago, I'd slipped uncomfortably back into my former position as loner. But I wasn't going down without a fight. My eyes were trained on Maggie. She sat between Shelby and Bridget, girls who didn't make friends with people like me. Shelby and Bridget wore black eyeliner that they heated with a cigarette lighter. They did back flips and hand springs and had pool parties. They were like book covers on a banned book. Everyone wanted to get in, to read their secrets. Even me.

Before I'd eaten half my sandwich, Maggie had glanced three times at me from across the cafeteria. I tried to hook her gaze, but she looked away and took a bite of her apple. I peeled apart my peanut butter sandwich and ate the rest open-face. It lasted longer that way. Her Nutter Butters and Babybels sat untouched, like she was taunting me. I wished I'd told Daw to go to the Gulf station for groceries before he passed out last night.

Maggie wiped her mouth with a napkin. I wiped my mouth with my sleeve.

Maggie laughed at something Shelby said, then tried to look at me in secret. I could tell she was stealing glances even though she tried hard to disguise it. I stared back at her, not meanly, but hopeful. Like when you're fishing, and there's something pulling at the end of your line, and you're there holding your breath, waiting.

I chewed until the bread turned to mush in my cheek and waited for her to look at me again. When she did, I raised my eyebrows. She gave me a half-cocked smile, and my insides went slack and the reel-line was spinning out of control. There was my best friend's smile again.

I set my half-eaten sandwich on the plastic bag. If she looked at me once more, I made a deal with myself, I was going to walk over to her and ask her to ride the bus with me. If she said no, Shelby and Bridget would smile and cover their mouths. But if she said yes...

A warning bell clanged through the cafeteria, jarring me from my thoughts. The principal's voice crackled through the intercom.

"Alert! The school is on lockdown. This is not a drill."

I froze. Some teachers standing along the walls shushed everyone, but they didn't need to. We were already motionless in the cafeteria, the echoing space filled by Mr. Hanken's voice.

"Teachers, lock or bar your doors. Shelter in place. Lights out. Shelter in place."

The school bell rang three times, and then his voice repeated the announcement in a hoarse whisper that made the hairs on the back of my arms rise.

For a second, everyone in the cafeteria stared at each other. I looked at Maggie – her gaze was already locked on me. Two creatures frozen, eyes bulging, hearts thumping. Then the teachers waved their arms like wings, mother ducks shepherding us to the edges of the room. The lights went out in sections – one, two, three – and left us in the shadows beneath the high windows. A few people were crying. Others shushed them angrily. "Be quiet! Shut up."

We all hovered close to the floor. I tried to make sense of our bodies, of the enemy outside. If a gang came through, we could pretend we were dead, but it wouldn't make sense if we were all dead before they even came inside to kill us.

I wondered if Sheriff Burnet was on his way and if he'd use his sirens. He'd be coming alone because Daw was all the way over in Dallas applying for the Rangers again.

"Third time's a charm," he'd said as he left this morning, the screen door banging shut like a clap.

"Daw, it's happening," I whispered aloud.

We'd never had a gang shoot up a Blessing school, but it had happened in Waco. And in Sherman. And Austin. It happened enough that we'd all imagined it unfolding here, in the gym, the library, home room.

I found myself on the floor near the double-door exit, my arms around my knees. Maybe I could trip whoever came through the door and jump on him. That's what Daw would tell me to do. But I knew I'd pretend like I was dead or run out the door, whichever gave me a better chance. The cafeteria lady ran toward me, fumbling with the giant key ring, and tried to fit one of the keys into the door. Her hands shook so hard the keys rattled as she whimpered, "Jesus save us. Jesus save us. Jesus. Jesus."

"Shhh!" the kids begged. "Hurry!"

I looked over my shoulder for Maggie, and then there she was beside me. It took all my strength not to leap at her and hug her tight. A long roll of thunder boomed outside.

"Do you hear that?" I whispered.

"I know. Shh," she whispered back.

The thunder rumbled louder until it wasn't thunder anymore. Half-sputtering, half-roaring, the engines of dozens, or hundreds, of motorcycles rolled through the street outside, yards away from us.

"Mother," breathed Maggie.

"Mother," I echoed.

I'd heard about Mother on the news. Such a strange name for a gang that stirred terror in everyone. The name was always followed by something terrible that the police couldn't stop. "Human trafficking." "Drug cartels." "Mass murder." The kids in Blessing were all used to the dangers in the Republic – that's why we carried guns. That's why it was required by law. Like most small towns, we only had one sheriff and one deputy. But even the big cities couldn't stop the gangs, especially not Mother. It was up to the children, apparently. President Apato had looked straight at me through the television and said, "You have a responsibility to defend our independence. You sing the anthem every day, 'O Empire wide and Glorious, you stand supremely blest.' Now you have to do your part."

I placed my hand on the cold floor beside Maggie's and considered reaching out to her. But she leaned over to her other side to say something to Shelby, who was crying like a toddler. The noise swelled outside the school, a chorus of hovering demons. They seemed to converge in the parking lot just outside the cafeteria doors. A lone gunshot echoed above the rumbling, and men shouted above the din in clipped commands. I strained to understand them, but couldn't make out their words.

But then, without warning, the motorcycle engines started to fade, and like the fleeing hooves of wild horses, the roar disappeared as quickly as it had come.

There was a long silence as we turned to each other.

"Students and teachers," the Principal's voice crackled, "you can resume your activities. The lockdown is over. Let's get back to work, Rams. And remember: Rams are respectful, courteous, and obedient."

The lights flicked back on – *one, two, three.*

"Really?" I asked. I stood up and brushed my hands against my jeans. "Are Rams really respectful, courteous, and obedient? Isn't that exactly what actual Rams are *not* supposed to be?"

Maggie curved her lips up into a nervous smile. But Shelby pulled her back toward the lunch tables, and our chance was lost in the explosion of chatter and excitement echoing through the cafeteria.

The third row behind the bus driver was the best seat on the bus. First, nobody wanted to sit that close to the driver and have her eavesdropping all over them, so I had the seat to myself. Second, I could see a few rows behind me in the bus driver's long mirror above her head. Daw says you can never be too aware of your surroundings. Today, I was aware. I think all of us carried our awareness around like bullet-proof vests. On the surface, we laughed when kids tripped, and teased each other about the size of our guns. The boys, especially, liked to make jokes about what they packed and who'd like to stroke their barrels. But inside, we were all on a high dive. Inside, we were standing there shivering on a wobbly, thin plank, waiting for someone to yell, "Jump!" And we knew that day was coming. We couldn't stay up there forever. We were going to have to take the plunge, all by ourselves, and hope we didn't drown.

I swung my backpack onto the plastic seat, pulled out my pencil and sketchbook, and sunk down so I could have a better view into the bus driver's rear-view mirror. The handle of my pistol dug into my side, so I took it out of the holster, checked the safety, and set it under my backpack as other kids climbed on the bus. A few boys tackled each other and hooted and whooped. One boy jumped on the back of another boy, who laughed and said, "Get the hell off, freak." Girls huddled their heads together or shrieked at the boys. The bus driver yelled at everyone to sit down and be quiet so she could count people.

The rowdy boys slid into the seat behind me and jerked the back of my seat as they wrestled. I slouched down lower and hoped they wouldn't notice me. Their wildness made me uneasy.

I opened my sketchbook, which wasn't a real store-bought one, but some folded sheets of blank paper I'd swiped from the library printer when nobody was looking. I was never any good at drawing people from my imagination. I pulled Marla's photo from my pocket and smoothed it out on top of my sketchbook.

As the bus pulled away from the school, someone yanked on my seat again. I looked up at the mirror and saw the blond-haired boy behind me, half-standing and leaning against the window, facing the aisle with his hand on my seat back.

"That lockdown was crap," he announced.

"I know," another boy said.

"Why the hell they make us carry guns if we can't wear them in school?"

"I know, right?"

A girl's voice shouted, "Maybe because you're immature and would shoot yourself in the butt."

"Screw you, Katie," he said.

"Sit down, Jeremy!" the bus lady barked and scowled in the mirror. The kids smiled. Jeremy didn't sit.

He leaned on my seat back with his elbows. "We wasted like two frickin' weeks on that summer safety class. But the moment an opportunity comes and we can actually defend ourselves, they treat us like kids. It's bullshit."

The bus lunged to a stop, and I wondered for a moment if the bus lady was going to start lecturing us about the language and the standing. But she just frowned into the mirror and shook her head.

The bus groaned forward again, and Jeremy kept talking. "Y'all, we got to defend our own safety, 'cause the police sure as hell ain't. We got a sheriff who's frickin' ninety-two, and Deputy Drunk. That's it."

My fingers froze on my pencil at the mention of Daw, and I shrank down a little farther.

"Jeremy Jones," the bus lady suddenly shouted. "You watch that tongue or I'm gonna come cut it out in Jesus' name."

Jeremy laughed and slapped his hand on the top of my seat. His fingers caught a few strands of my hair, and the sting of it made my eyes water. "Sorry, Miss Bus Lady," he called out. I rubbed my scalp and glanced up in the mirror at his flashing smile.

"Deputy Drunk," the boy next to Jeremy hooted. "I like that. Deputy Druuuunk." He dragged out the word like he was belching.

"Jeremy," a girl said.

I glanced up again, and all the eyes in the mirror were on me.

"Whatever. It's not like it's a secret." Jeremy shrugged. "Her dad's out there giving my dad a ticket for speeding, but then he goes and gets a DWI hisself. So he's gonna get fired, and now we're down to a hundred-year-old cop for the whole town."

I closed my eyes and squeezed my fingers on the photo of Marla. Blacked them all out for the rest of the ride. Daw couldn't help it. It was Marla's fault he was that way. She came to my dreams herself and told me so.

It was always the same dream. We were at the airport, and I was four. Daw and Marla were nervous because more and more flights out of Texas were getting canceled. Marla paced the airport floor and watched the giant screen of letters and numbers, blinking red, and I ran in circles around her, yelling "Look at me!" The borders were closed, and people were shouting at the airport workers, threatening them with fists because we didn't all carry guns then. But we made it onto the last plane. I could feel the brush of my mother's skirt as I tiptoed down the narrow aisle. It had to be true because I'd never been on an airplane since – how would I remember the orange lights along the aisle? I looked up at the strangers who had already buckled their seatbelts and were mumbling to each other, and all around us the air was filled with a nervous hum. Marla buckled herself into a seat beside an oval window. She was smiling. She pulled back her shoulders and then let her head fall back against the headrest. I was up in Daw's arms, looking down on her, those happy eyes, that long heavy sigh.

And then: "I can't do it. I'm not going." Daw said it without warning.

"What?"

"I'm not doing this. This was never my idea."

"Mark, no." Marla's eyes turned white-wide. She shrank down into her shoulders.

He tightened his grip on me. "This was a mistake. I'm stayin'."

"Well I'm not. It's crazy here, Mark. It's not safe!"

"It's not safe anywhere, Marla. At least here, we're unified. We were born here. It's our country."

"No, please," Marla pleaded and looked around with wild eyes.

Then I was up and moving backwards with Daw, his arm still tightening around me. "You comin'? You can't take her with you."

And Marla's crying. "What are you doing? You promised!"

Suddenly, Daw was shouting. "We have to get off the plane. We're gettin' off!"

"Mark, please!" Marla was shaking her head, leaning over the seat, reaching out to me. "Let me have Blue. Please let me take her! Blue!"

"Come on! Marl, come on!" Daw shouted.

Daw's whiskers rough against my cheek as he retreated. We bumped and jostled our way off the plane, but I could hear my mother's voice crying for me even after Daw stopped running. "Where is she?" he whispered. Even after we stood in front of the giant window and watched the plane race down the runway, I could hear her. Blue. Blue. The plane lifted up and flew away, screeching like a bird. Blue! I clutched my ears with my hands and looked at Daw. His face was wet with tears.

And every time, I'd wake with my hands over my ears and know it was true.

THREE

Daw came home in a mood. He wasn't drunk. I knew because I smelled him. I figured it had to do with Dallas.

"What, you think I wouldn't come home?" he said as I leaned on him for a sideways hug. We didn't hug much anymore, hardly ever. It was nice when we did. He smelled like sweat and leather and coffee and the road.

I leaned back and took in his surprised eyes. "You always come home at some point," I said.

"Yeah well, I'm a cop, so you been lucky so far."

I opened the fridge, knowing there wasn't much in there to eat. Maybe tonight we'd sit on the couch and watch TV together. I didn't want to ask him about what happened in Dallas, but I needed to know. He was wearing that same dark mask he came home with every time he went up there.

"How was your day?" My words came out so shaky I had to clear my throat.

"Fucking Dallas," he said, pulling a Lone Star from the fridge door. He held up the beer can and peeled his index finger from it to point at me. "I don't ever want you to go there, you hear me? Or any of those other big cities. Full of crazy people."

"Okay." I backed up and sat down at the table. Pulled my backpack from the floor and found my English spiral. It helped to bury my face in homework when Daw talked about politics.

"I mean it. You don't want to turn out...' His eyes glazed for a second, but then he looked at me. "You know why I went there?"

I figured he'd applied for the Rangers again, but I shook my head and opened my spiral on the table to a clean page. I wasn't going to say it out loud.

"Diversity march," he sneered.

I looked up.

He took a drink, appreciating my interest. "Bunch of commies who don't understand everything that President Apato has done for the Republic. The Rangers know. The force knows. Diversity is just a code word for illegals and gays and Muslims, which is not what the Republic stands for. They know that, everybody knows that."

He scoffed and took another sip. It was the last beer in the fridge, so he took his time. "I'm not taking away their rights, but I'm the one they're spitting on. Literally, they spit on me right there." He pointed to his name badge. "I'm there to protect them. Meantime, who's protecting me?"

"Why'd they spit on you?"

"'Cause they can. Nobody respects people more than I do. I know lots of blacks and whatnot, and as an officer, I'm sworn to protect them from the bad guys. And sometimes from themselves." He nodded, like he'd stumbled on a deep thought. "It was the women who spit on us. Animals."

I tried to imagine those Dallas women frothing at the mouth, spitting at Daw, screaming about...what exactly?

"Why were they marching?" I asked.

"Hell if I know. Never seen so many whiny people in one place."

"But what do they want?" I spun my pencil between my thumb and index finger.

He glowered at me. "What they're not gettin'."

I'd heard about the marches. In the big cities, people wanted to make all sorts of things legal again. Abortion, gay marriage. I never understood how anyone could march about killing babies. And there weren't any lesbians or gays in Blessing, so I'd never met one. Living in Blessing protected us from those sorts of people.

"I say keep the crazies in the city." Daw pointed with his beer hand. "With the Scalers and the Islamies and the homos." He paused. "Actually, I got nothing against homos. What they do in private is not my business. Long as I'm not forced to agree with it. Long as they're not trying to spread their agenda. To the kids and all. That's when it's dangerous, you know."

I nodded, although I didn't know. I flipped the pages of my English spiral, and suddenly I was staring at my drawing journal. It must have slipped into my spiral when I stuffed it into my backpack. Daw could not see my drawings under any circumstance. I couldn't bear it if he made fun of them. I put my feet on my chair seat, and propped the spiral on my knees like I was about to write something that required concentration.

Daw kept talking. "I try to love my neighbor and all that. But I'm not going to invite them all over for supper, you know what I mean?"

I slid my drawing journal out of my spiral slowly, like the secret it was, and let it fall silently down past my thigh and into my open backpack.

"We all voted for these laws," Daw was saying, "just like we did for Secession. And those that don't like it shoulda left before the borders closed."

He threw back his beer and finished it, wiped his mouth with the back of his hand, and then placed it carefully under his heel and crushed it. I knew he was thinking about Marla, the one who did leave before the borders closed. The one who didn't love me enough to stay.

I hunched over my English spiral and wrote "Illustration with Words" at the top of the page. Mrs. Theroux told us to describe our favorite room in our house. I couldn't choose my bedroom because it was a mess. Clothes on the floor, and the wall seams coming apart just enough to let the ants in. If I lived in Maggie's house, I'd describe her room. That four-poster bed, her white dresser and cowhide rug, and the little jewelry box with tinkling music and a spinning quarter horse inside. The pink and purple tin sign hanging on the wall that said Jesus Forgives, but Trespassers Will Be Shot. I smiled. It never hurt to imagine. I began the essay with my white, four-poster bed with a feather down blanket and pillow so soft and thick that when my head sank down into it, I couldn't even hear my own thoughts.

I'd filled the page when I realized how quiet Daw was. I looked up. He was holding a tiny bottle, the baby-sized ones you find in baskets at the liquor store. Another bottle was on the table, already empty. He must have had them in his uniform pocket. Daw's eyes were wide, staring at me.

He looked at my bare legs and feet, then at my hair, like I had a spider up there. I touched my head, just to be sure. He was kind of frozen with horror, like he didn't even recognize me.

"What?" I finally said.

"For a second, you looked just like…" He stopped and stood up. "Never mind. Give me that." He swiped the English spiral from me.

"No, give it back. It's just homework."

"Homework, huh? Let's see what you got here." He held out the spiral at arm's length and squinted. "My. Favorite. Room."

He muttered as he read. "This ain't your room."

"I'm using my imagination."

"I see that. Leaves painted on the… Why'd you want leaves on your wall? What's a four-poster, anyhow?"

"It's a kind of bed with tall poles at the corners."

"Oh yeah. I seen them. The kind for kings and queens. You gonna skin that cowhide rug yourself?" He laughed and tossed the spiral back at me. "Don't waste your time dreamin'."

I closed the spiral quick and stuffed it into my backpack, not sure why I was embarrassed. "It's just an essay."

"So, your teacher's telling kids to make up crap. To lie?"

"No. I was trying to illustrate something… normal."

He scoffed. "There ain't no such thing as normal, you got to learn that. And making up crap is not what you're going to school for. This is the Republic, not some art school in California." He scraped the chair backward and stood up. "I'm beat. You hungry?"

"No. I can make some mac and cheese if you want."

"Maybe later. I'm lying down. Wanna watch something on TV?"

I didn't want to anymore. I tried to ignore him so he'd go away and I could pull out my sketchbook in peace.

"Why're you doing homework, anyway?" He untucked his shirt, scratched his stomach, and lumbered to the couch. "It's Friday. Shouldn't you be at a ball game or something? Ain't you got friends?"

I tucked my sketchbook and the nubby pencil at my side. "I'm just gonna sit on the porch for a little bit and read."

"Use the porch light. Don't run out them flashlight batteries."

"I don't have the flashlight."

The TV clicked on noisily and filled the living room with blue light.

"Take your firearm," he hollered.

"I'm just sitting on the porch," I shouted back.

"It's night. There's copperheads. Safety first!"

I set my gun under the plastic chair, hiked my knees up, opened my sketchbook, and drew a picture under the dim cone of light. This was my peace offering to Maggie. Something I'd never been able to draw before. I could see her face in my head, and I drew it, with the freckles across the bridge of her nose and her pointed chin and the star of light in her pupils. It was good.

Then I turned the page and drew her standing like a statue, her rifle into the air. I sketched her outline, her strong, lean muscles, one knee bent on a rock and her toes on the other outstretched leg gripping the grass. I didn't know why I'd sketched her naked, except that I'd done the proportions so good and her legs and arms so realistic, it was a shame to add clothes. You could hardly call her naked in this drawing because I'd covered up her privates with her bent elbow and her hitched leg, and it was very tasteful. But when I closed the sketchbook, my hands were shaking.

FOUR

The Wisdoms' house was the biggest one in Blessing, up at the top of the hill in the new neighborhood where all the houses were enormous. The older neighborhood was downtown, two miles up the road on the other side of the floodplain, where the schools and the post office and the McNealty Grocery and the church and the karate classes and the police station were. There, the original houses were made of wood and painted pink or yellow or blue and had wrap-around front porches so river-wide that whole families could eat dinner on them in the spring, but hardly anybody did that anymore. All the rest of the houses in Blessing were sprinkled among the pine and oak trees on their own little acres, a few made of bricks but most, like ours, rusting mobile homes on cinder blocks.

The new neighborhood had caused a flurry of excitement because it was owned by the Wisdoms from Austin, and everyone talked dreamily about what if they could build their own house from scratch, but at the same time complained that the new construction would make everyone's taxes go up.

I stopped by the Gulf gas station for some cherry sour belts, which Miss Olsham gave me in a sealed plastic baggie if I picked up the litter around the storefront. The old people out front smoked cigarettes and talked about Maggie's daddy being the "de facto Mayor" ever since Mayor Haggard died, and what good luck that he showed up right when the Mayor passed, and what good news that he was a big name in crude oil, and what an influence he was already having on the schools and the trash pickup.

I rode my bike across Farmroad 3891 to the new development. Behind me, the pop-popping of gunshot echoed, maybe coming from the firing range or someone fed up with a stray dog or a neighbor. In front of me, everything was neat and smelled of cut lumber and resin from soldered fences.

Mr. Wisdom's white teeth and blue suits made me nervous, so I was glad I didn't see his red truck when I biked around their pond and up to the concrete lions that guarded their steps. I sat there on my bike outside of Maggie's house, screwing up the courage to face her. I wiped the sweat from my forehead and eyed the sour belts and sketchbook in the basket. It was Saturday and still early. Early enough, I hoped, that Maggie didn't have company.

It wasn't that I hated her new friends. Maggie was the best at everything, so it was natural that the cheerleaders liked her. But she was my friend first, and I needed her more than the others did. I'd never be like them. Maybe Maggie didn't understand that. Maybe she thought I could just sit with her and Shelby and Bridget, like it was normal. But that wouldn't happen.

I nudged open the kickstand and grabbed my sketchbook and candy. I flipped through the pages and looked at the drawing of Maggie the Skeet Shooter. It was my best drawing ever. But now I wondered if she'd like it.

The door smacked open and Mrs. Wisdom took a step onto the patio and shaded her eyes as she looked out at me. I clapped the sketchbook closed and stiffened. Mrs. Wisdom was the kind of person that, when she came into view, you'd stand up straight out of respect. Her hair was always whipped into place, every strand behaving itself no matter how she moved her head. She had shiny pink nails and white skin and apple lips. Most Blessing people didn't look or smell that good, even on Sundays, much less Saturdays.

I waved at her.

Her squinted eyes and puckered mouth relaxed into a smile, and she waved back.

"Hi, Bluebonnet. I haven't seen you around for a while." She pulled two large bags from inside the house and looped the handles in the crook of her arm, then flipped her sunglasses down on her nose and jangled her keys. "I'm just heading out."

Her pearly opal SUV glimmered in the driveway. Lone Star Beauty, a giant magnet on the passenger door said. Makeup, Youth Serum, and More! Become a Beauty Consultant today! Make Money – Ask Me How!

How? I wondered, but never asked.

She swung open the passenger door and set the crisp white bags inside. "It's good to see you," she said with a tight smile, and then peered over at the woods and the pond, where some dog had started nosing around.

"You there!" she hollered at the dog. "You! Shoo, get on!"

The dog looked up and then dashed away.

Mrs. Wisdom tilted her head at me, smiling again. "Is it good to see me, too?"

"Yes, ma'am." My cheeks turned hot.

She nodded. "Is Maggie expecting you?"

I looked up at Maggie's second-floor window. The blinds were open, but no Maggie. Mrs. Wisdom took a breath, but kept standing. Waiting for something. In her presence, I always felt like I'd been raised by chickens.

I cleared my throat and found a few words. "I need to talk to her about something important. It'll only take a few minutes."

Mrs. Wisdom nodded. "Well, you do that." She pointed to my pistol in the bike basket. "I see you have your firearm – that's good, especially riding all over by yourself. But it belongs in your holster. Really, Bluebonnet. What would your daddy say?" She shook her head. "Riding with it in your basket. You're going to shoot yourself."

"Sorry," I said, and holstered the gun.

"Good girl. It's for everyone's protection, you know." Mrs. Wisdom smoothed her white shirt and dabbed her hairline with the back of her hand.

She turned and took a few steps to her truck before swiveling back to me. "How do I look?" She adjusted her thin white belt and put her hands on her hips. You could just barely make out the little pistol on her thigh under her skirt.

I smiled. "Pretty. You always look pretty."

"Oh, not always!" she said, and flicked her hand. Mrs. Wisdom clicked her high heels back to the SUV. "You have to work hard to look pretty. Beauty is my business, after all. Remind me next time – I've got samples you might like, and our summer clearance line is very reasonably priced."

I nodded and waved.

She backed out the driveway along the crayon-green lawn, then I walked past the lions and up the stairs. My cheap holster-belt dug uncomfortably into my side, but at least I was wearing it and I hadn't shot myself in the foot.

I tapped my boots on the base of the door to fling off the dried mud, then brushed them against the welcome mat. "Howdy", it read. And in smaller letters of loopy rope: "May all who enter here be Blessed".

If blessings were a sign of God's approval, then the Wisdoms were his favorite family in Kellman County. As soon as they moved to town they joined the Covenant Church, donated to the school PTA, and bought a truck for the volunteer fire department, so everybody loved the Wisdoms, in heaven and on earth.

I pressed the doorbell, and when Maggie didn't answer, I started knocking. I knocked so hard that my knuckle scuffed open. I sucked on the tiny bulb of blood.

I backed up, shaded my eyes, and squinted at Maggie's bedroom window.

"Maggie!" I pounded the door and hollered. "Maggie! Maggie! I know you're up there. I'm just going to keep calling your name until you answer the door. Maggie!"

A yippity dog down the street barked, and I looked over to see a white-haired woman scowling at me from her brand-new front porch. I frowned back. She was old and still wearing her pink robe and pajamas. A rifle hung from her left hand, barrel pointed at the ground.

"It's just me," I yelled, "Blue Andrews. I'm not a stranger!" I didn't believe the old lady would really shoot, but you couldn't be too sure. "I'm Maggie's friend, remember?" I waved.

"That's debatable," someone said behind me.

I turned around to see Maggie standing at the door, hand on her hip.

I held my breath and stared back at Maggie. Took in her long blonde hair, her smirk, and her pajama pants and T-shirt.

"Still in bed? It's like nine o'clock." I held up the baggie. "I've got candy."

Maggie sighed and peered over my shoulder at the old lady. "You're going to get shot yelling like that."

"By that old woman? She wouldn't."

"She shot a dog yesterday."

"Really?" I looked at the old lady, who was bending over some potted plants.

"Stray dog. But still." Maggie walked back inside, and I stared at the doorway before realizing that this empty space was Maggie's way of saying *Come in, I guess.* I made an ugly face at the old lady and then stepped into Maggie's house.

I kicked my boots off and lined them up square next to Maggie's in the entrance. Under my damp socks, the marble floor was cold. I took a look around, like always, because it never didn't stump me to be in a house that looked like a museum of dead animals. There were three sets of antlers mounted on the walls, a cougar head, a wild boar head, and an entire black bear on its hind legs, walking like Frankenstein. I wandered into the kitchen, where Maggie stood at the open refrigerator.

Maggie pulled out a carton of orange juice and poured herself a glass. Daw never bought orange juice because of the import taxes, but it was hardly ever in stock at the stores anyway. I set the sour belts on the counter and nudged them toward her. Then I smoothed out my drawing journal.

"I'm here to say I'm sorry," I told her.

Maggie set a second glass on the counter and held up the carton. It was a test. "For what?"

"For...saying that Shelby's brother eats dog food."

"And?"

"And...for saying that Bridget is so dumb she'd fail a blood test."

Maggie cracked a smile and poured orange juice into the second glass. "I forgot about that."

I grinned, too.

"But anyway, it's not nice to say things about people, Blue."

"I know."

She studied me seriously. "You can't decide who my friends can be."

"I didn't mean to."

"Yes, you did."

"Well, you were my friend first. And I was just trying to protect you."

"From what? Birthday parties?" She nudged the glass toward me. "Drink your juice. I need to go upstairs and finish cleaning."

I drank it all in one go and wiped my mouth with the back of my hand. Then I licked my hand to get it all. "Gosh, that's good."

"I know, right?" She shook her head. "I don't know how Daddy gets orange juice. Probably with my college fund money." She opened the sour belts and planted one in her mouth, letting the belt hang down her chin like a sugared tongue.

"Can I go up with you? I could help you."

She shrugged. "I don't think you can help, but I guess you can stay for a little. I'm cleaning my guns. Competition's on Monday."

I would have cleaned her toilets if it meant we could be friends again. I took my sketchbook and followed her to her room.

Upstairs, Maggie had spread a towel on the white rug where her two shotguns – Browning and Benelli – were laid out ready to take apart. She tied a short apron around her waist and picked up a cleaning cloth.

She explained how to disassemble each one and how she ordered each piece as she cleaned and oiled the barrels. I only knew what I'd learned at gun camp, which was mainly about keeping the safety on, aiming straight, and watching the recoil. Maggie had a private tutor and had already won a blue ribbon at the skeet shooting contest in August. As Maggie finished the Browning, she handed it to me, and I slid it carefully into the gun bag and zipped it.

Sun streamed through the window above her bed. The room was already sweltering, and soon sweat ran down my back.

"Jesus, I'm burning up," Maggie said, shedding her pajama pants under her apron. Her fancy pink boy shorts peeked out from behind it.

"Why is it so hot in here?" I fanned my shirt away from my damp skin.

"My mom. She's always turning the air off, like we can't afford it." Maggie peeled off her T-shirt and shoved it under the bed behind her. Her sports bra had dainty red flowers, the same pattern as Mrs. Wisdom's skirt, but smaller. Reminded me of tiny blisters.

Maggie hopped up and disappeared for a few minutes.

I looked around her room. Her laptop, her gaming system, her flat-screen TV – things that were fun and expensive and completely impossible on a deputy's salary. Daw would spit beer laughing if I ever asked him for those kinds of things.

A snapping sound came from the attic, then the air conditioning hummed awake. When Maggie came back, she flipped through her hangers and chose a tank top that she tossed on the bed.

"Hey." She nodded at my holster. "You're actually wearing your gun. Nice to see you're following the rules."

"It still feels weird carrying it."

"You'd get used to it if you practiced."

"I just don't like it." I tugged on the holster. "We're only in ninth grade. Even *I* don't trust fourteen-year-olds. Why does the Republic?"

"I like it. I feel safer with mine."

"Did you hear about what happened at The Pump?"

The Pump was the other gas station in Blessing. It had more expensive gas than the Gulf, but the candy and soda selections were bigger and so it drew kids from the next county.

"Everyone heard," Maggie said.

"That boy died."

Maggie glanced at me, then lay the barrel piece on the towel.

"He died because he stole a Snickers," I reminded her.

"I know," she sighed. "He shouldn't have stole."

"He was eleven."

"That's old enough to know better. He probably looked older. And he could have had a gun." She sounded irritated.

I held out my sketchbook to Maggie. "Look inside. I drew something for you."

She gave me a puzzled look. "What's this? A present?"

"Yeah. Not the whole book. Just open it."

She opened the stapled cover and flipped through the book until she froze at the last drawing, which I'd torn out for her. I tried to see whether she was horrified or happy, but her blonde hair hung down around her face as she stared at the page.

"It's like a...like a...Greek statue," I stammered. "I'm trying to practice anatomy. If you don't like it—"

"It's nice," she said.

"It's you," I told her.

She looked up and nodded. "I know. Thank you. It's really nice. Why am I naked?"

I looked down at her sports bra and her bare legs, which seemed to be the way she ended up nearly every day in the summer.

"I was focused on getting your arms and legs right, and it just seemed more...heroic or something to leave it like that. It's not showing your privates."

She nodded.

"I can draw clothes on it if you want."

"No, it's okay. Thank you." She folded it and put it under her bed. "I like the face one. Can I have that one, too?"

"Sure."

She tore the portrait of herself out of the sketchbook and propped it on her mirror above the dresser.

"It's too bad you can't go to an art college," she said, not looking at me. "They just do art and nothing else. They have all kinds of colleges in America."

"How do you know that?" I asked.

"Don't tell anyone, but Daddy's computer can get around the firewalls," she said. "Sometimes I use it when he's out, just to see what's out there."

"What *is* out there?" I was fascinated. Most everyone had old computers that were pre-Secession because no one could afford to import new ones that met the Republic's requirement for firewalls that prevented access to American websites. We had so many firewalls, it seemed like everything beyond the border was as far away as hell itself.

"A lot of stuff. Wicked stuff. But some good things, too. Lots of people go to college there, still. But I'm sure you'll be a great artist even if you have to go to school in Texas." She pointed to her sketch and grinned. "You're already making masterpieces."

She was being so nice. It made me bold.

"So... I've been wondering." I said, carefully. "Are we friends again?"

Maggie took a breath and hitched her shoulders up like a question mark.

"The thing is, I think we've... changed. I've got new friends now I'm settled in high school." She met my eyes directly. "We're just different, Blue. You know that. Summer was a long time ago."

Her words were like weights on my shoulders, crushing me. "I can be different." My voice was small.

"Well, I think you should be you. It's just, we've grown apart, and I'm just not sure we have that much in common." She

44

was so confident. So not sad to lose me. "We can still be friends. I'll say hi to you in school. Okay? You just won't be coming over much because I'm getting busy with competitions and Shelby's club." She patted me on the shoulder like you might pat a puppy. "Now. Look at this beauty." She handed me the gun receiver – a long, angular piece of metal.

The sides of it were etched with feathered swirls and leaves. I barely glanced at it.

"It's pretty." I handed it straight back to her, my voice stiff.

Her words had stung.

She held it up and examined it. "Don't get nervous just because it's a weapon. Jesus, no one would know your dad's a cop. Think of it like a work of art. Like your drawings. My work of art got soaked last weekend, so I've got to degrease it. Oil the firing pins and trigger. The first thing you do is remove the firing pins. Then you degrease the action, forend iron, and barrel assy." She pointed to the parts spread out on the cloth.

Numbly, I handed her the alcohol and the gun lube when she asked, and watched as she cleaned the receiver, stopping briefly to turn on the small air compressor she kept in her closet. She chattered away the whole time, but I said nothing. My heart ached, knowing that it would never be like this again. I'd lost her. Weeks ago I'd lost her.

Finished with her weapon, Maggie switched off the compressor and glanced at my holster. "When was the last time you cleaned your gun?"

I shrugged.

"Seriously?" Maggie held out her hand.

I hesitated. "You don't have to clean it."

45

"I know I don't. But I kind of do. Empty the cartridge."

I unsnapped my holster, released the cartridge, and handed over the pistol. Maggie sat on the floor and studied it doubtfully.

"This gun is ancient. Your dad can do better than this."

She drew the oilcloth across the barrel, but paused and set the pistol on her lap. "Hey. You're not mad, are you? You'll find other fr—"

The explosion was deafening.

I jumped at the noise – a *boom* that shocked my ears. We both sat frozen. Then my gaze drifted down to Maggie's hands.

They were trembling, hovering over a gray-ringed hole near her stomach.

"Oh my God," I whispered. "What happened?"

Maggie looked down and touched her skin. Her hand came away red with blood. "You emptied it," she stuttered. "I thought..." She gasped. Blood seeped out of her skin, oozing through her fingers. "You emptied it, right?"

My heart twisted.

"Don't talk," I said. "I'll call 911." I jumped up and spun around, patting my shorts, looking wildly around the room. "Where's my phone?" I searched every flat surface as I stumbled toward her door. I must have left it in the basket of my bike, if I'd brought it at all.

When I glanced back, Maggie's face was already gray.

"Maggie? Where's your phone?"

She gazed up at me and said nothing.

I scanned her room, but didn't see her phone anywhere, either. The Wisdoms didn't have a landline – almost no one did.

There was nothing to do but run down to my bike to see if mine was in the basket. Had I even brought it? What if it was at home?

I kneeled beside Maggie. "I'm going to get my phone. I'll be right back, okay?" I kissed her forehead. "You're going to be okay." I rushed out, but stopped at the door to glance back.

Maggie slouched sideways on the white rug, a smear of blood on the bedspread behind her. We locked eyes again.

"I'm bleeding," Maggie whispered, bewildered.

I took off, sailed down the stairs, flew through the front door, tripped down the porch. My bike basket was empty.

"Please God," I whispered. "Please please please please." My heart raced. "Where's my freaking phone?"

I scanned the grass yard – nothing – then ran back up the porch steps before swiveling around and freezing, hands splayed in the air.

"What do I do? What do I do?" I asked nobody.

I had to get help from somewhere. I kept seeing that look on Maggie's face. The terrified, unspoken question.

I leaped off the porch and rode my bike to the old lady's house and pounded on the door.

"Hey!" I yelled. "Hey! Open up! It's an emergency!" I pounded again in a fury. The woman was there, I knew it. She had to be there. "Open up! We need help!"

As I beat the door and screamed, I imagined the old woman cocking her shotgun on the other side. Raising the barrel. Pulling the trigger. Shooting right through the door.

Do it! I thought madly. *Do it!*

I looked down the long winding street and all the trees and empty lots of the new neighborhood stretched out so far, too far from Maggie. It was a long way to the next house. I picked up my bike and coasted downhill to another house near the entry and the stone Pleasant Valley sign. I banged on the door but again no one answered.

You've been gone too long. My mind raced. I biked up the hill to Maggie's house again, fighting for breath and chanting *don't die, don't die* inside my head. I threw my bike to the lawn and ran through the front door and up to Maggie's bedroom. Her body slumped over to the floor. I dropped down on the rug beside her.

Her eyes were closed. Her eyebrows were pulled together by some invisible stitch.

"Maggie," I whispered. "Maggie. Maggie." I gently shook her shoulder. Nothing.

I choked on my words. "Maggie, please wake up. Maggie?" I lowered my forehead on Maggie's cheek and cried. Something sharp dug into my knee, and as I lifted my leg, I saw my own gun, half-tucked under Maggie.

The sirens called me out of the house. Someone must have heard my screams and called for help.

I stumbled down the stairs, out the open door, and onto the porch. I stopped and looked for the flashing lights. There, on the left side of the porch, was my cell phone. I must have dropped it when I came in.

I was just reaching for it as the sheriff's car pulled into the drive, Daw's eyes wide on me from the passenger seat.

FIVE

The police station was dusty and cold and smelled like old hamburgers. I'd been in the two-room office many times before, when I was little and had a fever or strep throat and couldn't go to school but couldn't stay home because Daw had to work. I'd spin myself dizzy in Sheriff Burnet's rolling chair, and when I was bored of that, I'd walk to the end of the block past McNealty's and the post office, then turn around and walk back to the station. Miss Jenny, the receptionist, would sneak gummy bears and sour balls into my pocket, and I'd get sugared up and climb into the rolling chair again until Sheriff Burnet kicked me out.

Miss Jenny had died a few years ago. An old lady I didn't recognize typed at a computer, squinting down her nose at the screen. I slumped in the chair and stared at the dust particles that spun up when I traced my finger across the file cabinet to my right. The front window had a dark tint to keep out the glare, but the lightbulbs inside the office buzzed and made my eyes ache. My bare feet were coated in dirt.

Across the room near the front door, an older girl slouched in her chair. I didn't look at her for long because she was the kind of girl you didn't stare at. I stole glances at her boots instead – thick black ones with a leather strap over the top and silver buckles on the sides. In little pieces, I made a picture of her. Motorcycle boots. Black tank top. Jeans with the knee-flap peeled away and her tawny

49

skin peeking out the rips. Shiny black hair shielding her face like a veil.

She glanced up at me and I pretended to be concerned about something out the window.

The blinds were broken. Maggie was dead. I stared into the other smudged window, the one without blinds, and saw in the reflection a ghost watching me.

Then the door behind me opened and Sheriff Burnet cleared his throat.

"Blue." He held up his hand and waited for me to stand up. I couldn't look him in the eyes. The sheriff was old and doughy with a white mustache and a kind voice. He nodded toward his office.

"You," he said to the dark-haired girl. "Don't you go nowhere. Your uncle's coming."

I rose and trudged inside. His office smelled of old ashtrays and yellowed paper. The black padded vests on the wall were new, as well as the gun safe that took up a third of the office. The whole station looked smaller than I remembered. How long had it been since I'd sat in the sheriff's chair and sang into the police radio microphone? Ages ago. A hundred years.

Daw stood there, too. His wide eyes stayed with me. As soon as I sat down he started pacing.

Sheriff Burnet sat down behind his desk, then stood up again and opened the minifridge under the window.

"You thirsty?" he asked, raising those white-bush eyebrows. "Water? I got buttermilk. Maybe prune juice. Might be turned."

I shook my head.

Daw raked his hands across his temples and worried the strip of space between the door and the window.

"You just never mind, okay?" Daw spoke finally. He planted his index finger on the desk. "You're going to be fine, Blue. I'll make damn sure."

"Mark," Sheriff Burnet said.

"What were you doing..." Daw began, but the sheriff cut him off.

"Mark, I think you better go outside."

"She's my daughter."

"Which is why you should step out." The sheriff's voice was low but firm. "Just procedure is all."

Daw looked at me, then at Sheriff Burnet. He nodded and opened the door. But then he turned back.

"She's only fourteen."

"She'll be okay." Sheriff Burnet held up his hand like a priest. "A few minutes, all right?"

Daw set his hand on my shoulder and lowered his mouth to my ear. "Just tell the God's truth."

The God's truth was the truth the Republic lived by, the truth on the TVs and at schools, the truth written all over our constitution after the Great Secession. The Plain truth, which Daw grunted about at home after a few beers, was a little more raw. The Plain truth always seemed to be followed by bribery and lies and corruption, which made Daw fume. I didn't understand half the things Daw ranted about, but I knew that the God's truth wasn't always the whole truth.

When he'd closed the door, Sheriff Burnet took a deep breath and coughed. "First off, you're probably addled still, I know that. But I have to ask you some questions about Maggie. Okay?"

I nodded, but my brain was full of questions. Where was Maggie now? Was she at the hospital? Was she at the cemetery behind the church? Where do they take dead people? Was she cold?

I shivered.

Sheriff Burnet pecked at his laptop, then sighed. He closed the lid and grabbed a yellow pad on his desk instead.

"Tell me now, why did you go over to Maggie's house?"

"I wanted to see her."

"You wanted to see her." He jotted something on the pad. "'Bout what?"

I inhaled, and a heavy ache spread across my chest. How could I explain?

He cleared his throat. "Tiffany Wisdom said you two was fighting?"

"No, we made up. I went over to apologize."

"To apologize about what?"

I shook my head to clear it. None of this made sense. "We made up," I explained again.

He kept on watching me. "Made up over what, Bluebonnet?"

"Nothing. Just...she made some new friends and we weren't..." My voice was a feather falling. I looked down and pulled on my frayed shorts.

The sheriff scratched at his notepad. "What time did you arrive at the scene? At the Wisdoms' house."

"I don't know. I think nine?"

"Nine or thereabouts." He paused and glanced up past me. I could hear voices before the rap at the door. "Damn. I thought we'd have more time." The sheriff stood.

A man in a cowboy hat and a woman in a suit walked in and then stopped because there wasn't anywhere to go. Daw pushed his way in too, his eyes darting around the room like he was tracking a fly. The five of us in the cramped office left no space to breathe.

"Sheriff." The cowboy nodded at Sheriff Burnet, then nodded at the woman. "This is Agent Rayna Johns from the Houston office."

The sheriff shook their hands. "Ranger Kern, this is my deputy, Mark Andrews."

Daw nodded his hat at the Ranger, then took the woman's hand in both of his and pumped the handshake until she pulled her hand away. Compared to the Ranger's straight edges, his sunglasses and crisp shirt and beige cowboy hat, Daw seemed shrunk up and withered.

"Seems like our plans have taken a detour," Ranger Kern said.

"I know you wanted to talk about the gang activity," Sheriff Burnet said. "We're dealing with a tragic occurrence right now, but I can still meet with y—"

"Where's the girl?"

"What girl?"

The Ranger waited like a statue. Like he didn't have to explain and he wasn't going to.

"Oh." Sheriff Burnet waved his hand at the door. "She's out there. Her uncle's picking her up."

"No. She's not there." He fixed the sheriff with a disbelieving look. "You didn't lock her up?"

"What do you mean she's gone?" Sheriff Burnet took a step, but the room was so crowded it was no use trying to get to the door and check. He craned his neck like he was trying to see through the frosted glass. "Well, I'll be."

The Ranger turned to the agent and took off his sunglasses. His eyes were like water.

"I'll go check the premises," the woman said, as if he'd given her an unspoken assignment, and slipped out.

"Now. I need to take a statement from—" Ranger Kern looked at his cell phone. "Miss Andrews." A thick gold bracelet slipped out from under his cuff. I stared at the shiny links of metal peeking out, a glimmer in the haze of my head.

"A statement from Blue? Why?" Sheriff Burnet's eyes widened.

"That's privileged."

The sheriff considered standing up for himself. "You don't have jurisdiction."

"I'm a Texas Ranger, Sheriff. The whole country's my jurisdiction."

The sheriff tossed his pencil. "What is going on? Is this Mayor Wisdom's doing? He ain't the law."

But the Ranger wasn't moved. "We need five minutes alone. You can wait out there," he said, nodding at the door.

Sheriff Burnet's face reddened. "This is *my* office."

But he stood up, scraping the chair backward along the floor, and thumped out of the room.

Daw leaned down to my ear. "Don't be afraid." His voice was hushed and low, and reminded me of the Rabbit and Bear stories he used to read to me. It was a century ago, that book, his voice. "This is just protocol. You done nothing wrong."

I nodded, but his confidence was like his sour-sweet alcohol breath – a little too much.

Ranger Kern squinted at Daw, calculating his wrinkled shirt, sniffing the air he stirred up. He waited until he was gone before turning to me.

"Bluebonnet Andrews," the Ranger said and took off his hat. His gray hair was mashed and damp.

"Blue," I managed to say.

"I will call you Bluebonnet, as that is your name on record." He paused and cleared his throat. "This won't take long."

I stared down at the oak desk and saw Maggie's pale face again, beads of sweat along her hairline, blonde cords that fell across her cheek. And Maggie's hand, cool under my lips. *Wake up, Maggie. Wake up.*

"Did the girl in the lobby talk to you?" the Ranger asked. He spoke low and monotone and stared a hole in me.

I shook my head.

"I'm actually in Blessing to investigate the incident this afternoon. The motorcycle gang passed through here again. You hear about that?"

I nodded.

"That has nothing to do with you. But I got a call from the Mayor's office."

"Maggie's dad?"

He unlocked his gaze from me and looked around the office in a sort of bored way that caught me off guard. "You see, your father being the deputy, and the only sheriff a close family friend..."

"He's not that close," I said, quickly.

He gave me a jaded glance. "Close enough not to fire a deputy who's terminally drunk."

I recoiled. "He ain't... most times. Not on the job."

He leaned in, lowering his voice. "I know all about your daddy. I interviewed him. He's not cut out. He needs to understand that."

What do you mean? I wanted to ask, but the words wouldn't come.

"Now. I just need to ask some questions for the Mayor's office and then I'm gone."

The Mayor's office *was* Maggie's daddy. My heart thudded against my chest. The Ranger pulled a small device from his pocket, pressed a button to start recording, and dropped the device on the desk. He stood at the dirty window.

"What happened today? What led up to the gun going off?"

I pulled at my fingernails. There was still blood under the edges, dried black and trapped there. I said, "I was at Maggie's house."

"You two were arguing?"

"No. I mean, she shot herself. It was an accident."

He sighed, still staring out the window. "Back up. When you first arrived at the Wisdoms' house..."

"I said Hi to Mrs. Wisdom – she was on her way somewhere – and then I went in."

"You opened the door and went in?"

"Yes. No. Maggie opened the door."

"A neighbor across the street says you were pounding on the door. Yelling. Said you were irate. Said you frightened her."

"I wasn't irate. I just wanted to see Maggie. She was my best—" the word caught in my throat, and my nose burned. It was already clogged from crying, and I'd just begun to breathe again. I took a tissue from the desk.

"And then?" he said.

I tried to remember what we'd talked about, but a few hours ago seemed like years. "We went to the kitchen and she poured us some juice. We made up. And then we went up to her bedroom because she wanted to clean her guns. She was supposed to compete soon."

"Was that your idea or hers – to clean the guns?"

"Hers. She was already set up to clean, and she wanted to clean my gun. I never clean it. I emptied the cartridge. I had it in my hand." I shook my head in confusion, trying to remember where the cartridge went. I wanted to go home. To fall on the couch and sleep for hours.

"Then what?"

"The gun went off." My voice was flat. I'd already told this story so many times. "I ran for help, but nobody would come to the door. And when I got back to the house, she... she wasn't breathing anymore."

"Why was your friend Maggie undressed?" the Ranger said slowly. He cocked his head to the side and narrowed his eyes.

"What?" I shook my head and jarred the memory. Maggie had taken off her shirt. Yes, she was wearing the poppy bra. "It was hot upstairs. Her mom turned off the air."

He didn't blink. "People don't normally go around taking their shirts off when it's hot. Not good girls."

"She was good," I said, suddenly angry. "It was a sports bra. Like a tank top."

"Are you a good girl?" He said it like I wasn't.

I narrowed my eyes back at him. "Yes."

The Ranger shifted his weight and checked the recorder. "Did you take your shirt off, too?"

I stared at my fingernails, confused about where this was going, but scared. "No."

"Did you convince Maggie to take off her shirt?"

"No."

"And yet she was in her bra and you were not."

I twisted the tissue around my finger, wanting this to stop. But it didn't stop.

"Maggie was a pretty girl," he said. "Were you in love with her?"

My stomach clenched. Did I love her? Yes, I loved Maggie, but I didn't love-love her.

I whispered, "I'm not gay. That's illegal."

"Then what's this?" the Ranger said. I looked up. He was holding my sketchbook in his hand. He opened it, and the two drawings of Maggie fell to the desk. I hadn't felt ashamed when I drew her portrait, all muscle and skin and hair, but in his hands, the picture was something shameful. A lump of guilt crawled up into my throat.

"Did you draw this?"

I wanted to say yes but the words wouldn't come.

"Why would you draw something like this?" he demanded, genuinely perplexed. "Especially after what happened to those boys down in Tyler. You hear about them?"

I'd heard. "Those boys" had been stripped naked, roped back to front, and hung from a tree in front of the library. The news said there were rumors. The kids at school said it was a warning.

A mix of panic and anger bubbled up inside me. Still, I didn't speak.

"Bluebonnet. Everybody has secrets. You were jealous. You convinced her to get undressed. Maybe you were angry."

I felt gut-punched. "No. *No.*"

The Ranger looked out the window and spoke calmly. "Your violent commotion at the door, Maggie's state of undress, your bullet that killed her. And this... pornographic drawing. Evidence tells me it wasn't an accident. You shot Maggie Wisdom."

"What? I didn't!"

"You did. I can see it. By accident or not – and I suspect not – you shot her."

"I didn't." My throat knotted, and I fought against the hot, angry tears. "She shot herself. You don't even know me."

"I know all I need to know." He put his hat back on and tucked my sketchbook in his vest. "I know all sorts."

"I'm supposed to have a lawyer," I said. "Right?"

The Ranger suddenly laughed, probably because there weren't any lawyers for a hundred miles. But I didn't back down.

"Can I go now?" I asked.

"Where you going to go, Bluebonnet?" he asked, with new interest.

But I was done answering questions.

"Are you going to arrest me or not?"

He stared at me unmoving. But I took the dare.

"Then I want to go home."

The Ranger gave a small, cold smile. "You know, at first I thought the Wisdoms were overreacting. But not now. I see the fire in you." He tapped the desk and spoke so low his voice turned to gravel. "Somebody's gotta put it out."

Before I could respond, he turned and opened the door. Sheriff Burnet and Daw were standing near the threshold, craning to hear.

"We're done for now," the Ranger told them. "Sheriff, you'd best keep your eye on her." He glanced at Daw. "And on your deputy, too."

Outside, a cool breeze shrink-wrapped my skin. It stirred me awake and calmed my head at the same time. When we reached the truck I saw my bike in the back. Someone must have picked it up outside Maggie's and brought it to the station.

"Where's Maggie?" I asked Daw.

He took my hand, such an awkward gesture for us both.

"She's dead, Blue."

My throat strained. "But *where*? Is she in the hospital? Is she in a freezer somewhere?" I imagined a cold, dark place. Cabinets of dead bodies. "Some people wake up, you know.

Everyone thinks they're dead but they're not, and they wake up, and what if she's not dead and she wakes up and no one's there to help her?"

My heart began to race. I imagined Maggie pushing on the cabinet walls, landing her fists in desperation. And even though my brain told me I wasn't being reasonable, it seemed so horribly possible.

Daw looked away and cupped his hand to his mouth. He cleared his throat and said, "Blue, Maggie's not waking up. Come on." He pulled me under his arm and led me out of the station.

We didn't go straight home like Sheriff Burnet told us. Instead, Daw parked the truck at the Cotton Gin at the edge of town and got out.

"Five minutes," he said, not looking at me.

I tucked my knees under my chin and didn't say anything because I knew what five minutes meant.

While I waited in the truck, I replayed the day. The sweet orange juice, so cold down my throat. Maggie's white skin and the red blood on the grease apron. The Ranger's eyes that cut my heart right out. He was right to blame me. It was my fault that a bullet was in the chamber. I didn't check it right. It was my fault that Maggie was dead. I balled my fists in my eyes and tried to stop crying, but it felt good, so I tucked up my knees and cried and cried into that dark, hollow space.

I woke to the sputtering ignition. To Daw stinking up the cab with his breath. I rubbed the crick in my neck. It was black outside except for the flickering neon Cotton Gin sign.

"I just had a couple shots – see, that wasn't long," he said, already drawing his s's out too long. I sat up and crossed my arms.

"Dang, you fall asleep?" He chuckled and nudged my shoulder. He waved a bottle of Balcones whiskey and grinned at the blue corn label. "Look-it what David the bartender gave me for like, hardly nothing."

I was exhausted. Desperate to be asleep again. "You're drunk. Why do you do this?"

He lurched the truck backward over the gravel lot, but took the main road at a crawl. "I'm fine. See? You're fine, too."

Every time we were fine he was drunk.

"Listen. I got to thinking inside the Cotton Gin. That's why I needed a drink – to clear my head. Fella in there, he comes up and fuckin' prays for me. Hand right on my head. I was like, 'What the hell?' And then all I could hear was this voice. This voice. *Soon your sins shall seek you out*, that's what it said."

He reached over and poked my the thigh. I recoiled.

"Didn't I used to say that? Soon your sins shall seek you out. And it struck me. We can't escape God. We got to get right again. That's why this is happening. It's part of God's plan."

The memory of Maggie's slumped body flashed in my brain. I could feel her hair again, wet from my tears, and I was so so tired. "God's plan. How?"

"That's the thing!" He slapped the steering wheel. "We don't know. But how would we? We haven't been to church enough to know."

I turned to the window, gazed out on the dark fields. It was my fault that Maggie died. My bullet. God wasn't supposed to check the chamber. That was *my* job. The truck veered onto the shoulder, but Daw jerked it back into the lane.

He was still rambling. "That man said to me, 'You got to go lay it at Jesus' feet. You got to bow down and humble yourself at the feet of Jesus. He knows what to do.' We got to pray, Blue. I haven't prayed right in years. God knows I'm not a perfect man, but I'm a Christian, goddammit. He's gonna listen. He's got to listen to us."

The whole conversation unfolded like a dream.

"What do we pray?" I asked.

"You are not going to jail. God's not going to let that happen." He reached out to pat my leg, but missed and his hand landed on the seat instead. "Tomorrow, we're going to that church up on FM 3189, or 3981, or 38 – whatever the hell it is. We're going to pray, get the whole church to pray for us. Church people got prayer-chains. You'll see. We'll be okay."

But I knew nothing would ever be okay. I wasn't against prayer, but it seemed like something you did when you'd already given up. The pin-dot headlights of another car flickered miles ahead of us. "Maybe I'll ask God why Maggie had to die."

"Why does anybody have to die? We won't ever know. We're just human people. Our brains are too small to understand God's ways. Right? Maybe…maybe this all happened to bring us back to Him. See, I was handed this bottle of Baby Blue – see right there on the label – that's a sign, that's you. Bluebonnet. Baby Blue. After this last bottle, I'm done drinking. Not. A. Drop. We got to trust in God and the law. That Ranger is gonna save you, 'cause the Rangers… there's nothing better. Nothing better."

Daw's words jumped from one thing to the next. First we were going to church, then he was complaining about the pastor's voice, and then he threw up on the side of the road. One thing was clear: Daw wasn't capable of taking care of himself, much less me. I'd been taking care of him for years. Tucking him in, sewing him up, hiding the bills. Cooking, cleaning, tossing out dead mice and resetting the traps. And I hardly ever got angry with him because Daw was cracked and it wasn't his fault. But I was cracked too now, and it was like my insides were leaking through. All the love and worry and fear and regret, all of everything I hoped Daw would do for me one day, was floating away.

Was this the way my mother felt when she left for California? When she abandoned me? Did we crack her until her there wasn't nothing left inside of her that belonged to us?

Daw talked on and on – about God and the Rangers and fine whiskey and damned potholes – until we got home. On the steps of the mobile home, he tipped back the bottle with the sort of desperation that the last inch always stirs up.

"You comin'?" he hollered.

I slammed the truck door shut and stood in the weeds. A breeze licked my thighs and made my skin shiver. Daw turned around and stared at me.

"God almighty, you looked like your mother just now. Stubborn, too." He opened the green door and stumbled inside, letting the door slam on the spring hinges.

I made the decision to leave about two seconds after Daw passed out on the couch. He'd never had the answers to our problems, and it filled me with equal parts anger and shame.

While he snored, I pried the empty bottle of whiskey from his fingers and set it on the floor. Kneeled beside and touched his hand. He exhaled clouds of sweet liquor breath.

"Goodbye, Daw," I whispered, against his cheek. "Don't be sad."

I didn't know where I was going, but I knew I had to leave while it was dark. As long as he didn't know where I was, he'd be fine. They couldn't hold anything against him.

I slung my backpack on and looked around for Daw's phone. It was on the coffee table. I shut it off, and then searched for mine before realizing it was still at the police station, taken as evidence, along with my gun.

"I'm not leaving you," I whispered to Daw.

Then I eased the door closed so the spring wouldn't give away the lie.

SIX

I dragged my bike out of the truck bed as quietly as I could and rode away, still in my cut-offs and boots, with Maggie's blood still on my hands. I had a backpack full of peanut butter and water bottles. I knew it wouldn't last long but it was the best I could do. It was gone midnight, and the late September air was unusually chilly. My sweater wasn't thick enough, but as long as I kept pedaling, I didn't get cold. I didn't know exactly where I was going. I just wanted to get away. From the Ranger, from Blessing, from the truth. West, I figured. West was Dallas, and after that a lot of cows and land, and then El Paso and the border. Somewhere in all that space, I would find a place to disappear.

I pedaled for hours. Getting off and walking when the seat bruised the bones in my butt, and climbing back on again when I heard creatures rustling nearby. I avoided the main roads and cut across so many yards and pastures, I lost track of who'd be pointing a shotgun at me if I got caught. In the black before dawn, coyotes howled and dogs everywhere worked up a frenzy, but they were familiar sounds and I convinced myself they were distant and small. When the sun rose, I was so exhausted I could barely see the road. But I kept going. Clinging to the handlebars and pedaling until my legs were weak. I peeled off my sweater when I got hot, and pulled it back on when the sun got low. I cut across to the road again and biked parallel to the pastures, stopping ever so often for a sip of water and a finger of peanut butter. I had no idea if I was still going west, but I kept traveling with the sun, and that gave me something. And then the sun was down low between the trees again. And I was so tired I could hardly move.

When my wheel hit a rock and launched me and the bike into a pine tree, I kept walking, leaning on the wobbly bike like a crutch. My thighs were shaking, and every few steps, one leg or the other would buckle beneath me. I leaned against a tree and suddenly I could go no farther.

Spend the night in the woods, I told myself. You're far enough. Figure out the rest in the morning, when your feet aren't cramping. Nobody will find you here.

I wasn't sure it was true but I had no choice. I needed to sleep. I stashed my bike on the ground and tossed some leaves and sticks on it for camouflage. Shoddy job, Daw would've said, but I was too worn out to do more.

I searched for a fat tree with a sturdy limb and found one with a perfect Y to settle into. I was an expert at climbing trees. I'd practically lived in the mimosa tree in our front yard when I was in elementary. I hated the thought of tree ants but boars were the real hazard, so I brushed off my hands, climbed up into the branches, and stuffed my backpack under my head.

It was only then, as I was staring up at the night sky, that I let myself think of Maggie again. I wanted to think that she'd forgiven me, and that she was watching, maybe from those two starry eyes winking through the trees. I wondered what else she saw from up there. Could she hear the cicadas roaring, or the frogs croaking, or the other million noises that crowded around me? I wasn't normally afraid of night echoes but I didn't normally sleep in trees, either. And I wasn't used to the bushes swishing when some creature passed through or the leaves scratching each other. But I'd always been able to sleep like a dead person – drop off and wake up in exactly the same position. So I braced my arms and slipped into the dark hollow of my dreams.

★

We were at the airport. I was little, and running in circles around Daw's legs. Marla wore the same white robe from the photograph, one hand gripping the handle of a large suitcase. She stared at the departures screen and chewed on her fingernails.

"Mama," I yelled. I hooked my left hand around Daw's knee and circled around him. I looked up. He was tree-tall and handsome. "Look, Mama!"

Marla wouldn't look. Her eyes locked onto the board.

A sea between us, crowds of people weaved past one another like fish, darting around Marla and a few other frozen travelers who were gazing at the same board in horror.

I ran toward her despite Daw's sharp call. Jumped into that stream of people and bags and suitcases, and pushed my way toward my mother in her white robe.

"Mama!" I said as I pulled on the white belt.

She looked down at me, her eyebrows knit up to her forehead. "They're canceled," she mumbled, not to knee-high me but to herself or to God or maybe to the fourteen-year-old me, because I realized then that I was dreaming. People don't go to the airport in their bathrobes except in dreams. I looked up at the giant board with scrolling letters and numbers. Red words blinked all across the board: Flight Canceled. There were others standing beside us, and every few seconds, someone would groan, "Oh no," swoop up their bags, and rush away.

Marla rubbed her palms together and her gaze drifted back up to the board. "So many cancelled. Los Angeles. Los Angeles." Her eyes darted across the words.

"Mama, look at me." I tugged the hem of her white robe and fluffed it out like a wedding train.

"Los Angeles," she murmured, and then gasped as her eyes landed on it. Her lips arched into a smile.

"Mama!" I said again, and my impatient hands yanked at her belt again, and her robe opened up, revealing her thighs. Immediately I felt the shame of my impatience and of what came next: Mama standing naked in the airport, a swat on my behind, the word "Blue!" slicing through the air like a hatchet to my lungs.

But then Marla caught the edges of her robe as the belt fell, and she stooped over, and her face cracked into a smile and then, like hand bells, a laugh. She finally looked at me and her eyes crinkled just like they did in Daw's photo. She laughed and I laughed, and I twirled around and around, dancing for her. Each circle making her brighter, each circle blinding with light, until we were both drenched in starlight.

When I opened my eyes, the white world was falling up. I must have flinched myself awake and rolled off the tree limb. I landed with a thump on something animal, and the next few seconds sped by like a nightmare.

I lay there sideways with the breath knocked from my lungs and a knee jammed up between my ribs. My ears rang, and the ringing turned into someone yipping out.

"Owwww!" the person howled, long and steady.

I scrambled off a body and hugged my ribs, and suddenly we were both yelling "Aaahhh!" I clapped my palm over her mouth at the same time she clamped her hand over mine, and we stared darts at each other. That's how I knew that she was hiding, too. Neither one of us could afford to scream.

We both hushed and scrambled away from each other. There wasn't a sleeping bag around, and she had leaves and twigs in her hair from sleeping on the ground. She hiked up her knees and dug in her black boots to balance herself, and then grabbed at her leather jacket like she was afraid I'd steal it. Her black-black jeans were the color of new and matched her spiky hair. It was the girl from the police station.

"I know you," I whispered.

She rose to her knees, still clutching her arm, and peered at the woods around us, so I looked too. Seemed like a good idea. I didn't see any campers or hikers or police on the prowl, so I sat back on my heels and rubbed my ribs to stop them throbbing. The girl moved a hand down, fingers gentle on her gun that was strapped in a thigh holster. She laid eyes on me again, with one eyebrow cocked.

"I know you," I said again. I glanced at her hand. I wasn't afraid. You have to be more cautious about the people who don't rest gentle.

The girl shook her head real slow, that eyebrow still raised.

But I wouldn't accept this. "From the police station. Remember? I was there, too."

The girl gave me another once-over. "I have never been to no station."

She was lying.

I gave up and began rubbing my bruises again. "Okay."

It would have been nice to have the company of another human soul, but what did she matter to me? I brushed the dirt and leaves off my legs and reached for my backpack, still in the Y of the branches. I wrestled with the zipper and pulled out a bottle of warm water. It tasted so good I didn't stop for breath, and a good part of it ran down my chin. The girl was staring at me. Her hand had moved from her gun to cradle her elbow again.

"You want some?" I asked.

She looked away as if she wanted to refuse, but finally nodded, and I reached in my pack and gave her my last bottle of water.

"Thanks," she said.

I watched as she drank half of it in one long swig.

The pink sky was fading fast into blue, and the woods around us were speared with light beams. Made me feel like I should be moving, but I hadn't quite figured out where I was going yet.

"Sorry for landing on you," I said. "You hurt?"

The girl screwed the cap back on and arched her back in a long stretch.

"No. I am fine." Her words were choppy and strange. I'd never heard a real person speak with an accent before. She wasn't from Texas, I was sure of that.

"What are you doing here?" I asked.

Her gaze sharpened. "What are *you* doing here?"

"I asked you first."

"Well, I am not here for long. I am just passing through and I needed to sleep." She stood up and brushed the leaves off her jeans. Then picked up a cloth bag and slung it over her shoulder. "And it is getting light. So. I must go."

I stood up, too, and immediately felt the bruise on my hip. Every part of me hurt. But I didn't want to be alone again, so I spoke quickly.

"Where are you from?"

"You ask a lot of questions. Plus, you did not answer mine."

I tried to remember what she'd asked. "What question?"

"Why are you sleeping in a tree and falling down on people?"

I was pretty sure she wouldn't be running to the police about me, but it was always good to verify. "Are you gonna tell on me?"

She looked around us and raised her hands. "Who am I going to tell?"

I swatted the ants off my backpack. "I'm running away."

I thought her shoulders relaxed, just a little at this. "Oh. Well, nice to meet you and have a good time running away." She kicked away the branches that covered my bike. "That yours?"

I nodded.

She pulled the bike upright and examined the bent wheel in silence. Then she turned the whole bike toward the path and let the handlebars fall to the ground. She walked away, like she wasn't even curious about why I was running. She knew what she wanted and where she was going and nobody was going to stop her. I swung my backpack up on my shoulder, yanked up the bike, and hobbled after her.

"Wait! Can I walk with you?"

She glanced back briefly. "No."

It wasn't mean. But it wasn't nice either.

"Please? I don't really know where to go."

She leaned her head to the side and said loudly, "How about home? I am sure whatever you did is not so bad. What could be so bad that you cannot go home to your nice mommy and daddy and your own bedroom and your own bed and your dog and I am guessing your one hundred video games?"

With that, she began to walk away faster.

"Murder." It slipped out so easily it had to be true.

The girl stopped and turned back. She scrunched her brows at me. "Murder. *You* murdered someone."

She didn't believe me.

All the hope and anger and fear and hunger whooshed through a little hole in my chest. I could hardly speak. "No. It was an accident. But they think I shot her."

My nose burned, and the back of my throat was strung taut, making it difficult to talk or swallow or breathe. I shielded my eyes with my forearm so she wouldn't see me cry. I'm not sure how she ended up beside me so fast, but there she was with her forearm under mine, guiding me back to the tree. She looked around the woods again, a little more cautiously this time.

"How old are you?"

I sniffed. "Fourteen." My nose was running, so I wiped it on my T-shirt.

"You look twelve."

I shrugged. "I'm short."

"What is your name?"

"Blue. Like Bluebonnet, but shorter. What's yours?"

"Jet."

"Jet?"

She nodded. "Like an airplane, but shorter." She gave me a thoughtful look. "Where are your parents?"

I shook my head.

Her eyes grazed my hip. "Where is your gun?"

"They took it away."

She heaved a breath and looked around the empty woods again. "Okay. You can walk with me. For a while. But we have to get rid of the bike."

"Can't we just leave it here?"

"Stay here," she said, and within a few seconds she'd run ahead so fast and so quiet she was out of sight. I stood amid hundreds of trees and waited and watched. The birds screeched at each other, their echoes zigzagging off the trees. I looked back up the dirt trail and listened for Jet's footsteps.

Somewhere in the distance, a motorcycle roared down a road, its engine whining like a strange bird call. I pushed the bike's handlebars forward and back. Kicked the bent wheel and caught the tip of my boot in the spokes. She probably left you, I told myself as I yanked my boot loose.

The path I'd come from was covered in yellow-orange leaves. In a few weeks, the fall colors would all drop to the forest floor and there'd be no more hiding in trees.

A faint whistle sounded. I turned, and Jet's dark head leaned out from behind a big oak farther up the path. She motioned for me to follow her. I ran stiffly, yanking my bike through the muck of damp pine needles and oak leaves that coated the floor. After yesterday's walk my boots had split at the soles. Now the black forest juice was seeping into the cracks and around my toes. I slipped a few times on the muck, and again when the bent wheel hit a rock.

"Where are we going?" I tried to whisper.

"Shh." She shot a hard look at me. I didn't like being shushed but I clamped my mouth and focused on keeping my calves away from the looping pedals. Sometimes I looked up and Jet was gone. She walked ahead without ever seeming to look back, and I began to wonder if she was going to get rid of the wretched bike or of me.

We finally broke through the forest and came to a clearing. It looked like someone had taken a chainsaw and chopped a straight line down the middle of the woods.

The soil sloped down into a ravine. At the foot of it, a shallow river swirled. When I stopped to catch my breath, the ripe smell of the water and algae and tadpoles filled my nose. Only a month ago, I'd been fishing with Maggie and digging for earthworm-bait on the bank.

We walked across a wooden bridge to the middle, where Jet stopped and looked out over the railing. Beneath us, the water sloshed over a boulder and into a swirling current.

"That will do," she said. She took hold of the back wheel and the bike seat. "Lift up the front," she ordered.

I followed her instructions, and a few seconds later, we tossed the broken bike over the railing. I watched it fall like a shot bird into the stream. It hardly made a sound, just a gentle *ploosh*. I expected it to be carried away with the water, but it sat there crumpled. The bent wheel stuck out like an elbow.

Jet brushed her palms together, as though she'd buried the bike in the ocean or something.

"What's the purpose of that?" I asked, not bothering to whisper. "Anybody can see that."

"It is the best we can do. This way."

I had a million questions for Jet. Where did she live? Who was she running from? Where was she going? What kind of name was Jet? Was she a Scaler? But I didn't ask, because I didn't want to scare her off. I had no idea where I was, and not being alone felt good.

Once we'd dumped the bike, we walked in silence, her always a few steps ahead of me, until we hit a road. Jet held up her hand. "A car is coming. Hurry, go back."

We hustled back to the tree line, watched the car speed by, and then continued to walk under the trees, parallel to the road. To keep the ghost of Maggie from wandering the rooms of my brain, I conjured up reasons why Jet was on the run. I followed her movements – her quick steps, pushing ahead with the purpose and focus of a bird dog on the hunt. What was she hunting? The longer we walked without talking, the curiouser I became.

I skipped ahead and walked in step alongside her. "I like your name. Jet."

She gave me a startled glance, as though I'd interrupted a conversation she was having with herself. Or maybe she'd forgotten I was following her. But she didn't slow down or say thank you.

I tried again. "Where are we going?"

"Up here." She nodded ahead at some imaginary place in the trees.

"I'm thirsty," I said.

"Me too. I think we are close, though."

"Close to what?"

"A gas station."

"Why do we need gas? Are you running from the police, too?"

She didn't look at me. "No."

"You're not." I doubted it.

"No."

"But… I saw you at the police station." I didn't tell her that the Ranger had asked about her.

"You were mistaken." She walked faster to punish me. "People like me get shot, not arrested. Only white people get arrested."

"That's not true." I could name five white people who got shot in Blessing in the past year alone. But I didn't know much about arrests. Still, it would have been some comfort if she understood what I was feeling. What I was running from. And why I had to run.

I tried again. "You're not from Blessing, right?"

She spat out a "*puh*" in disgust. "God, no."

"Then where are you from?"

She didn't answer.

"I'm from Blessing," I informed her.

"I figured that."

"Are you running away from home too?"

"No."

When she stooped to avoid a branch, her black jeans dipped and revealed a small tattoo on her lower back. It was a flower with barbed wire. Someday I'd have a tattoo too, and I'd design it myself. But not with spikes.

"I like your tattoo," I said. "I want to get one someday. Did it hurt?"

"Not really."

"It's a rose, right? Is that a gang symbol? I'm not judging."

Jet snorted. "It is not. There is no rose gang."

We walked a little more without words.

"Don't you want to ask me questions?" I asked.

"No."

"Why not?"

"The less I know, the safer we both are. Trust me."

It seemed to me the wall around Jet was ten feet high.

"You're not scared?" I asked.

Her steps didn't slow. "No."

"Where are you going?"

"I told you – the gas station."

"No, I mean after that. Where are you going? I won't tell anyone."

She gave me a steady look. "You won't? Because you are kind of a chatterbox."

I shook my head.

"If I tell you, you promise to stop asking me millions of questions?"

I nodded.

She stopped and faced me. "Fine. I'm going to my aunt's house."

"Ont?"

"Yes, aunt."

"Ont?" I searched my brain, but came up empty.

"Yes, aunt. She is really the best friend of my mother. But I call her my aunt."

"Oh, aunt," I smiled. "It's pronounced *aunt*. Like an ant. Why—?"

Jet held up her hands. "No-no! No more questions."

I spent the next chunk of time imagining what Jet's aunt looked like, where she lived, and what her name was. I decided her aunt was married to a tall man with a mustache, and she painted her nails coral and wore a long skirt that swooshed like a broom. She hadn't seen Jet for ten years, and so wouldn't recognize Jet right away, but she'd be nice, with a laugh like bubbles, and she'd serve warm cake and invite all the neighbors to celebrate her arrival.

I swallowed and realized I didn't have any more spit. I needed water. Just as we cleared the tree line, I saw a gas station the size of a matchbox down the road. We both walked faster. But at the last second, Jet stopped and pulled a dark blue baseball cap from the battered cloth bag hanging from her shoulder.

"Here, take this," she said, handing it to me. "Keep your head down."

But I barely listened. I stuck on the cap, raced inside, and hugged the water fountain. I was a beast, slurping at the stream, getting my shirt half-soaked while Jet went to the restroom. I was still hogging the water fountain when Jet passed me again and went to the man behind the cash register.

"I am supposed to pick up a money order here," she said to the man.

He was like every other gas station cashier – wrinkled shirt, bored eyes, mussed-up hair that suggested showers weren't a priority. The man leaned out to squint at me, and I knew what he was thinking. But I hadn't even considered stealing anything until he squinted at me.

I slipped into the restroom, and when I came out, Jet was arguing with him.

"But I am sure the wire came here. From Juanita Grace. Will you check again?"

"Juanita, huh? Sounds foreign. We don't accept business from Scalers."

"She is not a Scaler. She is American."

The man cocked his head to one side and sucked his teeth. His lips curled into half a grin and he spoke slowly. "You girls traveling alone?"

Jet stiffened. "That is not your business."

"Ouch." The man laughed at Jet. "You're like spicy salsa. I like a little bite in my sauce."

"Juanita with a J. Please look again." Jet's voice was low, but it carried back to me like a warning. I looked at the door, measuring the shortest distance in case we needed to run. I stepped backwards to the next aisle so I could watch them from the hedge of corn chips. The man's eyes roved over Jet's body.

"I'll tell you what. I think I saw something from Western Union in my manager's office. It's probably there in the back. Why don't you come with me, and we'll check together? Won't take more than a few minutes. Five or six if I have to…dig around." He lifted his hand. A ring of keys was looped around his index finger. He shook it, then looked straight at me. I ducked down.

"You stay here, girl. Keep an eye out for customers. And don't steal nothin'."

Jet slapped her palms on the counter and leaned in. "I am going nowhere. What is that?" She pointed to a slip of yellow paper behind the man.

"What?"

"That paper. That is Western Union, no? Is that my money?"

The man sniffed and glared at Jet, but eventually turned around, picked up the paper, and looked at the ceiling. "Nope. This ain't it."

"You did not even read it. Let me see."

He jerked the paper up when Jet reached out to grab it.

"Read it," Jet demanded. "Or maybe you cannot read?"

The man's face tightened instantly. "The *fuck*? You sayin' I can't read?"

Jet stood her ground. I gripped the cold edge of the water fountain. The stronger she looked, the more scared I became.

"You listen here." The man leaned back his head, and even from where I stood I could see his nostrils flaring. "My dad and my grandad and my fucking great-great grandad were here in Texas before you Scalers snuck in here with your drugs and babies and Mary idols."

He tore the yellow paper in half, then again in halves, and again before releasing the pieces like a magician. The fragments fluttered down and disappeared behind the counter. Jet thrust her fist along the counter, her forearm launching cartons of gum and cigarette lighters across the floor. I held my breath, wondering if she was going to pull his hair out, because that's what you'd expect from a tattooed girl with spiky hair and a black leather jacket and motorcycle boots.

The man stared at her in disbelief. "You're crazy." He picked up the receiver from a phone under the counter and waved it. "You'd best leave right now, before I report your ass for attempted robbery."

"What?"

"You heard me. Cops know you Scalers are all the same."

Jet turned and stared at me for a moment. Her eyes bore right through my chest, as if I weren't there. She shoved her fists into the pockets of her leather jacket, and I could see the tip of her gun barrel poking out against the seam. *Don't*, I said to her in my head. *Don't.* As if she'd heard me, she lifted her gaze and met my eyes.

"You better git," he called to her back. "Nine. One...."

I turned and hurried to the door, panicked by his threat. I couldn't go back to a police station. I knew what waited for me there.

Jet's body brushed against mine as we shoved out the door. The cowbell jangled as the door swung shut, and the man's voice followed us. "That's right. Y'all git. This is my land. Not yours."

Outside, Jet kicked the gravel and muttered curses on the man. I kicked the gravel, too, although I wanted to run.

"Did that guy steal your Aunt Juanita's money?"

"Yes." She stomped in a circle, the dust coating her boots.

"Where does she live?"

She glanced at me like she was deciding on how much information to give. Finally she said, "El Paso."

"That's a long way, right?"

She gave me another inscrutable look, and then said, "Come on. We cannot stay here."

She hadn't taken ten steps before she stopped in a beam of sunlight, as if blessed by some goddess, protector of travelers. I followed her gaze to the black, glossy motorcycle propped up by the men's restrooms.

As if I'd asked her a question, Jet gave me a firm nod. "I would say, yes, that bike is worth the money he stole from me."

It took her two seconds to find the key under the seat but she didn't start the motor. Instead, she began rolling the bike down the road, away from the station. I followed silently, thinking about the look on her face when he'd torn the money order up into little pieces.

After a while, she stopped and pulled the gun from her pocket, jamming it into her thigh holster before climbing onto the worn leather seat. She waited motionless for me to get on behind her.

I couldn't see her face when she said, "I will take you as far as Dallas. You can get lost in big cities like that. The good kind of lost."

Daw had made me promise not to go to Dallas. Big cities were places you ended up if you were rich or godless or homeless. But when you're running from the Texas Rangers because you shot your best friend, Dallas makes sense. But I didn't shoot her, did I? It was my gun that shot her. I was hungry and tired. My brain was fuzzy, and my memory darted from Maggie's limp fingers to Daw to the Gulf gas station and its steady supply of sour belts and gossip and you-can't-hide-from-Miss-Olsham. Dallas was a place to disappear.

But I already felt lost.

SEVEN

We didn't have motorcycle helmets, which was all the better because when you're flying down the highway, your hair is rippled feathers and your teeth are dry as a beak, and if you put your arms out, you feel like a bird.

"Are you crazy?" Jet turned her head and yelled at me. Her black cords of hair whipped across my cheek. "Hold on!"

I wrapped my hands around her waist again and tucked my head on her shoulder. The gun in her thigh holster had shimmied around and the weight of it pressed into my leg.

"Why don't we take the big highway?" I yelled over the wind.

"We would attract attention, especially without helmets."

"But nobody wears helmets."

"We are not nobodies."

She said something else, but I missed it in the wind that roared in my ears. After that, we didn't talk much. The baseball hat wouldn't stay on my head so I'd shoved it into the front of my shorts, pressed between us.

Highway 80 spread out before us like a lonely river, safe as long as we kept moving. Once, a police cruiser pulled up beside us, sirens blaring, and made me nearly jump off the seat. But it passed us and howled up the road toward some other fugitive. Afterward, every time a car passed us my chest tightened and I closed my eyes as if that would protect me, as if they couldn't see me, a killer, running from her crime.

After a while, the tall pines and evergreens slurring past made me drowsy. Twice I thought I was falling off the motorbike and caught myself drifting asleep. I jerked up my head and let go of my grip around Jet's waist only to grab her again even tighter, which sent our balance off kilter. Jet yelled something that the wind carried away. I rubbed my eyes on her leather jacket and started counting highway markers to keep myself awake.

My butt grew numb – the kind of numb accompanied by a thousand needle pricks. At some point, we pulled off the highway and rolled into a gas station. I jumped off the bike and stomped my feet to stop the stinging. Jet turned off the engine and stared at a white-haired man at the pump next to us. The old man wore a wrinkled shirt and a baseball cap. He fought with the pump handle until it caught the lock and stayed in place. Then he massaged his knuckles and looked over at us. The patch on his cap had a Republic flag with an AK-47 stretched across it.

Jet leaned back and whispered in my ear. "Go ask him for money."

"Why me?"

"He will not be scared of you."

I didn't want to beg for money, but Jet had got us the bike. It only seemed fair that I should at least try to get the gas. From the looks of the old man's wrinkled clothes and whiskers, he probably didn't have much more money than we did, which was nothing.

"Can I borrow a few dollars for gas?"

"Borrow?" he asked, giving me a once-over and then looking over my shoulder at Jet, who was standing by the motorbike. "You planning on paying me back?"

"No."

"Then why'd you say borrow? You mean give."

I felt sorry for his grandkids.

"Who's that?" He nodded. "She don't look like she's from here."

"Oh," I glanced back at Jet and thought fast. She turned to study the labels on the gas pump like they were magazines or something. "She's our maid."

"Maid?"

"Yeah. We're supposed to meet my dad in Dallas 'cause it's his weekend. But I forgot to get the gas money on the counter that Mom left me."

"Divorced, huh?"

I nodded and tried to look appropriately somber.

"Divorce ain't right in the eyes of God. Makes the whole country unstable. I suppose it ain't your fault, though. Where's your mom? She just let you run off?"

I hunched my shoulders, trying to come up with a place that wouldn't make him so angry. "Church."

He sniffed and put the nozzle shakily back in place. Then he dug around in his pockets and pulled out some coins and a few wadded-up bills that he poked at on his palm for another minute, like he was still deciding if I was worth a few quarters.

"That's all I can give you." He handed me two coins and two crumpled bills.

"Thank you so much. God bless you." I added that last part because it felt right, my mom being a church-goer. The old man slammed his door shut and pulled out of the station.

"Jesus," Jet said when I brought the money back. "You are a natural."

"Thank you. A natural what?"

"I'm your *maid*?" She unscrewed the gas cap and watched the old man's car disappear. "What kind of fucked-up racist shit is that?"

"What?"

"That story."

"I just made it up. I'm not racist." I was offended but also confused. I wasn't racist. I'd just said what I thought the man might want to hear.

Still, something hot spread over my skin, like a blanket of fever. I didn't say anything as she paid the clerk, filled the tank, and started the bike. I climbed on and barely touched her jacket until the droning highway lulled me against her back again.

At the edge of Rockwall, we pulled into a Granny's Table parking lot. I'd lost track of how long it had been since I'd had a meal. Days. When I smelled the cooking scents coming out of the kitchen, I didn't feel hungry. I felt empty.

"What if someone recognizes me?" I asked as I climbed off the bike.

"You think you are on the news? With a big reward or something?" Jet asked.

"Maybe. Maggie was the mayor's daughter."

Jet stopped smiling. "You will be in the news. Wear your hat."

I shoved the flattened baseball cap on my head as she opened the glass door of Granny's Table and the smell of bacon and eggs slapped us in the face. "Here is the thing." Jet pulled me toward the restrooms and lowered her voice. "If they are searching for you, we have to do something about your looks."

"Do you smell those eggs?" I looked back longingly. "They've still got a breakfast buffet."

"Focus," Jet ordered.

In the restroom – which smelled like grease and pee and chemical air freshener – Jet checked all the stalls. We were alone. She set her backpack on the counter, unzipped the side, pulled out a pocketknife, and pinched the blade out.

"Take off the cap."

"What's that for?" I asked.

"Disguise. They are looking for a girl with long hair."

I looked at the knife doubtfully. "You want to cut my hair with that?"

"I would use scissors but I lost them, along with the hair dryer and the expensive shampoo."

"Fine." I looked in the mirror at my hair, which hung just below my shoulders. It turned blonde in the summer and brown in the winter, so now it was an in-between September shade. I worried that cutting it wouldn't be enough. "If we're going to do it right, we should dye it a different color."

Jet rolled her eyes. "I will remember that the next time I help a fugitive."

She tugged hard at my scalp as she sawed with the knife but I said nothing. I just watched the long fistfuls of hair fall into the sink.

"Head up," Jet said, after a few minutes. I stared at my reflection, marveling at the weary, dirt-smudged, short-haired girl looking back at me. In my faded shorts and baggy shirt, I could have passed for a boy.

"You're good with that knife. Make it shorter." I held up my fingers and pinched them to an impossibly small gap. I wanted to chop away everything about me. "Real short."

"Okay. I cut mine off too, but not this short."

"How long was it?"

"Like a horse's mane. Down to my ass."

She held my hair tight to cut it closer at the scalp. I tried to imagine her straight, spiky hair as a blue-black mane, but I couldn't.

"Blue, I know I will regret asking you this, but where are you going? What is your plan?" she asked.

"California." I blurted it out before I had time to think about it. But as soon as I said it, I knew it was true.

"You will cross the border alone?"

"Sure."

Jet's brow furrowed. "You know there are border soldiers. With guns. And the wall is twenty feet high in some places. And do not forget the dogs. How will you get past them?"

"I'll do it when they're not looking."

"What is in California? Someone to help you?" Jet persisted.

"My mother." The words came out so naturally, it surprised me.

"Your mother. Does she know you are coming?"

"We have a plan." I didn't have a plan, of course, but it felt good to say I did.

Jet sawed away and after a few minutes most of my hair was on the floor or in the sink. Shaved nearly to my scalp, I didn't exactly look like a boy, but I didn't look like any girl I knew either. Given how short I was, she'd also shaved off about two years.

"I will take you as far as Dallas. No farther," Jet said and stuck the baseball cap back on my head. I leaned in to the mirror and wondered what Maggie would have said. She would have pulled her head back like a turtle, trying not to laugh. She'd have said, "Girl, there ain't nothin' my mom's makeup can do for you now."

"Put this on." Jet pulled a white T-shirt out of her bag and frowned at my boots. "Boys do not wear boots with shorts."

"You have jeans I can borrow?"

"No. Two of your chicken legs could fit into one leg of my jeans. We will fix it later."

We gathered up the hair on the floor and trashed it. Jet's face turned pale as she stood up, and she screwed up her mouth.

"Are you okay?" I asked.

"Yes, just standing up too fast." She slapped her hand to her mouth and made that sound I hated. The sound of old lemonade coming up into your throat and burning your nostrils, just before you threw up, and knowing that you're going to throw up, you swear you will never drink lemonade again. She stepped into a stall and retched into the toilet.

"Are you okay?" I asked again, my words already stupid and useless because of course she was not okay. She was throwing up.

She waved her hand at me and shut the stall door.

"It is okay. Just wait for me out there." And then she threw up again.

I covered my ears so I wouldn't hear the vomit splash into the toilet.

I didn't know what she could be throwing up. She hadn't eaten any more than I had.

In the dining room, the smell of Hot Breakfast All Day made me forget the misery in the restroom. I stood next to the buffet and stared at the metal trays of eggs and bacon and biscuits and gravy with lumps of sausage and grits and syrup and little pancakes, and I memorized the way they looked. Then I closed my eyes and inhaled, counting to five six seven, soaking up every last ounce of smell before letting it go.

"Smells good, huh?" A woman's voice punctured my food-dream. She was about fifty. Or sixty. Old enough to have a map of wrinkles around her eyes and lips. She had the voice of a thousand cigarette cartons, and like most people with throaty voices like that, her words were packaged in kindness.

I nodded.

She set her tray on the metal buffet and started spooning scrambled eggs onto her plastic plate. I thought I might faint.

"You getting the buffet?" she asked and took two, three, five slices of bacon from another metal bin. "This here bacon is the business. My business." She laughed and took more bacon with the tongs.

92

I looked around, first for Jet, and then for my imaginary family who had ordered a breakfast buffet and somehow had slipped out of view.

"Where's your plate?" she asked.

"I don't know," I finally mumbled.

"Here, take this." She held out her second, smaller plastic plate. "Take it. I can't eat both these plates without bustin' my gut. Although I usually aim to try."

I stood there not knowing whether to take the plate. My stomach answered for me with a loud gurgle, and I covered it in embarrassment. The old woman smiled and shook the plate, so I took it and stepped up to the buffet line.

"Thanks," I whispered.

I heaped scrambled eggs onto the little plate, and then balanced six bacon strips on top of the egg mountain, three for me and three for Jet. I looked at the restroom door in the corner, but she hadn't come out. The old woman seemed to have disappeared, too, so I carried my tower of eggs and bacon to the bar, closest to the television on the wall. It was barely audible over the people chatting and the clinking silverware, but I needed to see if my picture was on the news. If I was, Jet and I would have to sneak out fast, but at least we'd have a full stomach.

A news lady with white teeth and pink eyeshadow smiled at me behind her wide desk and said, "Now for the daily dissolutions. Linda?" Linda stood outside and stared blankly into the camera. She held her microphone with one hand, while the other shielded her face from the sunlight. Behind Linda was a gray cinder block wall, which the cameraman tracked upward and down to give us a sense of height. After a few seconds of silence, she smiled and said, "Yes, Candace. As you can see from the screen, today's number seven seems to be lucky indeed. Seven dissolutions today, seventy-seven for the year. We asked Deputy Chuck Sherman if seventy-seven dissolutions is indicative of a steady decline in border-related deaths. Deputy Sherman?"

The camera turned toward a man in a beige cowboy hat, and Linda repeated, "Seventy-seven dead this year. That's a pretty good number, right?"

"Yep. I think so." He cocked his hat up to his hairline. "I think Scalers are getting the message finally. 'Specially with the help of volunteer border militia. They got very good aim." He chuckled.

"Personally," the deputy continued, "I think the seven today is still too high, specially 'cause one was – they say he was eleven. It don't feel good to aim at a kid, no matter where they come from." The deputy's cheeks sagged on both sides, hound-dog-like, and he spoke even slower than we did in Blessing. "But it's pretty good considering."

"Scalers have been a real problem here on the eastern border, right?" Linda asked.

"Even more so than down south. I mean, down south we're protecting our border from the Mexicans scaling the Wall in. But up here, we got to worry about mules and cartels scaling out."

Linda nodded and said something I couldn't hear because a few people in the restaurant had begun to chant, "Scalers! Hook'em dead! Scalers! Hook'em dead!"

I leaned in to hear the deputy.

"—some are just impatient Republic citizens trying to cross over without paperwork 'cause of the delays, you know, down in

Houston. It's a real shame when we end up shooting our own. Borders guards've got feelings, too, and sometimes it's tough. When we encounter Scalers or anybody for that matter, we try to shoot to maim, not kill, but it don't always work out. But yeah, seventy-seven's not bad, not compared to last year."

"Thank you, Deputy Sherman. And thank you for keeping our Republic safe." Linda smiled and faced the camera again. "There you have it. Good news, live from Waskom, Texas. Back to you, Candace."

Candace said something about a festival fundraiser for Marshall Baptist Church, and then delivered news about an artists' colony in Austin that had taken over a condemned hospital downtown. The camera panned across a gray, vandalized building with windows like empty eye sockets. Laundry hung on thin ropes behind a woman who was pointing to a statue of a bird made out of old car parts. I leaned in and squinted at the art, but I was too late. The car-birds were replaced by Candace's face.

"For now, the Republic is allowing the artists to stay, as long as the crime rate stays low. It's not a stretch, though, to say that the police aren't excited about the Neighborhood, as it's called. Looks more like a haven for the homeless to me, Mack."

I looked down to see I'd eaten all the eggs on my plate. Most of the bacon, too. Jet still hadn't come out of the restroom, and an uneasiness fluttered in my stomach. I was about to refill the plate for Jet when the woman with the cigarette voice sat down beside me, her own plate full of pancakes and grits smothered in syrup.

"This is seconds. You getting seconds, too?" She winked at me and took a bite of pancake.

I nodded and looked at the TV, trying to avoid eye contact with her.

"I saw you sitting alone and thought '*that* one needs company.' I'm Suzanne. What's your name?"

I gave her a polite smile, but inside I felt the beginnings of panic set in. I almost forgot that I was a boy. I cleared my throat and spoke in the lowest voice I could muster. "I'm B...Billy."

"Billy?" She nodded and wiped her sticky hand on a napkin, then held it out to me like old people do.

I shook her hand, and she took in the whole dining room, like she was on guard.

"Nice to meet you, Billy. You're all alone?"

"No. My friend is in the restroom."

Suzanne nodded, but I could tell she didn't believe me. I added some non-maid details, hoping she'd go away and stop being concerned about me.

"She's like my babysitter, if I was a baby. Which I'm not. Of course." I needed to stop talking.

"Ah," she nodded. "I can see that."

I stuffed the last piece of bacon in my mouth and we both looked at the news lady on the TV.

"That's a shame about those dissolutions," Suzanne said. "I wish people would stop breaking the law and killing themselves."

I nodded, but kept my mouth shut.

"Oh my God," Suzanne said, pointing her fork at the TV. "I been following this story. Hush a sec, look."

I looked up, my heart racing, half-expecting to see my own face plastered across the screen. But it wasn't my face on the TV. It was Jet's. Her white-gleaming smile and beauty-pageant makeup made her almost unrecognizable. The camera widened to reveal the whole photograph of Jet, standing in a white gown that looked like a giant vanilla cupcake with lacy frosting, long black hair falling over her shoulders.

She's married? I thought, confused. But no. It was a birthday party. Two silvery balloons shaped like a one and a five floated behind her.

Candace's voice deepened and her eyebrows knit together as she described Jet's predicament, as if her disappearance were a personal tragedy.

"The search is still on for Julia Gonzales, sixteen-year-old runaway from Marshall. Distraught by her disappearance, her family is asking the Republic for help, saying she may be a danger to herself. Her uncle is a frequent donor to the Freedom Party and assures Channel 7 that they are here legally."

"Scalers!" the rowdy table yelled again.

"Shush your mouth!" Suzanne yelled back. "I'm trying to listen."

"At first," the news droned, "the authorities were looking east, but after tracing cell phone pings, they've now shifted their attention west. If you know the whereabouts of Julia, please call the hotline on the screen."

"Dear Jesus," Suzanne muttered. "Please protect that child and send her home safely." She eyed me and waved her fork at the photo of Jet, who smiled at us from her strange cupcake-dress photo. "I've been praying for that girl. I think she's been trafficked. I just know it in my gut. You know, you can always trust your gut. You aren't in school today?" Suzanne asked, switching topics abruptly.

I swallowed the lump of bacon at the back of my throat. "I have strep."

Suzanne nodded. "Most people with strep can't eat anything but soup. You on antibiotics?"

I nodded, glancing again at the closed bathroom door. I had to warn Jet before Suzanne spotted her.

On the TV, Jet's photo had disappeared, and Candace was talking about problems with tariffs and exports, which the news people complained about every night.

"You can't be too careful these days, Ben. It's Ben, right?" Suzanne asked.

I nodded, wishing her away.

"'Cause these drug and people traffickers, they don't care about us. And sad to say – and I'm not racist when I say this – but sad to say, those traffickers are mostly Mexicans and Asians. And Blacks. The Mexicans used to be good, hard workers. Decent people."

I looked at Suzanne, not sure what to say. She leaned over and lowered her voice.

"But they changed after the 'cession. You can't trust them, you know? The ones still here, all most of them care about is drugs. They're not like us." And here, she leaned in closer, so close that I could feel her breath on my ear.

"I know you're a girl, Ben," she whispered. "Or Billy. Or do you have a real name?"

I shrank a little into my shoulders, but she didn't back away.

"I can help you. You're all alone, aren't you? You got no money. Is someone trafficking you? I can call the police."

My heart was racing faster than I could breathe. I prayed that Jet would stay put – that she'd do anything but wander back into the dining room and collect me, because Jet was the one in danger now, not me.

In my heart, I'd thought Jet was illegal. But it sounded like her family was working with the police. Didn't that make them decent people? Scalers hid in the shadows and didn't ask the police for anything because they didn't want to go to jail.

I glanced at the restroom door for Jet again. I swiveled my whole body toward Suzanne and blurted something desperate. "Yeah, I'm not a boy. People are just always mistaking me, and I didn't want you to feel bad. But don't worry about me. If anybody tried to traffic me, I'd punch and scream."

"That's right." Suzanne pointed in my face. "Right in the balls. That's where it hurts. The balls."

"Right in the balls," I agreed.

"Good girl."

"And it's not my babysitter in the restroom," I revealed. "It's my sister."

"Your sister?"

I nodded. "Adopted. From South America."

"South America?"

"Yep." I kept nodding, unraveling the story as fast as it would come. "She looks different from me, and I just get ashamed sometimes because she looks so…different. You know, darker. And kids tease me, call me a Scaler, too."

Confused by my passionate confession, Suzanne said, "Oh, kids can be cruel."

"So sometimes I say she's my babysitter so people don't tease me. Suzanne, if you could pray for me to be nicer, and not so mean to my own adopted sister, I'd appreciate it."

Her eyes flashed with sympathy. "I certainly will pray for you. I'll put you right on the prayer chain. What is your real name, dear?"

"Elizabeth."

"That was John the Baptist's mother. That's a nice name."

"Thank you."

I asked Suzanne if I could trouble her for a small apple juice, which made her even happier than the prayer chain. As soon as she turned the corner toward the cash registers, I ran as fast as I could to the restroom.

I pushed the door just as Jet was pulling it open, and she grinned when I almost fell on her. But then she saw my wild face and her grin disappeared.

"Jet! We have to git, now! Now!"

I yanked her hand and dragged her out the side exit.

"What happened?" she asked as we ran to the motorcycle.

"Give me your cell phone," I demanded.

"Why?"

"They're tracking it. It was on the news. They're coming for you."

She pulled an old cell phone from her jacket, threw it against the brick wall with all her strength, and jumped on the motorcycle and revved the engine.

I gripped the ball cap in my hands and buried my head in her back, ready to fly away.

EIGHT

We arrived in Dallas just before the sun set. We couldn't risk riding on the highways, so we took the smaller roads all the way. Sometimes Jet would slow down and point at a pretty house with a perfect green lawn or I'd point at one with purple shutters and we'd grin. The neighborhoods changed from matchbox houses near the lake, to mansions with chimneys and gas lights, to rotted-out houses near rusty cars on cinder blocks, to clean red-brick townhouses, row after row, like something out of a picture book. Then the city's tall-tall buildings, and everything all lit up in greens and reds and twinkling whites – it was enough to catch my breath. I leaned my head back to take in the dizzy buildings that scraped the purple sky.

"Pretty, huh?" Jet said at a red light.

I nodded and felt a shiver ripple down my skin. How could Daw have ever hated this place?

Here I was and nobody had spit on me yet. But I was about to be on my own here. What next? My stomach clenched. I needed food and a place to sleep – and to figure it all out fast because this was the end of the road as far as Jet was concerned. She'd made good on her promise of bringing me to Dallas.

"Where are we going now?" I asked. But the wind was rushing and she couldn't hear.

We pulled into a dirt lot underneath a maze of bridges that separated the skyscrapers downtown from smaller buildings. Jet killed the engine, and we both climbed off and shook the buzz from our legs. People huddled under the highway in groups. I knew right away they were homeless from their clothes. I kept my eyes peeled for "brim full of crazy," like Daw said, but all I saw were people shuffling around after a long day.

Everything about them was scruffy. In a way, I liked it. The way they hovered around a trash barrel that breathed fire. The way they put their tents up in little rows facing each other. The way they talked too loud and laughed too loud and let their dogs run free.

"Stay here for a minute," Jet said. Then she walked over to a group of people sitting on lawn chairs in front of a blue tarp. I couldn't hear them – could barely see them in the dark – but I knew Jet was talking about me because they all leaned out and gave me a once over. Jet waved to get my attention.

"Bring the bike," she called.

I heeled the kickstand and walked the bike up. Three men and an old lady nodded at me. I'd never seen a real live homeless person this close before, but I wasn't scared because Jet was armed, and people tend to respect each other when everyone's armed. They seemed friendly.

"Hi," I said.

"Good evening," the old lady said. She grinned, and even in the dark I could tell some of her teeth were missing. "What's your name?"

I glanced at Jet. Was I a boy or a girl now? Jet just bugged her eyes to make me speak, so I chose a safe one.

"Chris."

I stretched out my hand and the lady gave me a bony handshake.

"Nice to meet you." Then she turned to Jet and said, "If you go on down there, over by that second bridge column, there's a man named Scooter should be there. Ask him."

"Sorry, we ain't got nothing left," one of the men added. He wore a thick beanie on this head and spoke through a silver beard. "But hey, I got a mint. You like mint?"

He fished in his jean pockets and pulled out a peppermint. When he handed it to me, it was still warm in the wrapper.

"Thank you, sir."

I popped it in my mouth, and Jet and I walked the bike toward the columns that held up the bridges above us.

"What were you looking for?" I said.

"Food. Are you not hungry?"

"Yeah, but they're homeless."

"So are we," Jet said. "And they eat whether they have a home or not. The homeless people I have met – the ones who live in groups like this – they are usually nicer than people who live in mansions."

We walked past crowds of strangers, huddled around makeshift fires. Past a few scary ones who paced and grabbed their hair or rocked back and forth or yelled at other people or themselves. Past quiet ones sitting cross-legged. A few dogs curled up on blankets.

Gunfire ricocheted around the city streets – *rat-a-tat-tat* – something automatic, like a machine gun. It reminded me of the Hawley's firing range in Blessing. Someone was playing music, but you could hardly hear it with the roar of the cars above us.

I smelled the hot dogs before I saw them.

It was Scooter who was cooking up wieners on hangers over a fire can. A big man with an army jacket and a beard, he was standing alone there like a hot dog king. Jet introduced herself as Cher and I said I was Chris. Sure enough, Scooter gave us two hot dogs. Jet was right. They were nice.

We finished the food in seconds. I licked my fingers, wishing for more.

"You know someone who might want to buy this bike?" Jet asked when we finished.

"How much you selling it for?"

"A hundred dollars."

I shook my head. Nobody here had that much money.

Scooter stroked his beard and looked at the bike, then at me and Jet, then back to the bike again.

"Is it hot?"

Jet didn't blink. "It is ours, fair and square."

"Hundred's too much. I'll give you fifty."

"Seventy-five," she countered.

Scooter looked at me.

"It's a real good bike," I said. "We rode here all the way from—"

"Seventy." Jet nudged me to hush up. "Final offer."

"Well." He squinted at the bike, then looked at the people all around us. He lowered his voice so the others couldn't hear. "I just got sixty." He pulled the money from his pocket and carefully peeled the bills open. I was surprised at how straight and unwrinkled they were. He handled the money delicately, like butterfly wings.

He counted out sixty and handed the stack to Jet. He had a few more bills in his hand, but we didn't say anything. Jet gave him the keys and the bike. He leaned over and whispered to Jet, but I heard him.

"How much for the kid?"

"What?" Jet asked.

"The boy. How much?"

My heart lurched.

She glared at him. "The boy is not for sale. Sick bastard."

Scooter rubbed his chin and sniffed. "All right. Don't get your hackles up. I wasn't serious anyway."

Jet took my elbow and we hurried out of the maze of tents and plastic lawn chairs. We crossed the street and sat on the curb facing the homeless camp.

"Here," Jet said, handing me thirty dollars.

"Thanks." I folded the bills into my fist.

Jet frowned at me. "I was going to leave you here, but now I am not sure. It is not safe. But I do not know where to leave you."

Hope leapt in my heart and I scrambled for good reasons to stick together. "We could help each other. I *know* you're running from something, even though you won't tell me. And you know I'm running. We should look out for each other. Anyway, people are looking for Julia and Bluebonnet, not Cher and Chris."

Jet fixed me with a look. "How do you know my name?"

"Because it was on the TV back at the restaurant."

She took a deep breath and looked away. "Do not call me that name. Ever."

"Okay," I said.

"Julia was another girl. She let other people push her around. I am Jet now. Anyway, how could you help me?"

"What?"

"You said we could help each other."

"Well…" I searched for a convincing argument. "You might not fit in places. You got an accent that might raise questions. If a stranger stops us, we could pretend you can't speak, and I could talk for you. And if you weren't offended so easy, I could keep saying you're my babysitter, 'cause that's what a lot of Mexicans do here. That'd work good."

"Do you mean that would work *well*? And by Mexicans, do you mean Hispanics? Because not every brown person you see is from Mexico."

I had offended her again without meaning to.

Her eyes blazed. "Blue, I have never stepped inside a Texan school, and I know how to speak English better than most of you."

I hesitated before telling her the simple truth. "That may be so. But you still have an accent. And people will notice."

"Yes," she said bitterly. "Nothing is fair here, is it?"

"Can't we just keep pretending we're what other people think we are until we get to the border? It could protect both of us."

She studied the homeless encampment, the crackling barrel fires and the murmuring people, and then replied as if I hadn't spoken. "I will show you where the bus station is. You can catch a bus west. The lady gave me directions."

I nodded because that was better than sleeping under the bridge. At least on a bus, I'd be going somewhere. And I'd have a place to sleep for a few hours.

Across the street, two men in black uniforms approached the old lady and her friends under the blue tarp. They had to be city cops. Rangers wore beige cowboy hats. They handed the lady a sheet of paper, which she glanced at and shook her head.

I nudged Jet and whispered. "Look straight ahead. Under the blue tarp."

The old lady talking to the cops pointed to her right, the opposite direction of Scooter. The police strode away, hands ready on their holsters. The old lady watched them leave, then turned her head and looked our way. I couldn't see her eyes from so far away.

"She looking at us?"

"I think so." Jet's voice had grown cautious.

The old lady lifted her hand slightly and flicked her fingers. *Go*, the gesture said. *Quick*.

We hurried away along the darker edge of the sidewalk, putting as much space as possible between us and the cops. In the deep shadows, we cut an arc around two men fist-fighting like real men, as Daw would say, and a woman begging them to stop. We took the long way, I suspect, to the bus station, which turned out to be only a few blocks from where we'd started.

"Give me your money," Jet said when we got inside, and when I gave her the cash, "Stay here."

As she walked away, I leaned against the back wall. Were those cops looking for me or for Jet? Across the big room, she approached the clerk and leaned in with her questions. I had questions, too. What the heck was I doing here? What would I do when Jet left? I didn't want to be alone in Dallas.

Jet turned away from the clerk and jogged toward me with a smile.

"Let's go!" She pushed open a nearby door and raced through.

I ran to catch up.

"Where are we going?"

"Bus! It is leaving now! We have to catch it." She waved two tickets and hesitated at the line of busses, scanning their lit numbers above the windshields.

A surge of happiness spread across my chest. We were going together. I wouldn't be alone. Not yet. But I also wouldn't see Dallas. And I was disappointed by that.

Jet waved at a bus that had already begun to pull away from the curb.

"Hey!" she hollered and waved the tickets. "Hey! Hey! Wait!" The brakes squealed and the driver opened the door. We climbed in, sweaty and tired. The driver didn't even glance at our faces. One less person to recognize us.

We sat in the back row where the seats were taller. The bus wasn't even half full, which gave us more room to stretch out and sleep if we wanted. I slouched down low and propped my feet on the velvety seatback in front of me. Jet kicked her feet up, too.

The bus pulled out into the street, and the night closed around it. I felt strangely safe.

I rolled my head so I could see Jet. "Thanks," I said.

She shrugged, like it was no big deal. "I could not just leave you there. With men like Scooter. It was not safe."

"Can I ask you a question?" I whispered.

She turned to me. Our faces were inches apart in the quiet privacy of the back row. "Sure."

"Are you a Scaler?"

She took a breath and let it out slowly. There was disappointment in her eyes. "You should not use that word, Blue. It is not nice."

"Sorry."

"No, I did not climb the Wall. My mother brought me here when I was nine. I did not have a choice, but she did not have a choice either. She needed money. A job. And my uncle was already here, so he helped us past the border."

"So you *are* an Illegal?"

Her eyes widened in the darkness. "I am a person."

"I know. I just want you to know that I don't care who you are. Or who your family is. I'm not going to tell anyone. I'm not racist. I'm your friend."

She was quiet for a moment. And then, like she'd made a decision, she answered. "Thanks."

I'd so needed her to believe me. I almost collapsed against her when she did. The wheels whirred and lulled us into a kind of daze. I folded my legs up on the seat cushion and let the vibrations rock me. The interior lights flicked off, and the whole bus was as quiet as sleep.

A gurgling thrum of motorcycles pulled up beside us. Everyone's heads popped up, and murmurs filled the bus. Jet and I watched the gang, some thirty bikes, many of them doubled up with riders hooting and howling in the night and pumping their guns in the air. It was as though the air itself shook and vibrated down to my lungs. My blood rose up my scalp, my whole body charged with electricity.

"Is it Mother?" I asked Jet.

"Shhh." Jet pulled me down lower in the seat.

As the bus slowed, the passengers started to panic.

"Go!" they yelled at the driver. "Drive! Run 'em over!"

"Get us the hell out of here!" an elderly lady shouted.

I imagined that everyone had their guns drawn, even the old lady. But nobody wanted to shoot first. You'd have to be crazy to shoot first. They had us surrounded, with semi-automatics that would rip right through the metal and glass.

The bus punched forward a few times as the bus driver tried to exit the highway, but the gang's bikes kept thundering around us, and the longer they kept at it, the more fun they seemed to be having. They were laughing and hollering and slinging curses. Drunk, maybe.

I stretched up to get a better look, but the bus braked again, and I ducked at the movement. The driver seemed to find a weakness in their shindig because somehow we lurched onto a ramp and sped off quick.

The entire busload erupted in claps and cheers and too-late threats. "Lucky bastards," an old man shouted. "I would've shot them all to hell." Someone else said, "I shoot to kill."

Jet wasn't looking so good. She didn't even look relieved.

"We're okay. They're gone," I said. After a few minutes, when she still hadn't spoken, I noticed her set mouth and blank eyes. "You look pale. Are you going to be sick again?"

"No." She sighed. "I'm pregnant."

"What? Oh my gosh, you're going to have a baby?" I loved babies. Their tiny fingers, their peach-fuzz heads that smelled like fresh dough. It wasn't unusual for girls to get pregnant in high school, but not having friends I hardly ever got to see a baby. They were like forbidden treasures.

Jet gave me an empty look and scooted down in the seat. "Stop. I do not want it."

"Don't want what? The baby? Why not?"

She looked away. "Because of all the reasons, Blue. There are too many."

"When you see it, you'll change your mind," I said, confidently.

"No," Jet said. "I am going to have it finished. That is why I need to go to the border."

"You mean an *abortion*?" I whispered the word, shocked. "That's illegal."

"I don't care."

I was horrified. "But you can't. Can you? You'd go to jail. Or…"

I didn't finish the sentence. But I didn't have to. Everyone knew the punishment for abortion in the Republic was death.

She still wasn't looking at me. "I can do it in New Mexico."

Suddenly, it all made sense. I looked out the window at the city lights and cars in the darkness. Jet had a baby inside her, a teeny tiny thing, and she just wanted to wash it down the toilet. Mothers were supposed to protect their babies, even the tiniest ones. In school, they called abortion murder of the worst kind. And she wanted to do that.

Everything blurred. I had tears in my eyes and I didn't know why.

"Can't you just have it and give it away?" I heard myself ask. "Maybe to someone who can't have their own baby?"

She didn't answer. I wouldn't give up. "Jet, it's murder."

The word had edges that hurt.

She looked at me again. Her eyebrows were knit up, wounded.

"Thank you, Blue. I feel much better now that you have explained that to me."

I didn't say anything after that. I just turned to the window and watched the world turn black until I fell asleep to the whir of the highway.

Maggie dug a hole in the mulch with the toe of her shoe. We were on the swings in the park near the elementary.

"How come you don't have other friends?" she asked.

"I don't know," I said. I wound up my swing and let the links twist and groan.

"Maybe you don't try hard enough."

"I don't want to try. Have you seen the way they are? They're not nice, Maggie."

"They seem nice enough to me."

"That's because you're rich and pretty. I mean, shit. If your dad was the town's drunk deputy who couldn't keep the lights on in his own house, they wouldn't be so nice to you."

"You shouldn't use curse words."

"Why?"

"'Cause." She shrugged. "I don't like cursing is all."

"Sorry."

"It's okay. You don't have a mom to teach you how to be a lady."

I gave her my I'm-going-to-punch-you look. She gave me her You-know-I'm-too-pretty-to-punch look. Then we both cracked up and let our swings go, spinning the sky round and round.

★

Jet's body flopped down on the seat cushions and jogged me awake. Maggie wasn't alive anymore. I was on the run. Jet cupped her hand over her mouth and took a whiff. "Gross," she muttered.

"Are you okay?" I asked.

"I just threw up. It is the bus moving. Do not go to the toilet."

"Car sick?"

"Stupid morning sick—" She clapped her palm over her stomach and grimaced.

I rubbed my eyes. "It's not morning yet. The baby must be confused."

Jet looked out the window.

"What time is it?" I asked.

"I do not know. We fell asleep."

It was dark outside the window. No more blur of city lights. We were in the countryside again. Everything around us was flat and barren.

"How long does it take to get to El Paso?" I asked.

"A long time. Go back to sleep. When you wake up, we will be close."

I bundled my backpack into a lumpy pillow and stretched out on the velvety seat. My head nearly hung off the edge. I stared down the aisle at yellow lights on the floor. At people's feet sticking out. The vibrating seat in front of me. The road and the bus engine roared in my ear. I looked down to the end of the yellow lights, at the bus driver's door handle. The EXIT sign. And at the very top, words that scrolled across a screen in lights. Waco. Temple. Pflugerville.

"Jet, where's Pflugerville?"

"Shhh. I am asleep."

I had too many questions – about the border crossing, about dogs and machine guns and the next bus and the bus after that – and no one could answer them anyway. I stared at the orange letters until they blurred into my sleep.

"Wake up," Jet said.

I rolled over. Jet's hand was on my shoulder, her face so close to mine that I smelled bubble gum on her breath.

"What? Are we there?"

"No. It is a nightmare. We are on the wrong bus."

I looked toward the front of the bus. "Austin?"

"Yes. How did you know?"

I pointed to the orange letters scrolling above the driver.

For the first time since I'd met her, Jet looked shaken. Like she'd lost her map of options. She leaned back into the seat and hunched her shoulders and for a second, I thought she might cry.

Everyone else made sleeping noises over the whir of the engine.

"Maybe we can ask the driver."

Jet shook her head. "I spoke to him already. We are going to Austin, and there is no way to turn around."

"Maybe we can buy another ticket in Austin to El Paso."

"With what money? I am so stupid." She heaved a sigh, and her throat hitched as she spoke. "I should have been more careful. There is *nothing* in Austin."

I looked out the window at the black shadow-trees scrolling past us. The moon was a fingernail floating in the sky. I couldn't tell what direction we were going. I didn't know if Austin was north or south.

"Austin," I mumbled. "Jet, remember when we were at Granny's Table and I saw you on the news?"

"Shhh."

I lowered my voice. "There was this other thing on the news. There's a group of people, like artists and poor people, who all live together in an old hospital. An empty hospital. It's like a free hotel. They just took over the rooms, but they also made the whole place into a little village. They call it The Neighborhood. They have a restaurant and a store. And the artists make stuff and sell it, which is exactly what I want to do when I grow up. And I think I saw a big garden that everybody has to help with."

"They are squatters?"

I shrugged. "The mayor said they can stay until the building comes down, as long as the police don't have to come out and deal with crime. It looks cool, and they probably have a jillion rooms there."

"Where is it?"

"Somewhere in Austin. It's an old hospital – it can't be that hard to find. And we'll have a place to stay 'cause they're not going to tear it down for six months – that's what the lady on TV said."

"I do not have six months."

"Right. Well maybe somebody there can help us. That's something, right?"

"Maybe...that is something." She sighed.

I reached over to pat her, and my hand landed on her stomach. I patted it twice before she lifted my hand between her fingers like a mechanical crane and moved it back to my seat.

After that we didn't talk for a while – each of us lost in our own worried thoughts. I had just drifted off to sleep when the bus pulled into a gas station. The bright lights of the parking lot stirred everyone awake. By the time the bus groaned to a stop in front of a Waffle King, half the people on the bus were standing.

The driver stood up and his voice crackled through the speakers. "This is a pit stop. We're not far from Austin, but if you want to stretch your legs while I refuel, go on and do it. There's coffee at the Waffle King. If you want to surprise your devoted bus driver, I take two creams, one sugar."

Someone laughed, another person groaned, but everyone got off.

Jet and I were the last. We didn't have any money for food or drinks, but Jet said she'd rather vomit in the Waffle King than the bus toilet.

"You okay?" the driver said as we passed. He had a round belly and a white mustache and looked like somebody's grandpa.

116

"We're fine," I said. "She's just bus sick, but we're meeting my great aunt in Austin – Aunt Bea – and she'll help us to get back on the right bus. I just love Aunt Bea."

Jet tugged me off the bus. "Too much, Blue. You do not always have to make up stories."

"But he was suspicious."

"He asked if we were okay. That is not suspicion."

"Well now he knows we're okay, too."

"Girls!" The bus driver limped after us, waving his hand in the air. "Wait!"

I froze, though my brain told me to run instead. He had money in his hand.

"Here." He gave Jet a five. "Go get yourself a ginger ale. It'll settle your stomach."

Jet kept her head down. "Thank you."

"And your Aunt Bea?" He looked from me to Jet and back to me. "Well, in case she doesn't show up or, you know, well…" He pulled his wallet from his front pocket and fingered through the cash. "I'd feel better if you took this." He paused, then held out a handful of bills – everything in his wallet. His hands trembled.

"What?" Jet's eyes widen in shock. My mouth dropped open. We were like two fish gasping for air.

The old grandpa thrust the money at us again. I took it, hesitantly.

"You two were heading to El Paso. That might help you get back on track."

"Thank you," I said. "It will help a lot."

He nodded, turned around, and walked back to the bus. We marveled at the cash in my hands, at his kindness that seemed almost reckless, and we hurried into the Waffle King. I longed for food, but we ordered two coffees to go from the bar. Jet ordered a third – two creams, one sugar – for the bus driver, and then we stood at the plate glass windowfront while we emptied more packets of sugar and cream into our styrofoam cups. I stirred the cream around, releasing the heat so I could take a sip.

"How much money do we have?" Jet asked.

I pulled the wad of bills and change from my pocket. I'd seen some twenties when I paid for the coffees, but I didn't want to attract attention, so I'd stuffed the money back in my pocket quick. Now, we huddled over the mound of money as we counted and smoothed out the bills.

"Seventy-two dollars and eighty-four cents," I said.

Jet looked at the money in disbelief. She didn't trust men or free money. I stacked the bills and coins into a single tower.

"Is it enough? For the bus tickets?"

"I do not know. We will find out in Austin."

"And if we don't, maybe the artists will help us."

"What artists?"

"At the Neighborhood. You know."

Jet raised her eyebrows and took a sip of coffee. "Maybe."

"I'm an artist. I could draw you if I had good pencils. I'm pretty good. You want me to draw you?"

"Sure," she said absently as she unstacked the coins into smaller stacks.

"That was real nice of that bus driver."

Through the window, I spotted Grandpa fussing over the gas pump. He'd driven the bus to the far end of the parking lot where the pumps were wider for big rigs. Now he leaned in to read the numbers on the pump screen, played with the pump handle, wiped at a window smudge on the bus behind him. He was like a bird on an elephant, picking off insects and keeping things just so.

Half of the people were shuffling out of the Waffle King, Styrofoam cups and small white bags in their hands, toward the bus.

"Let's go," Jet sighed.

But as I scooped up the money and Jet pressed the cap on her coffee, an ominous rumble in the parking lot caught our attention. And then froze us in our tracks.

Outside the plate glass window, a wave of motorcycles had begun to descend on the truck stop. I don't know how it happened – how it could be silent and calm one minute and then all at once, a thousand drums thrumming in your ears. The engines backfired and rumbled and grunted. Bikers circled the lot like wasps, like they were trying to figure out what this place was and who was in charge. Their bandanas zipping by in greens and yellows.

I heard myself say, "They're back."

The passengers who'd already wandered back toward the bus were now screaming and backtracking to the gas station or toward the Waffle King. Our grandpa driver, still standing at the gas pump, looked around, confused, but didn't move. His hand froze on his holstered gun. In the commotion, everything slowed down. He stood like a statue beside the bus as the motorcycles closed in.

Run, I pleaded silently as I watched him lift his hands. Then his head jerked back and slammed against the side of the bus a half-second before the *bang* of gunfire echoed across the pavement. Grandpa's body slunk down and met the pavement. Jet flinched back from the window and grabbed my arm, but we didn't run. We just stared in horror as though the driver's bowed body had frozen the whole world for a second.

In an instant, gunfire was everywhere. People didn't run fast enough. As the motorcycles circled, they began to fall. *Rat-a-tat, rat-a-tat.* An old lady in a pink shirt fell face down near the gas pumps. A man wearing a red cap grabbed his leg and dragged it a few steps toward the Waffle King before falling. But the bikers were falling, too. They were shooting at each other, and the bus people were shooting at the bikers. Muzzle flashes glinted from all sides, sending shock waves against the glass.

"Get down!" someone shouted from the kitchen.

Everything happened in a matter of seconds, but the details fell like water droplets, magnifying everything. Styrofoam coffee cups strewn across the parking lot, white leaves in the darkness. A woman in a leather vest falling off the back of a motorcycle, bouncing off the pavement and then lying still. A car screeching away with the pump handle still inside, gas spewing out behind it. Two bikers shooting each other right off their bikes, their bodies collapsing in tandem.

Someone turned off the lights in the Waffle King just as Jet and I dropped to the floor. It was a battlefield outside. Shotguns, semi-automatics, motorcycle engines, and screams. Inside the Waffle King, people hunched in their booths mumbling curses and shushing each other, their weapons at the ready but no one to shoot.

Outside, a barrel-chested man in a leather jacket and red bandana dragged himself on his knees toward the front door. There was blood on his hands, and bright red swaths of it in his matted gray hair and beard.

His gruff voice came right through the windows. "Help me. For God's sake. Help me!"

But another biker got to him before he could reach the building, circling him like a vulture. A green bandana flapped like a flag from his handle. The engine revved and taunted the wounded man, who'd ducked his head under his forearms.

"Back up!" Jet pulled my backpack, and I scooted back with her away from the glass.

We crawled across the floor until we reached the cash register, then around behind the serving counter. In the chaos, a waitress had bolted the glass door even though more people were scrambling toward us to be let in. But all that glass wouldn't protect us for long.

"The back," Jet hissed in my ear. "Kitchen!"

I followed her on my knees, sliding across the greasy kitchen floor.

"Where are we going?" I whispered.

Rising to her feet, she pointed ahead to a solid door with a small "Manager" sign.

When we reached it, though, the handle wouldn't turn. Behind us we could hear bursts of gunfire and the first faint sound of sirens in the distance.

"I can't get the door open," I said, panicking.

Pushing me aside, Jet tried the handle. "Locked."

We stood at the door and knocked, begging through the crack, hoping someone was on the other side.

A loud *boom* shook the room behind us, followed by sounds of shattered glass and screams.

"Do you have your gun?" I asked Jet, but she ignored me and pounded her fist on the door, pleading, "Please."

"Open the damn door!" I said, pressing my lips against the door. "I got a pregnant lady out here."

I don't know where my plea came from. Maybe from an old movie I'd seen, but it did the trick. A second later, the handle turned and the door cracked open to reveal a brightly lit room. We scrambled through, and a bald man locked the door behind us.

Inside, three other people were already huddled in the corner of the small, windowless office. All wore Waffle King uniforms. The wheeled chair in the office sat empty. I turned to the bald man, who wiped his sweaty forehead with his tie.

"There's another waitress out there," I said.

"Jennie?" He gave the others in the corner a grave look.

"What if other people want in?" I asked. *What if we let in the bad guys by accident?* I shivered and braced my own spinning thoughts.

He didn't answer. His attention was on Jet. "You the pregnant one?"

Jet glanced at me. "Yes."

"Well," he sighed. "Leastways, I saved a baby. With all this bloodshed, least I saved a baby."

He glued his ear to the door, but we could all hear the gunfire from where we sat. The distant shots like punctured balloons, the closer ones a shock of *booms* that rattled our bones.

"It's Mother, ain't it, Mr. Johnson?" a young waitress in the corner asked.

Mr. Johnson hushed her.

"More'n that," the guy in a white apron said. He couldn't be much older than Jet. He held a waitress in his arms, but seemed to be clinging to her rather than the other way around. "It's like two gangs. Or three."

"I saw them shooting each other," I whispered. "Maybe they're not after us."

The waitress sobbed. "They kill anyone who's in the way. They kill for fun."

"Shhh!" Mr. Johnson spat.

"Shut it, Donald," the other waitress said. "You can't boss us around now. We're in a god-damned siege. She's just scared is all."

"I'm the manager. You're still on the clock, Arnetta. So all of you *shut up* so we don't get shot."

Arnetta squinted at him in disgust.

I looked down at the pistol in the manager's belt. "You have a gun."

"It's not loaded," he hissed.

I looked at the others huddled together. They shook their heads no.

"Doesn't anybody have a working weapon?" I whispered.

"Don't judge us," Arnetta growled at me. "Lots of people carry guns, but cheap ammo ain't easy to come by." She nodded at Jet, who was staring at her own hands. "What about her? She don't talk much."

The manager turned to Arnetta. "That's because we're hiding! She knows how to hide. Shut. Up!"

After that we all shut up and our silence made the sounds outside even worse. The gunfire was more sporadic now and came in short bursts of three or four. People from the bus, the ones we'd seen cowering in their seats, were whimpering. Suddenly, someone pounded on the manager's door with a frantic but muted cry. The manager put his finger to his lips and shot his other hand out to us in warning. The pounding stopped. A few seconds later, the sound of shattering glass, followed by a flurry of gunshots and guttural screams.

Each time we thought the gunfire outside had stopped, another burst rang out. Finally, though, we heard sirens growing into a glorious chorus.

The manager turned to us, wild hope in his eyes. "At last! Police."

The sirens, one upon another, were just outside.

"Oh please," the young waitress whispered.

The popping gunfire stopped, replaced by a staticky official voice through a megaphone. "Cease your fire!" someone shouted over and over. "Cease your fire! Cease your fire!"

I'd heard rumors that cops wouldn't stop bikers if they might be members of Mother. If you so much as thought about Mother, you'd wake up and find your tires shot and your car on fire, even if you were a cop. They just let them roll on by, as long as they weren't causing any trouble. And now the cops were using megaphones to stop a gang battle.

"Never!" another man's voice boomed, and I jumped. He wasn't on a megaphone. He was in the Waffle King, not twenty feet away from us. In response, another round of automatic gunfire, louder this time. It sounded like it was just outside the office door.

We threw ourselves to the floor. I looked at Jet, who shook her head. *Wait*, her expression told me.

The younger waitress whimpered, and the cook clamped his hand over her mouth.

Then silence. We waited, holding our breath. Jet's hand found mine, and I squeezed it. And then, someone's footsteps on the other side, slow and methodical. In the quiet, we all heard it. The cracking of glass underfoot.

I searched Jet's face, and her eyes searched mine.

The door handle turned and moved slightly toward us until it bumped against the lock.

"It's the police. They're here to save us!" Mr. Johnson scrambled up. "Don't shoot!" he called as he scrambled up, turned the bolt, and swung open the door.

Jet jumped to her feet to stop him but it was too late.

"Don't shoot!" he said again, flinging his arms up in the air like a kid.

Outside stood a man in a green bandana, pointing a rifle at Mr. Johnson's chest.

Two shots cracked the air within moments of each other. The first, a split second after Mr. Johnson opened the door. The force of it sent him stumbling two steps back where he collapsed on Jet's boots. I jumped up to pull her back just as the man in the green bandana turned his gun on her.

He met her eyes and I saw something in his face. Something like recognition. He half-laughed, half-grunted, like he'd just figured out something.

The second gunshot popped like a fire-cracker right through the bandana-man's left eye, splattering us with his blood. The man dropped, a grin frozen on his face. The cook screamed, and now two dead bodies were heaped on the floor of the tiny office.

"Shit," Jet whispered, wrestling her foot from under Mr. Johnson's weight. She nudged the lifeless body away with her boot. In her hand, her gun trembled.

A cop in a black uniform ran toward the office, his rifle raised. "Hands in the air! Hands in the air!"

The waitress screamed, "Don't kill me! Don't kill me!" In the confusion, I grabbed Jet's gun from her and shoved it into her back waistband in a swift movement before throwing my own hands up. She gave me a startled look as she slowly lifted her hands.

We scrambled over the two dead men as the cop kept shouting, "Hands on your head! Hands on your head!" His rifle motioned us toward the front of the Waffle King.

I hopscotched over the broken glass and clamped my hands hard behind my head.

Outside, the night was lit up in red and blue flashes from the police cruisers parked crisscross on the pavement. "Single file! Stay in line!" someone yelled at us as we scurried out into the lot and past upended motorcycles and burly men, handcuffed and splayed out on the ground.

Slowly, other survivors joined us – or we joined them – all of us in a row with our elbows sticking out.

Paramedics lifted a body onto a stretcher. In the distance, more sirens howled. The temperature seemed to have dropped ten degrees – either that, or it was fear that chilled me. Someone here was bound to recognize us.

I tucked my chin to my chest to hide my face.

Behind me, Jet whispered, "We have to get away. First chance, run. We'll meet up."

Even as she said it, though, another crowd of police cars swarmed the lot. Different paint, different forces, but all lit up with swirling lights and sirens. A black pickup truck with a yellow star emblazoned on the door came to a stop a few feet from us, and then I saw the word RANGERS across the side.

Shivering, I folded my elbows together and peeked from beneath them, half-expecting Ranger Kern to step out and point at me.

But a sudden barrage of shots echoed from the gas station next door. The police raced toward the noise. In the frenzy of police cars and sirens and bullhorn commands and whimpering people, Jet shoved my shoulder. "Now!"

She darted around the shadowed corner of the Waffle King into the darkness beyond. I tried to follow, but another police cruiser pulled up, cutting me off. I ducked and turned, my elbows still guarding my head.

"This way! Hands on your head!" a man in black gear yelled. I followed the survivors' line past the dead and the wounded, past a cruiser and a host of flashing blue lights, and across the darkened gas station parking lot. The overhead lights had been shot out and it was hard to see where we were going.

The survivors' line was bunching up as more people shoved their way in. When we reached the empty bus, I found my opportunity. I skirted around the bus and slipped under the front wheel, belly to the ground. Feet shuffled by – untied laces, barefoot women who had abandoned their heels to run faster, but were now limping across glass and plastic shards. I looked over my other shoulder and scooted down toward the center of the bus, then wiped my graveled palms on my cut-offs. There, a few feet from my boots, was the bus driver's body. He had slumped onto the pavement, and I could just glimpse the back of his white hair from my position.

"Thank you," I whispered to the kind man, and closed my eyes to give him two seconds of respect. Then I steeled myself. Now was not the time to cry. I waited a minute or two until a new ambulance pulled up, then scrambled out from under the bus and sprinted across the darkened lot to the line of tall shrubs on the corner. Without looking back, I cut across the hedges and trees, down a culvert underneath the highway bridge, where I stopped to catch my breath and steady the heartbeat thudding in my ears.

I decided to wait until things calmed down, and then go find Jet. I crouched at the top of the sloped cement beneath the highway and waited and watched and watched and watched – the police taking photos of the dead gang members and innocent travelers, the ambulances pulling away lights flashing, the fire engine hose spraying the blood from the pavement to the black edges of the buildings, where Jet must be hiding, too. Somewhere.

As time crawled by I shivered and grabbed my elbows. I was alone again. How did I keep ending up alone?

I leaned back onto the hard slope and closed my eyes. The whole world was throbbing behind my lids. After a while, exhaustion won out, and I slept.

NINE

I woke with a start, chilled to the bone. For a second, I blinked at the pink-fingered light and listened to the loud, steady whoosh of car tires above my head before realizing that I'd fallen asleep under the bridge. I rolled over to see what was left of the shoot-out from the night before. Yellow tape wrapped across the entire front of the Waffle King. Closed, of course. But the gas station next door was open again, and it looked like every other gas station on a normal weekday.

I opened my backpack and pulled out what was left of the jar of peanut butter. I scraped out a bit with my fingers and licked as I studied the commotion across the street: cars and trucks and big rigs filling up, people exiting the store with giant plastic cups and potato chips and powdered donuts or whatever food could fit in the crook of their arms. A policeman lingered in front of the gas station, probably to make people feel safe. He'd nod at a few people as they passed by, then look down at his phone screen.

I needed to get to the back side of the Waffle King. Jet was waiting for me – at least I hoped she was waiting. As I stuck the jar in the backpack, I saw the bus driver's money. I'd shoved it there before the shoot-out. Despite everything, my heart jumped. I could buy a hot chocolate. I could buy real food. A kolache, if Jet didn't mind me dipping into our bus money. I shivered as I made my way down the sloped underpass and across the street. The policeman didn't look my way once as I stole across the parking lot.

The pavement was rust-stained where the bodies had fallen.

I paused behind a blue Dumpster and felt the cold seep through my bare legs. I'd been so stupid to wear shorts. *Why didn't I wear something more reasonable when I ran away?*

But when I spotted the white sign on the metal bin next to me I thought God might be paying attention. "Lone Star Aid for the Less Fortunate: Donation Bin."

Well that's me, I thought. I am very unfortunate.

I pulled the lever and the heavy metal door creaked open a crack, but I couldn't see anything but darkness inside. The lock wasn't fully closed, so I jostled it carefully until it swung open.

Inside I found a mountain of clothes. The bin smelled like Daw's three-day old socks, but I'd rather smell like feet than freeze. Leaving the door open for light, I dug through the piles hastily, finding a pair of jeans that looked like they might fit. There was no time for caution, so I stripped off my filthy cutoff shorts and pulled them on. The fabric was soft and warm against my bruised skin. They were a little too long, and a bit too baggy, but they'd work if I rolled up the ankles. In the sliver of light, I also located a knit hat, a bulky blue sweater, a pair of socks, and even some worn out Nikes. I yanked the sweater over my T-shirt and replaced Jet's ball cap with the knit one. I stuffed the shoes into my backpack.

In my new, warm clothes, I made my way around the back of the boarded up Waffle King, practically tip-toeing around the ghosts of dead people. Half of me expected Jet to be waiting there for me with her arms folded and her eyes saying *Finally*. The other half expected exactly what I saw: nothing and nobody. Just the smell of cold grease and a red NO PARKING sign on the wall.

For a while, I leaned against the brick wall and watched for movement in the tree line across the way. The leaves rustled in the wind, and cars on the highway behind me whooshed by like waves. Outside the Republic, I'd learned from movies, people got on an airplane or in a car and didn't ever pack an emergency kit, much less a gun. But inside the Republic, most of the streets were pocked with holes. Gas was expensive. The roads ruined tires. And if you got into a wreck, who knew if an ambulance would show up? The rich city-people took the Star Airline to Dallas or Austin or Houston. But I wasn't rich. This was the farthest I'd ever been from Blessing in my entire life. If I didn't find Jet, I wasn't sure what I'd do. I didn't know how to travel like she did.

I scanned the tree line again. Gradually it dawned on me that, if she were hiding in the trees somewhere, she'd have seen me by now and come to meet me. A sick feeling clenched like a fist in my stomach. Hunger or fear, it was hard to tell. But I was alone now. And I needed something to drink. And maybe that breakfast kolache, if it didn't cost too much.

"I won't spend more than a dollar fifty," I whispered out loud for Jet's sake. I turned the corner and nearly ran into the policeman stationed there. He looked up briefly with a sort of empty glaze in his eyes, like he'd forgotten where he was and why. He muttered, "Mornin'," and then squinted out across the parking lot as if there was maybe something suspicious way out there.

I hunched my shoulders and hurried into the gas station. Some of the shot-out windows had a spider-webbing of tape, but other than that, it might have been a normal morning in the station.

Rows of snack food, an assortment of coffees, dozens of soda fountains and frozen slushies churning their way to creamy snow. My mouth watered. I picked up a breakfast burrito wrapped in white paper, then when I passed the donut rack, traded it for a cinnamon roll. Juice was too expensive, so I grabbed an orange fountain soda and carried my treasures to the front.

"On your way to school?" The cashier smiled at me like he was grateful he wasn't. His mustache and goatee were trimmed neatly, he had long tattoos on his forearms, and his pinky nails were painted blue.

"Yeah. I missed the bus."

"Hell, that sucks."

"Least I get my exercise." I didn't know when to shut up.

"My goodness!" a lady behind me exclaimed. "Don't tell me you're walking to school."

I turned around, and by the horrified look of the lady, I knew I'd made a miscalculation. The lady reminded me of Maggie's mom. Red lipstick, a handful of rings, a teeny rhinestone belt on her teeny waist, and big hair, except hers was fiery red.

"It's no big deal." I shrugged.

"Well. You are not walking this morning. It's not safe, especially after all the commotion round here last night." She waved her jeweled fingers toward the parking lot, and I wondered if she'd seen the shootout on the news and that was exactly why she chose to stop by here for gas and the bottled coffee in her movie-star hands.

"You want a bag?" the cashier asked me.

"No, thanks."

132

"You just stay right there," the lady said to me, and then to the cashier, "I had twenty dollars on pump seven and this mochalicious." She handed him two crisp bills and smiled sweetly. "Keep the change, and you have a blessed day."

"Come on, now." She motioned for me to follow as she sauntered away. "You'll let me drive you to school, or I'll tell that officer out there to take you. My Lord, what are people thinking?" She glanced back at me. "You don't even have a gun."

"You don't have to bother that cop," I stammered. "You can take me."

This is bad, I thought as I followed her to her fancy white car. I had no idea where the nearest school was. The woman pressed her key fob and the car woke up with a *tweep*!

"So, thank you for the ride, Miss…."

"Stacey." She smiled at me. "And what's your name?"

"Chris." I couldn't tell if she'd pegged me for a boy or a girl. *Chris, Chris, Chris*, I chanted in my head so I wouldn't forget it. I stuffed my backpack on the floor mat between my feet, buckled the seatbelt, and clutched the cinnamon bun and drink awkwardly.

Stacey's car was fan-*cey*. Tan leather seats and polished wood on the doors. I'd never sat in such a fancy car before. Not even Maggie's mom's car was this fancy. I took a few sips of the orange soda and tried to peel apart the cinnamon roll with my teeth and not make a mess.

God, how glorious was that cinnamon roll after days of nothing but peanut butter. I wiped a bit of spittle that seeped from the corner of my mouth and said, "Wow. This car is nice. Are you rich?"

She turned the ignition and laughed. "I don't count my treasures here on earth, but I am rich in the blessings of Lord Jesus. My husband's a pastor at River of Glory. Do I look familiar?" She flashed a smile at me.

"Yes?" I guessed.

"What I thought. You probably recognize me from the billboard up the highway. We have the second biggest church in all the Austin suburbs, and our church members paid cash for that church. Our flock is very faithful. We just do our best to share our blessings with others. I always try to pass on little acts of kindness like this." She motioned at me, and the diamonds on her rings caught the morning sun, which sent fireworks throughout the whole car.

"That's nice of you," I said.

"You're going to the middle school up the road, I guess?"

I nodded, dry-mouthed. She thought I was younger than I was. That was fine with me. I took another long sip of the soda.

"My little boy would be going to the public school if we hadn't felt God's call to open up our own church school. Have you heard of the River of Glory Christian Academy?"

I shook my head.

"We provide the best education in the Republic, rooted in the laws of the Almighty," she informed me with pride. "That's the big difference between the public school and us. At the public schools, kids are coming from all kinds of messed-up home lives. Drunk parents, people scamming charities. You know how poor people can be. And the Republic letting those sorts of kids carry guns in ninth grade? At least we know when our kids go to school, God has His hand on their guns, protecting them from evil."

134

I slid my hand back and forth across the soft leather seats. Stacey's school probably had leather seats, too. Leather seats and nice teachers and enough books for all the students in every room. They probably didn't even have school bullies or embarrassing dads like Daw.

I looked out the window. At some point I'd lost track of the turns she took. The neighborhood was unfamiliar. My heart sank. Somehow I had to find my way back to the gas station to look for Jet.

Stacey hooked a right, and suddenly we were on a street full of small homes that reminded me of cartoon gingerbread houses. One house of screaming violet next to another of lime green next to another one half-covered in sky blue before the painters gave up and left the rest yellow. The Republic flag hung limply near most of the doors. I needed to keep track of the street names if I wanted to ever find my way out again. At the stop sign, I caught sight of where we were. Gingerbread Lane.

The cross street was Gretel. The next street was Hansel. I didn't like the general direction this theme was headed. When we stopped at the street called "Big Bad Wolf," a sense of doom set in.

"Aren't the names of these streets cute?" Stacey grinned. "Especially the Three Little Pigs Road. That's my favorite. What's yours?"

"Oh, they're all interesting," I said, vaguely.

"It's a shame the neighborhood has gotten so run down. A real shame, but most people bring poverty upon themselves because they don't tithe."

"What do you mean?"

"Well, for example, my neighborhood is very nice. Prosperous. Because we tithe to the church."

"Don't you own the church?"

"*God* owns the church," she corrected me. "We just run it. Anyway, when you tithe right, God pays it back twenty-fold, like the Bible says. That's the prosperity message. If you want to *receive* over and above, you have to *give* over and above. I've seen people put their whole paycheck in the offertory because they have that much faith in our message. They have to believe, of course, that God will reward them. That's the other half of our message."

I couldn't remember Daw ever putting money in the plate when it was passed around at church. But I hardly remembered church, either.

Stacey's voice rose like a sermon. "That's why most of Texas is in such a bad state. They're stingy with their tithe. Don't get me wrong. I love poor people. They're hard workers. The Pastor and me give them all kinds of jobs, babysitting and keeping up the yard. But look at that truck."

She clicked her tongue at a truck without wheels propped up on cinder blocks. Could have been Daw's truck on its broke-down days.

"They don't keep up their own neighborhoods and let the riff-raff move in, and before you know it, cute neighborhoods like Storyville here just go to pot."

At Pied Piper Way, she turned into the middle school parking lot. It was packed with cars. A few stragglers ran toward the school's front doors just as the bell rang.

"See now? You're barely even late. Hmm." She leaned toward me and peered out my side of the window. "Must be a parent meeting with all these cars. I'm surprised so many parents even showed up this side of town."

I stuck the roll in my mouth and grabbed my backpack, balancing the soda as I hopped out. "Thank you, Miss Stacey," I said through the dough.

"God bless!" She waved and drove off.

I stood on the sidewalk chewing. The sweet roll made my jaw ache, but I swallowed fast as I walked to the side of the building. In Blessing, the secretaries were always stomping outside the school, yelling at the late kids to get inside, so I knew to steer clear of the front doors. I hid behind a tree as I finished up the soda.

About three seconds later, I had to pee. I crushed the cup beneath my heel into a flat disk and left it a little guiltily there in the grass. Keeping my eyes on the throng of people, I waited for my chance to slip in the school unnoticed.

More cars pulled into the parking lot, so I followed a few parents through the front doors and crept past the front office while they lined up to check in.

I stepped on cat paws down the hall, searching for a restroom. I passed a boys' restroom first but couldn't make myself go inside, even with my buzzed hair. So I kept walking until I found a girls'. There wasn't even a door – just a little maze of walls you had to follow to find the toilets. But it was cleaner than any of the restrooms at my school. The whole bathroom smelled like lemons and bleach, so I sat down on the toilet for a pee and didn't even bother putting paper on the seat.

When I washed the sugar-stick off my hands, the soap smelled like the honeysuckle bush back home. So I lathered up a second time and kept lathering up my arm until I had sleeves of honeysuckle bubbles. I licked my arm because my teeth were fuzzy, and the soap helped slick them clean. Over the sink, I scraped my tongue, rinsed my arms off, and then used a fistful of paper towels to dry myself. As I bent over to brush off my boots, a glass shard tinkled across the floor. I searched my scalp and found another tiny piece of glass. People from the shootout flashed across my eyes. People I hadn't even remembered seeing. A dead man in the parking lot with his bloody shirt hitched up over a hairy belly. A woman face-down on the Waffle King floor, perfectly still in her ironed dress and pink shoes. I wondered what their last thoughts were. If they had any regrets. If it hurt to die.

I couldn't think about this now.

I ducked under the faucet and soaked my chopped hair and scalp. It took a fistful of paper towels to soak up the wet. When I straightened up again, I studied myself in the mirror. I wondered if I could really pass for a boy with my hacked off hair and blue sweater, courtesy of the Lone Star donation bin.

I borrowed a roll of toilet paper along with a handful of paper towels and stuffed them in my backpack in case I needed them later.

I headed out the bathroom holding my breath, and walked down the hall, looking for a side exit. I opened a set of double doors and stumbled into the cafeteria, chock full of grown-ups and commotion. Most were sitting at the lunchroom tables. Others were standing along the edges of the room, shoulders hunched forward. Most of them were mumbling or nodding or jutting their chins up in the air.

From somewhere on the right, a man's voice reached across the room. "Seems like everywhere I turn, people's still trying to take away my rights. Is this or ain't this the Republic of Texas?"

I searched the crowd for the voice and found it belonged to a man in a red ball cap. He stood near the front of the cafeteria, towering over the other people. He wore a checkered dress shirt and a pair of tan pants held up with black suspenders. The kind of man Daw would have slapped on the back and bought a beer for at the Cotton Gin bar.

"All due respect, Lloyd," a woman's voice called out. She was standing against the side wall, and tapping her watch. "But can we get to the point of this meeting? What happened yesterday with the gun, Principal?" she asked the woman on the stage.

Lloyd in the red cap kept standing, not ready to give up his position, but also clammed up by his own curiosity. A woman tapped my shoulder from behind, wanting inside, and I found myself standing along the back wall with a whole line of parents. None of them seemed to notice me. They were all focused on the debate.

The principal raised her arms in the air. "What happened is this: I've emailed letters the past several weeks about our little gun issue. For those of you not on the school's email list – first of all, y'all should all be on the email list – but the emails said we're having a problem with students bringing their parents' guns to school. Y'all know that they can't do that, and shouldn't be carrying until after eighth-grade camp. Our kids hide them in their backpacks and jacket pockets so they can show them off to friends. Some of them are pricey, too, way out of my salary range. Think about that. Your child sneaking your expensive gun to school and you know they're bound to lose it."

A few nervous laughs echoed across the room.

"It's not a laughing matter. Yesterday in the lower school, a second-grader pulled out a gun because he was mad at his teacher. He wouldn't put the gun down, and the teacher in question had to pull out her gun and direct it at the child."

I tried to imagine the teacher, a young nervous one, both palms tight around the butt of the gun, training the barrel on a skinny little seven-year-old.

"Jesus Almighty," a lady beside me muttered. "That's bad parenting."

The principal squinted at them. "Nobody was hurt, thank God. But parents, we've got to have your help securing your guns. We don't want our teachers to be aiming weapons at students. That's not the point of having teachers armed."

"I disagree!" Lloyd in the red cap interrupted. He was still standing. "That's exactly why we want them armed. Principal Huffman, that boy was a threat to the whole class – coulda shot anyone in the room. She shoulda shot the kid in the foot."

"Whoa now, what?" Another man half-stood, raising his dark hand into the air. He was probably the only black man in the audience. "That's a second-grader. We can't just shoot second graders willy-nilly."

Lloyd groaned. "I'm not talking about killing your kind. This ain't about race."

"Gentlemen." The principal held up her hands, "Let's not get sidetracked. My point is that our children are coming to school with guns, which they cannot legally do until they're fourteen *and*

140

in high school. Yesterday, Miss Andrea was able to disarm the student, but not before the gun discharged and shot a hole in the classroom speaker system. Now we've got a very expensive repair to make, one that frankly we can't afford."

A murmur of agreement rumbled through the cafeteria, money quickly distracting the parents from the gun situation.

"Our technology funds are tragically low. Now I've heard through the grapevine that many of you give your kids guns as birthday presents, but I'm trying to run a school here, and I can't have guns and whatnot on a daily basis turning up in children's jackets and desks."

Another man stood up beside Lloyd. His blond hair was neatly combed, his Republic or Die T-shirt ironed and stiff. "Why don't you focus on better teaching and not telling me what to do with my gun or my son? The whole reason the Texas Constitution allows for my gun rights is to stand up to oppression and tyranny."

I knew I should get going but it was warm inside and I leaned down and slipped between some elbows to get a better look. The whole room rumbled again – parents shifting around on the stools, the air groaning with agitation.

"Wait a minute." A mother stood up and turned her whole body toward the two men. She wore a sleeping baby in a sling across her belly. "Are you calling our Republic tyrannical? 'Cause you know, you can just leave if you feel tyrannized."

The man pointed his finger and said, "Don't question my loyalty to the Republic. You don't have no right." His hand wandered up to his hip and settled on the gun holstered there.

The woman bristled. "I got a right to speak just like you! We shouldn't be arming seven-year-olds. Clearly some people are more concerned about their rights than their own kids' lives."

"Well I'm sick and tired of people claiming the moral high ground." The man's fingers danced on his gun, and my stomach fluttered uneasily. "How about teaching your own kid the difference between right and wrong? Fucking idiot."

The woman's eyes flashed as she lunged forward at the Republic or Die man, but two or three people latched onto her arms and pulled her back. The room erupted. I'd never seen two adults duke it out in the cafeteria, especially with a baby tucked between them, and the thought of it filled me with equal parts terror and delight. It felt wrong somehow, getting excited about a fight, but I couldn't help it.

Still, I felt sorry for the principal on the stage, resetting her glasses on her small nose and raising her arms like Moses, while the seas were just getting stormier.

"Stop!" she interrupted the man. "I'm not asking you to do anything unpatriotic and I'm not telling you how to raise your children. We're here because we need to come together to deal with the problem."

"We need to have bullet-proof vests is what we need!" someone shouted.

A few voices shouted "yeah." A young woman hurried across the stage and whispered into the principal's ear. The principal sighed and shook her head.

"Okay, folks," she said. "We need to dismiss. I'll send you a follow-up email of resolutions. God bless us and keep us safe."

The whole room answered, "God bless." But that was the only thing they agreed on. The whole crowd lingered, barely keeping a lid on their outrage.

It seemed to me that nothing would ever get fixed when adults couldn't behave like adults.

I needed to get back to Jet. I shouldn't be here in the first place.

TEN

While everyone was arguing, I slipped out the side doors and headed back in the direction I thought might take me to the gas station and the Waffle King. I'd only gone a few blocks though, when I realized I was already lost. I tried cutting across a few back yards to make my way back, but that only made things worse. Every turn was unfamiliar and yet every street looked much the same. The Storyville street names mocked me. Riding Hood Lane. Goldilocks Road.

I walked until my toes were swollen in my boots. Just as I was about to give up and risk knocking on someone's door, I found Gingerbread again. At last. I was close now. Only a few streets away from the main road that would take me back to the gas station. I didn't have a real plan, but at the very least, I could check the station for Jet.

A truck sped past and honked at a squirrel dashing across the street. The squirrel leaped onto the curb just a few feet ahead of me, and stood on its hind legs to look at me. Then it looked down the street where the truck was disappearing. It turned around and chittered.

"Driving like that, he's going out of the neighborhood," I told the squirrel. I broke into a run, hoping to catch the truck's next turn. If I did, I'd follow him out to the main road. By the time I reached the stop sign though, the truck was long gone, but there was another car speeding down the road, and I raced after it. I was like a dog running after cars, my heart pounding with hope and excitement. The backpack thumped against my back, and I winked away the sweat that stung my eyes.

It worked. The neighborhood ended at the black-tar road, the same one I'd crossed earlier near the gas station. Tall pine trees lined it, one lane going in each direction, but with hardly an edge to walk on. I shielded my eyes with my hand and looked down the black-tar as far as I could see in both directions. I couldn't tell which way led to the station, and my pinkie toes were aching after days of walking.

I stepped away from the stop sign and walked back a few yards to where the sidewalk had ended. I'd sit a minute, give my feet a break. Figure out which way to go. Figure out what to do once I got there.

I was tired of figuring things out, tired of walking, tired of being lost and hungry and cold and dirty. It was all futile. I'd probably lost Jet for good anyway. Why would she hang around? She was capable and smart, and I was just a burden to her. She must have taken her chance back at the Waffle King last night and hit the road for El Paso. I couldn't blame her.

Suddenly, everything seemed pointless. I sat down on the curb and pulled off my boots. I peeled back my socks and examined my red heels and the blisters on my toes. They were still pink and soft, but not ready to pop, so I dug through my backpack for the old Nikes from the donation bin. They felt good on my feet – soft against my sore skin. I shoved the boots into the backpack. I wanted another orange soda. Another cinnamon roll. A hamburger.

I wanted Maggie back. I even wanted Daw.

Shadows danced across the sidewalk as the sun peeked out from behind the passing clouds. I wiggled my toes inside the sneakers. They were scuffed around the toes and the soles were worn down, but they were still a good find. Nike had pulled out of the Republic after the Great Secession, along with dozens of other big companies, and even though old people said good riddance, kids at school still talked about Nikes like they were distant, rich cousins. We didn't secede from basketball and football. We needed good kicks, not the shoddy ones made in Texas. I heard someone paid three hundred dollars for a pair of new Nikes on the black market.

I looked at my feet and smiled.

I was so lost in thought I barely noticed the dark blue car as it pulled up to the stop sign, and then rolled back slowly until it was right in front of me. My heartbeat quickened, hoping they'd just go away.

But the driver rolled down the dark window. It was a woman in sunglasses. She pushed them up onto the crown of her head and looked me over. It was Principal Huffman.

"Shouldn't you be in school?" she called out.

I blinked at her. "Uh, I don't go to school here, ma'am. I'm just visiting from out of town."

"Who you visiting?"

"Family."

"Ah." She nodded at my backpack. "Is that your lunch?"

"Actually, I was walking to the gas station for a hot dog, but it's farther than I thought."

"The gas station!" She looked as horrified as if I'd said I was walking to a bordello. "Well, first off, it's dangerous to walk on that road. There's no shoulder, and there's copperheads in the grass. And second, the hot dogs at the station are even riskier than the copperheads." Unexpectedly, she gave a wry smile.

She seemed like a nice one. This suburban town seemed to be full of nice, nosy rich women who couldn't leave a runaway alone.

"I'm the principal over at Storyville Middle School," she said. "You want to try a decent lunch up the road instead? My treat."

I needed to find Jet. But Jet, I increasingly believed, was gone. And it had been more than a day since I'd had a real meal.

I squinted at her. "How far?"

"Just a little ways past the gas station," she promised. "Not far."

But Jet, part of me thought.

Jet is gone, I scolded myself. You're on your own.

"I am kind of thirsty."

"Well, hop in." She nodded me over. "I could use some civil company."

"Bethany Huffman," she said when I opened the door. She shook my hand like I was forty instead of fourteen.

"Chris," I answered. Second nature now.

She looked older up close. A few grays nestled in her soft brown hair. Her eyelids slanted down at the outside corners, which made her look tired and wise and kind all at once.

"Buckle up. You like burgers and fries?"

"Who doesn't?"

She smiled. "Good. Now first thing you need to know is never jump in a stranger's car again. I happen to be a good person, but you never know." She pulled down her sunglasses and turned left at the stop sign.

By now, I figured I could take care of myself and she really didn't look very dangerous to me. But I nodded politely.

"I don't normally leave school for lunch, but today I had to play hooky. I literally could not stay there for another second. You ever had that feeling?" She glanced at me.

She had no idea.

"Yes, ma'am."

"Well, it's not supposed to happen to me. The principal."

I was a little surprised that an adult was talking to me this way. Like I was another human and not a kid.

I said, "I bet you have to deal with a lot of difficult people."

She nodded.

"Kids can be a pain," I added.

"Parents can be even worse," she assured me.

I liked her.

Ahead of us, the tiny shell-shaped sign appeared in the distance.

"You remind me of someone," she said.

"Who?"

"My daughter. Used to be a tomboy. Shaved her whole head when she was nine. Nine! Nearly gave me a heart attack. All that pretty hair on the bathroom floor." She chuckled, but it gave way quickly to a gulp. Part sob, part laugh. She smiled again, a little wobble in her bottom lip. "Anyway. You have similar features."

"Sounds like she knows what she wants and makes it happen."

We passed the gas station and turned near the culvert where I'd spent the night holed up under the bridge. The burger place was up the road beside a giant neon sign that was lit up even in broad daylight: DILLO BURGER. Under the flashing letters, a neon-green armadillo tilted back his cowboy hat and held up a hamburger.

Inside, the icy breeze from the A/C gave me goosebumps. The smell of french fries and hiss of seared beef made my stomach pinch so hard I caught my breath. After days of little food, it was too much for my senses. A cashier waved us toward the counter where you were supposed to order, but I didn't move. Principal Huffman looked back at me, her kind eyes encouraging me.

Standing in front of all those menu options, I wasn't sure what I was supposed to do, manners-wise. Everything on the wall was over ten dollars.

"Jesus," I mumbled. Principal Huffman ordered a burger, fries and an iced tea.

"I'll have the same," I muttered, hoping it wasn't rude to copy her. Daw hadn't exactly trained me up on manners, but I hadn't been bothered by it until now. God help me if I ever found myself at a restaurant with tablecloths.

We sat at a booth near the windows and slid up an armadillo flag – number seventeen – for the waiter to find us. The twang of country music echoed across the restaurant.

Principal Huffman stuck a straw in the lid of her sweet tea and let out a sigh. She settled her brown eyes on me and cracked a smile.

"So. What's your story, Chris?"

"My story?" I was dizzy from the smells and the noise, the music on the radio. The strange *normality* of it all. It was hard to think.

"Yeah, 'cause I *know* you're not on a family vacation." She winked and leaned in. "I've seen a lot of kids. Trying to make it on their own."

"Hmm." I took a long sip of tea and hoped there'd be refills. I felt dry through.

"Where are your parents? Don't worry. I won't tattle."

I sucked on my tea and let the cold shock my head before answering. "I don't know."

"You don't know?"

"I mean, I don't have any."

"Oh." She studied me for a long time. I couldn't tell what she was thinking.

I was glad when the burgers came quickly, hot and greasy, along with two baskets of fries. There was no way I'd be able to eat it all, but I'd sure try. I squirted a mound of ketchup in the corner of the basket and popped a hot fry in my mouth.

"You know," she said, watching me, "there's lots of children in foster care. Too many. You have relatives?"

I shook my head.

"Then…?"

I swallowed. "I'm sort of homeless right now."

"Homeless." She chewed slowly and nodded. "For how long?"

"For a long time."

She swallowed, then set her burger down and looked right into me, past my eyes and into the real Blue. "Every child deserves to have a home. Every child deserves a safe place to live and good food and clean clothes and an education and spiritual guidance. And love, Chris. It's not your fault that you're alone."

If only she knew, I thought. Maybe I could have been better if someone like Principal Huffman had been my mother. Maybe I would know how the word "love" feels.

I looked up, mouth full of hamburger meat, and there was Principal Huffman with her lips quivering and her eyes filling up with tears. At first, I thought her meat had gone down wrong because she was making muffled choking noises. But then she let out a sob and tried to cover her mouth, but the tears kept coming in spurts.

I didn't know what to do. I wanted to comfort her, so I handed her my napkin.

"Are you okay?" I asked. She'd seemed just fine a few moments earlier. It was a shock to see her crying.

She blew her nose and dabbed her eyes and turned her whole body away from the other tables. "I'm fine," she sniffed. "I'm sorry – I don't know what came over me."

"You're probably just tired," I said, because it was a thing people said.

She forced a smile. "Yes, definitely tired."

"You should eat," I offered. "Food is fuel, that's what my best friend used to say. She never ate fast food. She said it causes depression and pimples and cancer." I was talking too much again, but it seemed to help her.

"Your friend's probably right. Who was she?"

"Maggie."

Her name caught painfully in my throat. I'd hardly been able to think of her. She wasn't supposed to come out so easily in my conversations. It hurt too bad to stuff her back into my chest.

"She died," I said, letting down my guard. People were still looking for me. But this lady, she'd found me, and I wasn't afraid.

"I'm sorry. I bet you miss her."

I kept chewing, but my eyes filled with tears anyway. I chewed some more, then sucked up some tea, and washed everything down so my nose wouldn't run.

"Are *you* okay?" Principal Huffman asked.

I cleared my throat. "Yes, ma'am."

We finished our burgers and walked to the car without hardly saying anything. My stomach was so full, I longed for a bed, some quiet place to sleep off the ache. After the principal buckled her seatbelt, she sat with her keys in her hands and stared at the silent radio.

"I lost someone, too," she said. "My daughter."

"She's gone?"

"She died."

"What happened?" Her daughter was dead and my best friend was dead.

Death was like a thread pulling us closer.

She turned the ignition and sat for a moment, before turning to me. "Could I show you something?"

"Sure."

We drove up the blacktop to the top of the hill and turned down a tree-lined lane that wound around like a lazy stream, with tall, wild grasses and yellow boulders, until suddenly she pulled up to a pretty house with columns and a white garage with windows like winking eyes. Her house was straight out of a picture book.

"Come in," she said.

A golden lab, all tongue and teeth, bounded around the corner and greeted us on the front walk, slowing to wiggle his rear and slapping his tail from ear to ear, and then flopped down on his back for a belly rub.

"Hey, Buddy." The principal cooed and baby-talked him while I scrubbed his belly. Buddy smiled and slobbered and ran around in circles like every kid's dream. He nudged his nose under my hand as I stood on the front porch.

"It's like he knows you," she said and unlocked the door. I followed her inside, and immediately found myself in a museum of trinkets and books, surrounded by sunlit windows and soft armchairs and wood everywhere – on every wall and across the ceiling, and winding up two staircases on the opposite ends of the room. The house smelled like flowers or lemon, something clean.

"Would you like something to drink?" she asked and set her purse down.

"No, thank you. This is a real pretty house."

"Thank you. Please wait here – I'll be right back." She disappeared down a hallway, her feet silent on thick carpet.

I didn't feel clean enough to sit down on her velvety couch so I busied myself wandering by the bookshelves filled with ceramic bears and rabbits that I couldn't resist touching. I stopped in front of the fireplace. On the mantle between a set of candles and under a collection of hanging crosses was a framed photograph of a little girl and Principal Huffman holding hands on a beach.

"That's Kristin," she said behind me.

They were both smiling in the photo. "You've been to the ocean."

She nodded. "Galveston. Have you ever been there?"

"No. But I'd like to someday."

"It's nice. You look out, and all the ships are coming and going to all over the world, filled with all sorts of things. Whole ships full of mystery. Even more so today than back then." Her voice trailed off.

"Is this what you wanted to show me? Her picture?"

She smiled. "I guess. Kristin was ten in that picture. That was about five years ago. She was happy then, or I thought she was happy. I thought a lot of things that didn't turn out to be right." She sat down in an armchair and clasped her hands. "You can sit if you want."

I sat on the edge of the velvety couch, reluctant to let my whole weight fall on it because of the dirt and grime that seemed to pervade me after the last few days.

"Kristin wasn't happy. She was bullied terribly, and I didn't know. I really didn't know until someone found her one night at the playground. She'd hung herself. She was only twelve years old." She stared at the rug. "I wasn't just her mother, I was the principal of the school, and yet I couldn't see that she felt so desperately alone and unloved. She deserved better from me. From everyone."

"I'm sorry."

"I was so sad for a long time. So depressed I couldn't get out of bed. I just wanted to fall asleep and dream about her, but she never came in my dreams. I hated the world. Hated God in my grief. My husband left, and I couldn't blame him. I made a deal with God to save every kid I could but really, I was just praying to have my Kristin back again. I still feel responsible. It's a life sentence."

A little cry tugged at the bottom of my throat, but I forced it back. "I know what guilt feels like. It feels like a leech on your back," I whispered.

She looked at me, searching my eyes. "But something strange is happening. Last night, for the first time since she died, I dreamed about her. She was on a merry-go-round, and I was pushing her, and she laughed and laughed and told me to get on and ride. I woke up smiling. And then you show up, and your name is Chris! Maybe that's why I brought you here. That dream. And because I wanted to show you who Kristin was and who I was. A mother. In a big empty home." She drew a long breath. "Chris, you don't have to be homeless. Maybe neither of us has to be alone."

I looked around the living room. At the sunlight falling in speckled beams through the windows. The blanket draped across the corner of the couch. The neat pile of magazines on the corner table. The dog bed beside the fireplace, where Buddy chewed his purple toy. I could see myself here, with Bethany Huffman to take care of me. A warm, safe place. A mother.

When I didn't reply, she stood and motioned toward the staircase, saying, "Come with me."

I followed her up the stairs, our steps silent on the thick carpet. On the landing she turned left, and stopped in front of an open door. Inside was a four-poster bed with a creamy pink bedspread, a white dresser with five drawers and glass knobs, a small writing desk with a globe and a line of plastic horses frozen mid-prance.

I knew everything before she even spoke. "This was Kristin's." She touched one of the horses, lightly. "I couldn't empty it."

I walked around the dead girl's room and looked at all the things she'd left behind. Posters of horses lined the bedroom walls. Wild horses, sleek show horses, horses with cowgirls smiling at the camera.

"She liked horses," I said.

"Yes, she did. She wanted to raise them." She opened the closet and turned to me, clasping her hands. "Chris, you could stay here for as long as you like. You don't have to decide now. Do you want to get freshened up? Maybe change into some fresh clothes…"

I leaned into the bathroom. Kristin had her own bathroom, just like Maggie's. Glass doors above the tub, pink bottles of shampoo that probably smelled of roses or strawberries.

I thought of Jet. And then I thought of scrubbing my hair with that shampoo. Of being clean, and having regular meals. Of being warm and dry and safe. And I reminded myself that Jet was long gone, probably halfway to New Mexico by now. It wasn't my fault that I was standing here. My skin itched from days without a good wash. I was already getting hungry again.

I said, "Actually, a shower does sound good."

Principal Huffman broke into a relieved smile. "Good. Look, how about I take the rest of the day off? We'll figure everything out. I'll bring up some soap and fresh towels, okay?"

"Thank you, ma'am," I nodded. The house was dizzying. Her kindness was dizzying.

As if she knew this, she paused outside the door and turned back to me. "Take your time. Just… try it out."

I took the longest shower I'd ever took in my whole life. The hot water never ran out, the soap smelled like roses, and the towels didn't have holes. I wiped a circle in the steamy mirror and looked at my reflection. I looked ghostly in the fog – could hardly see myself before the steam covered me up again. I looked young to everyone else, but I felt older, much older than I'd been a few days ago.

Maybe death has a way of warping time.

When I was clean, I opened the closet. It was strange to slide the hangers one by one as I browsed through the dead girl's clothes. Dresses and more dresses. Half of them looked too small, but half didn't. I kept looking for a sign in all this, something that told me that I was meant to stay here. God talked to lots of people but He'd never spoken directly to me. Wasn't *this* a sign, that He'd put me in a warm, safe house?

I found a plain white shirt and some stretchy jeans. It felt strange to put them on, but they couldn't have fit better. Suddenly, I was exhausted. I sat on the bed, which was soft and cushiony and the very opposite of the concrete slope under the bridge. I leaned back to close my eyes for a few minutes.

Jet's face flashed across my eyelids, and she pointed to the gas station, saying "We have to sneak away. First chance. Run!" But I was too exhausted to hang onto her. And soon she was swept away on a gentle river of sleep.

★

When I woke, the light had changed and there was a thin blanket draped over me. I went downstairs and found Miss Huffman on the velvet couch reading a book. The living room smelled like warm butter.

"You looked so tired I didn't have the heart to wake you," she said. "You were out for a few hours. Did you sleep well?"

"Like the dead," I said, then immediately turned hot with embarrassment. "I didn't mean..."

She shook her head kindly and closed her book. "I've got a chicken casserole in the oven that should be ready. Are you hungry?"

I nodded and followed her into the kitchen, marveling at how starved I was in spite of eating that huge lunch. I wondered guiltily if Jet was hungry and how she was going eat without her share of the money.

Miss Huffman glanced at my jeans. "I see you found some clothes that fit."

I tugged at the shirt hem. "Yeah. Thanks, ma'am."

"You don't have to keep thanking me. I'm just happy I didn't save everything for nothing. There's some dresses, too. I bet you'd look so pretty in them."

"I'm not really a dress sort of person."

"That's okay. Some girls just like to wear jeans. It's more practical, anyway." She opened the oven and pulled out the casserole, wrapped in aluminum foil. "The glasses are in that cupboard, if you'd like some water. There's iced tea in the fridge."

The fridge was full of food, which made me happy even though it wasn't my food. She wouldn't let me help, so I watched her unwrap the casserole and spoon out two servings of soft rice and mushrooms and chicken.

"It's been way too long since I've cooked a casserole," she confessed as she filled the plates. "It's just been myself here for so long."

She showed me how to set the table. Clean tablecloth. Real plates instead of paper ones. Knives on the right, napkins and forks on the left.

"It's important to know how to set a proper table. You never know when special company will show up on your doorstep. Good manners are a sign of respect. They show that you care about other people."

I'd never set a table in my life, but Daw and I never had company, so I hadn't disrespected anyone yet.

There was a proper place for bread and for the glass of water and for other silverware, if we needed it. As we ate, I copied the way she held her fork and knife and dabbed the corner of her mouth with her napkin. Miss Huffman was kind and patient, but the more she talked, the more I worried that Daw had raised me every way wrong. I felt it deeply, like I'd been wrong all my life and never knew it.

She didn't ask me what I wanted to do until dinner was over. Then, when we were sitting with empty plates in front of us, she said, "So, what do you think?"

"It's a lot to remember. I've never heard of half these rules."

"I mean, what do you think about staying?"

I smiled, but my insides were like static. Without Jet, my compass was broken.

She leaned toward me. "Chris, I've been thinking. I know you've run away from something, and you can tell me about it when you're ready. Or maybe never tell me, it doesn't really matter. What matters is now. I can give you the life you deserve, that Kristin should have lived. It's my second chance, and maybe your second chance, too. I can protect you."

"It does sound nice," I admitted.

"You see it, right?" She smiled. "I think God sent you to me. He answered my prayers."

I nodded, but a sudden guilt rose up in me. I wasn't Chris who sounded like Kristin. I was an imposter. I'd fooled her and God, both.

"But I'm not Kristin," I said softly. "You don't even know who I am."

She didn't flinch. I had the feeling she'd considered this while I was sleeping. "The truth is," she said, "I don't want to know your last name. It would make things too complicated. I could enroll you in school using Kristin's social security number. I don't think the government would catch on until long after you've graduated, they're such a mess. You could be a Huffman."

"Maybe." I'd be lying if I said I didn't want a mother, a kind person who cooked dinner for me, a normal house, an invisible life. But I already felt a part of myself, the real Blue, slipping away, and it took me off guard. Something felt off kilter.

"You can stay here while I work for a day or two, just until I get the school paperwork and our story sorted." She took our plates to the kitchen. "Don't worry about cleaning up," she called. "There's plenty of time to help with that. Go relax. Turn on the TV."

★

After I brushed my teeth and slipped into Kristin's pajamas, Miss Huffman came to say goodnight and read me a scripture from the Bible.

"It's just something I remembered and thought I'd share it with you." She sat on the edge of the bed, opened the Bible, and read a story about a father of two sons. The younger son took the father's money and after he spent it all, returned almost begging to be a servant in order to come home. When the older son complained about the big party and the money the father spent on the younger son, the father told him not to complain. "All that I have is yours," she read, "but thy younger brother was lost and now he is found." She closed the Bible and smiled.

"I won't ask you for money," I told her.

"That's nice of you to say, but that's not why I read the parable."

"Oh."

"Good night, Chris." She said it so tenderly I was sure she'd forgotten I wasn't her daughter.

"'Night, Miss Huffman."

"Call me Bethany," she said softly.

Later, after I slid under the sheets of the dead girl's bed, I tried not to think about her body hanging from a set of monkey bars, or wherever she'd done that terrible thing. I tried not to think of Maggie's blood on my hands. I tried not to think of Jet, hitching a ride to El Paso or standing around in Austin, hungry and cold. But I failed on every attempt. My head was a prison from which I desperately wanted to escape. Was this the way Kristin had felt? That her head was a cell and her life was a sentence?

But Miss Huffman was gentle, like her name. Bethany, the name of a fairytale godmother. My eyelids grew heavy. If I stayed, if I hid here in Bethany's dream, I could be safe.

I must have fallen asleep because I woke with a start. It was 6 AM on the clock, and the house was quiet. A blue early morning light filtered through the window. And I knew, somehow I *knew*, I had to leave.

I tiptoed onto the landing at the top of the stairs. The smell of coffee filled the air and a dull murmur of voices came from the TV below. I could see the whole living room from where I stood.

There was Miss Huffman, cradling a cup of coffee and kneeling in front of the TV. The news report was about me. Bluebonnet Andrews, wanted for the murder of Maggie Wisdom. A photo of a mousy-haired girl hung on the screen, and although I hardly remembered that long-haired child, I knew it was me.

The news man spoke without emotion, his words coming to me in pieces: fugitive, dangerous, police, hotline. The principal lowered her cup to the floor, slumped her shoulders and bowed down her head.

Even though everything in my body wanted to run, I stood there frozen, watching the principal cry. Her daughter was dead twice now. The real one and the dream one.

I'm sorry, I wanted to say. In spite of everything – the haunted room and the fake name and resurrecting a dead girl – I wanted to believe that Principal Huffman still wanted me. I wanted to believe that she'd still protect me, but she was already reaching for her phone, already clutching it to her chest and sobbing. I tiptoed back to the bedroom, pulled on the jeans, slid my feet into my Nikes, and grabbed my backpack. I slid open Kristin's window and held my breath as I jumped, aiming for the flowering bush below. I cracked my ankle from the fall, but was able to hobble back to the main road without being seen.

Miss Huffman's neighborhood was still asleep, save for the birds calling their morning songs. All the houses so quiet and pretty.

That had been my mistake. I'd thought quiet had meant safe, but it only made my own presence louder. If I were to stay safely anonymous, I needed a place that was loud and packed. Like the Neighborhood. Even Jet had thought that kind of place was good idea. And it was the last place we'd talked about before we got separated.

My ankle got better as I picked up speed. This time I didn't get lost. The gas station was straight up the main road, easy enough to backtrack to.

I was going to get out of here. And one way or another, I was going to find Jet.

ELEVEN

The brick side of the Quick Mart was the best place to hide. I had a clear view of the cars exiting the southbound freeway and pulling into the station. My plan was to wander around the pumps and ask people if they were heading toward Austin, and could I have a ride if they were. Austin was the only place that made sense to go. If Jet wasn't at the Neighborhood, then I'd look at the bus station. And if she wasn't there, she might be in jail or sent back to her family. There would be nothing I could do then but make another plan.

I wasn't stupid. Hitchhiking wasn't the safest way to travel. I'd heard the rumors about kidnapped girls and boys. But I had little choice.

I began looking for another kindly, but hopefully less nosy, woman who might give me a lift.

A blue truck sped down the exit ramp and veered into the gas station. The driver was a bearded man who tucked a wad of chaw in his lower lip. He didn't look very welcoming.

A silver car came next, but I doubted the white-haired woman was driving down to Austin. I weighed my options without moving from my hiding place. Ladies were safer than men, but men asked fewer questions. After fifteen minutes, I still hadn't worked up the nerve to talk to anyone, and I was getting worried that Miss Huffman might come looking for me.

I took a deep breath, pulled on Jet's baseball cap, and walked toward a white car. But before I got there, the lady hurried toward the Quick Mart, leaving the gas hose in her car. I stood near the pump, pretending to be interested in the trash can. When that looked suspicious, I turned my attention to a tub of soapy water. I leaned against a brick column and scanned the lot. Up near the Quick Mart entrance, a black police truck with a gold star pulled in and parked. I edged behind the column and watched the door open, praying silently, *Don't be the Ranger, don't be the Ranger, don't be…*

It was Ranger Kern. I knew his straight-rod back and snakeskin boots before I even saw his unforgiving face. He unfolded a paper as he stepped up to the glass doors. I turned my back and looked out at the highway, held my breath and felt a cold sweat on my palms. He couldn't be looking for me. Maybe it was a coincidence he was here. Maybe he was following the gangs.

I searched my memory for his interrogation back in Blessing. He was here for Mother, not for me. Even so, his words rang in my ears. *Somebody's gotta fix you.* I peeked around again.

The Ranger held the door open for a woman as she walked into the building. For a second, he scanned the parking lot, and I caught those blue-white eyes. I hunched lower.

A Jeep pulled up beside me, blocking my view of the Ranger. I ducked behind the column again.

The Jeep doors opened and a group of older kids tumbled out loudly. It was hard to age them – maybe late teens or even early 20s. They were laughing and joking as they slammed their doors shut.

I tugged the bill of my cap lower and looked at my shoes while one of them wrangled with the nozzle and then jogged toward the station. I scanned the nearby cars in a panic, hoping to see a lady who looked like she was headed to Austin. That was when I noticed the bumper sticker on the Jeep: UNIVERSITY OF TEXAS AUSTIN.

My heart raced. I crouched down and, without waiting for doubt to creep in, sidled behind the Jeep and tried the handle on the trunk door. The door lifted without a sound. Moving slowly, I crawled in, carefully closed the door, and waited in a breathless panic under the tinted window.

"Stay still," I whispered to myself. "Don't look."

But I couldn't help myself. I inched up and peeked over the back seat. Through the front window, I saw the four laughing teenagers walk out the station, poking and dodging each other. The Ranger followed them out, observing them with suspicion.

My heart climbed up my throat, and I pressed my hand against my chest.

The Ranger turned away from the teenagers and followed the lady to her car, overtaking her like a bird dog on a fresh scent, his hand on the butt of his gun. It was good luck I hadn't approached her.

I was so focused on him that I didn't notice the teenagers until they were almost at the Jeep. Three boys and a glamorous girl – not much older than Jet – shoved each other playfully as they approached. In two seconds, I memorized their faces in case I was murdered. It didn't make sense, but you don't make sense when you're having a heart attack in the back of a strange car. Two of the boys had wavy brown hair. The other boy was shorter and

Asian. The girl looked like a movie star in a shark movie – blonde and all legs. All of them wore flip flops and shorts and carried Quick Mart cups. They didn't look like the murdering kind.

All the same, I curled into a ball and squeezed my eyes shut and wished myself smaller than my backpack. In my black cocoon, I prayed they wouldn't open the hatchback door.

Several doors whined open, and the friends climbed into the car. The seat jolted backwards against my head as someone jumped in the back seat. The smell of cheap gas station food filled the air.

"That was close," one of the boys said, which set them all into another fit of laughter.

"Dude, I was ready to turn you in to that Ranger. Legit, if he started asking questions I'd hand you over. I can't get my car impounded."

"Douchebag," another boy laughed.

Something light landed on my cheek. A potato chip? I didn't move.

"Hey! Stop wasting the food," the girl said.

"Man, I'm wasted." That was one of the boys, but I wasn't sure which.

"Just drive," another boy said.

Yes, drive, I urged them silently.

The Jeep revved to life, along with the speakers, blaring a beat that vibrated right through my bones. The car jerked forward and sent my balled body against the hatchback door. I scrabbled for something to hold on to, resisting the urge to raise my head enough to look out the window.

I had no idea where we were going, but anywhere was better than the Quick Mart.

After a minute, I opened one eye, then the other. The trunk was a mess. Empty Dr. Pepper bottles, fast food bags, a sock, a broken umbrella, and crumpled papers all around me. At first, I was afraid to move because I might rustle something and give myself away, but the music blared so loudly, I relaxed and unclenched my jaw.

As I lay there, I tried to figure out if we were really heading toward Austin. They looked too old to be in high school. I'd never met real college students before. Back in Blessing, kids usually went to trade schools after graduation. The colleges were for rich kids like Maggie. Teachers said that all young people were the future of the Republic, but we all knew the rich ones would run it.

It was hard to eavesdrop over the pulsing music, so I stretched up just a little.

"Wes, you'd better not make me late to Comp class," the girl said. "We were supposed to leave fifteen minutes earlier."

"Tame your tits, Hannah," the boy named Wes said.

"Shut up," Hannah said. "You know I hate that phrase. Just because I'm an honor student and I care about my grades—"

"Hey Wes," another boy said. "My Comp class sucks. Drive slower."

"Nooo!" squealed Hannah.

"Cash. You. Are going. To fail. Comp," Wes announced. "But that's okay, my man. You are a beautiful person of many other talents."

"Thank you!" Cash said. "Writing is not for everyone. Can't they accept that? Besides, I'm gonna have my secretary write all my emails. And I'll have a speech writer."

"Ooh, hire me, Cash!" Hannah said. "And pay me a million bucks."

"Damn straight I will. I'm gonna put you all on my payroll and we're gonna freakin' rule Texas. We'll fire all the old guys, and modernize...modernize? Mahhh-dernize is a funny word."

Everybody mumbled "modernize" several times.

I'd never been among such happy people in my life. Even their arguments were filled with laughter. They seemed a bit stoned.

"And modernize the Republic!" Cash stumbled back on track. "But only if we all meet at Hannah's lake house every month. Your lake house was dope, Hannah."

"Confirmed," Wes said. "I'll bring beats. David's got snacks. Hannah brings the lake house."

"And I'll bring the finest shit in Texas," Cash added.

They whooped and agreed and tossed bits of food around the car, some of which landed on me. I won't lie. I ate those bits. It had been a long time since supper.

"I'm coming down," one of the boys, probably David, said sadly. The others mumbled that they were coming down, too. They didn't seem dangerous to me, but one thing I was learning: you never knew what people were capable of being. Life keeps you on your toes that way.

"I'm so tired," Hannah said. "I'm gonna take a nap."

"Dude, what are you doing?" Wes asked.

"Chillin'. I don't have class Tuesday and Thursday, bro," David said. His voice was all syrupy.

"You are seriously not smoking in my car. Dude. It'll get all in the leather and my mom will smell it."

"Chill. I'll blow out the window."

"Don't waste it, man," Cash told him. "There's some serious second-hand pleasure in this shit."

The sick-sweet odor of pot filled my nostrils and almost immediately sent my stomach into coils. I hugged my knees as the speakers thrummed a steady pulse into my back.

"Aw, dude. You are paying for my car to get cleaned when we get back. Detailed!"

David and Cash, who were sitting in the back seat just a few inches from me, sang with the lady's high-pitch voice coming through the speakers. They made up lyrics that sent them into a fit of giggles. The air was thick in the car.

My nose itched. Then it tickled. I wriggled my nostrils and tried to hold my breath, but as soon as I breathed again, I sneezed.

David and Cash stopped singing. "Bro, was that you?" one of them said.

"Naw. Sounded like a hamster sneezed."

The music stopped. I looked up, and there were two faces looking down at me.

"Hey," the boy with David's voice said. He was the Asian one, I could see now. "We have a dude back here. A little dude! A little dude!" He bounced like he'd seen a leprechaun.

"A stowaway?" Cash peered back at me.

I sat up and half-waved, feeling a little light-headed. Hannah was looking over the front seat, too.

"Holy crap," Wes said, watching in the rear-view mirror.

"It's a kid," Hannah cooed. "Hi, kid."

"Hi...Hannah," I said. "David. Cash." I smiled and kept my hand up. If I was friendly, they might not kick me out.

Cash nodded and raised one hand. I tapped it with mine.

"Do you know us?" David asked, wide-eyed.

"I just guessed," I told him.

"You are the world's best guesser! Mind blown. I mean, your name is not that common, Cash."

"I think she heard us say our names, David," Hannah said.

He turned to gaze at me. "No way. Dude's not a she."

Hannah cocked her head and studied me. "I think she is."

David turned to me with concern in his eyes. "Are you a dude boy or a dude girl?" The ash on his joint dropped into his lap, but his focus was on me.

My stomach twisted again. I looked at all of them. They weren't like anyone I'd ever met in Blessing. But the way Hannah shook her head and smiled at me made me think *girl*. Still, I had a feeling I'd better ditch the name Chris for a while.

"My name's Riley," I said.

"See? Girl!" Hannah said.

"Is that drugs?" I pointed at the joint in David's hand. He looked at the joint and shook his head.

"Because I think I'm allergic to it." I hardly got the words out before I sneezed again. "I think I'm going to be sick."

"Aw, hell," Wes said. The car swerved over to the shoulder and the tires crunched to a stop.

"What are you doing?" Hannah asked.

"She's got to get out."

"What? You can't just dump her on the side of the highway. She's not a dog."

"Dude, that's cold," Cash told him.

171

Wes squinted at me in the mirror like he couldn't bear to turn around and face me. "We don't know anything about her. Look at her. What if the cops pull us over?"

Hannah looked me over.

"No way," Cash said, then turned to me. "Are you a thief?"

David was still slouched in the seat, holding in a drag. He coughed and looked up at me. "Is the dudette a street kid?"

"She looks like one," Wes decided.

"How can you see anything in here?" Hannah waved the smoke from her face.

My stomach turned again. "I'm not homeless. And I'm not a thief."

"Are you a sex worker?" Wes asked.

"*Wes.*" Hannah was horrified. "She's a kid!"

He didn't back down. "I will not get kicked out of school for trafficking a kiddie sex worker. You know who's getting in trouble if we get pulled over and this rando's in the car."

"She's not a sex worker," Hanna insisted. "Are you, Riley?"

"Excuse me," I interrupted and started to climb over the seat. "I have to get out."

My stomach was about to springboard.

"Well, go on," Wes told Hannah.

"Go what?" she asked.

"She can't be sick in my car. Go help her... you know... out there." He pointed to the grassy field that lined the highway.

Hannah got out and opened the door for me. As I got out she told the others, "Open the windows, y'all. It smells like a bong in here. And give me my gun. Poor kid. I'll be back in a minute."

172

She shoved a handgun in the waistband of her shorts and walked me all the way to the line of trees, picking out her footsteps carefully in the tall grass in case of snakes. The clean air instantly calmed my stomach. I began to feel foolish for making her come out here.

"How'd you get into Wes's car?" she asked.

"I opened the back door."

"Clearly. Are you running away?"

"No...."

"So... why were you in the car? You're *not* a thief, right?"

"No. I got separated from my sister." I whipped up a story, painting the details in my head. "We were on a bus to visit my dad, and we got separated. There was a big shootout at that gas station the other day. Huge."

"No way." Her eyes widened. "Was it Mother?"

"Yeah."

"Shit." She took the pistol out of her waistband and looked nervously back at the highway. "You can't go anywhere these days without those lunatics messing it up."

"Yeah." I stared at her gun.

Hannah was the kind that talked with her hands, so her gun danced in little loops. "The cops came, right?"

I nodded.

"Why didn't you tell them? They would've found her for you. Or," she gasped, "were a lot of people shot? You think she got shot?"

"No, I mean yeah, a lot of people were shot, but I saw her get back on a bus to Austin. I missed it, though. And I can't tell the cops because my dad would be mad. Real mad. My sister would get into so much trouble if he found out she lost me. He's waiting for us in Austin."

She looked excited. "We're going to Austin!"

"I was hoping you were. Because of the bumper sticker."

Hannah suddenly seemed outraged for me. "You know, it's not your sister's fault that you got separated. Parents can be such jerks."

"I know. And I'm gonna get in so much trouble for losing my gun. But the cops wouldn't let me look for it after the attack." I gave her a pleading look. "You think you could drop me off in Austin?"

"Yeah, we'll drop you off."

"What about Wes? He doesn't like me."

She put her gun away. "He's just scared. Let me worry about Wes. He'll do what I say."

I gave her a sideways glance. She was so pretty, with her honey blonde hair and slim ankles. Silver bracelets jangled on her thin wrists. "So... you're a real college girl?"

"Yeah, I know. There aren't many of us," she chuckled. "My mom's nearly gone broke sending me there. I'm going to be a doctor, just like her."

I blinked. "But if your mom's a doctor, aren't you rich? Don't you live in a mansion?"

"I wish. I mean, our house is nice. But, well you could say my dad screwed us over when he up and left. So, not rich. No mansion."

"But when you're a doctor you'll be rolling in money," I said, confidently. "What about a yacht? Do you have a yacht?"

Her smile widened. "No."

174

"Daw – I mean my dad says doctors all have yachts. That's why he doesn't go to the hospital. Says he won't pay for some doctor's yacht. But I don't mind," I added, in case I'd offended her. "I like boats."

She had a musical laugh. "You're funny, Riley."

I grinned at her, though I hadn't meant to be funny. "I want to be an artist. Do they have art classes at your college?"

"I don't think so. Everybody wants to be an artist or a singer or an actor when they're little. It's a nice dream, but you've gotta pay the bills."

By the time we found a good place for me to throw up, my stomach had stopped cramping and my head had stopped swirling. But Hannah gave me the napkins and I squatted to pee instead because I couldn't waste the opportunity.

Afterward, we trudged through the tall grass and stickers back toward the Jeep.

Hannah paused and turned to me. "Here." She held out her gun. "Take it."

I stared at it. I'd gotten this far without a gun, and I didn't know if I could ever touch another gun without seeing Maggie's face asking me why.

Hannah waved the gun at me. "We've got three other guns in the car in case we run into trouble and I've got two at home. Seems like you need it more than I do. I won't take no."

I took the gun, checked the safety, and tucked it in the back of my jeans. The metal was still warm from Hannah's body. Maggie's face danced before me. "I'm not really old enough to carry," I added as a last attempt to protect my identity.

"Doesn't matter," Hannah said. "Riley, you have to stand up for yourself. Don't let your dad – or anybody else – lay a hand on you. You've got a gun now."

"I couldn't ever threaten my dad," I told her seriously.

She kept walking. "Never say never. Most men deserve to be shot every once in a while."

TWELVE

The drive into Austin took less than an hour. Cash and David were all questions – how old was I, where was I from? Was I running away from evil foster parents who made me cook and clean for them and their real kids? Hannah didn't say a word.

"Where you going?" Cash asked.

"The Neighborhood. Have you heard of it?"

"Yeah. Cool. Is your dad one of those hippy artists?" David asked.

"Yes." Daw hated hippies.

"What's he make?"

"Paintings." I tried to imagine Daw with a paintbrush in one hand and a French beret tilted on his head. The image made me smile.

"Big ones?" Cash asked.

"Mm-hmm. Huge."

"Like those murals downtown. Abstract, or like longhorns and shit?" David asked.

"Longhorns," I decided.

"Wouldn't it be cool to be an artist?" David marveled.

"No, bro." Cash leaned back lazily. "Artists don't earn shit. No offense, Riley."

"It's okay." I wondered if he knew how little cops made.

"Hey, you think your dad can score us some more weed?" David asked, hopefully.

"Bro, don't be a douche," Cash said. "She's like in middle school."

David put his hands in the air. "Dude, never pass up an opportunity for networking. Rule number one in business school."

"You guys need to zip it because I need to study for class," Hannah said. She opened up a chunky fashion magazine and set it on her face. "I love the smell of print," she murmured.

Wes turned on the music again. My head vibrated with the pulse of the bass, and the scenery outside melted one image into another. David and Cash settled into their own worlds, humming to the music, laughing every once in a while about something or other. I propped my head against the corner and stared out the window. A girl on the radio sang about love and a time machine. I wanted a time machine that would take me back to that awful morning. I'd leave my gun hidden on the porch before knocking on Maggie's door, and she'd be alive again. How long would I need to keep running, keep talking, keep spinning stories to keep my brain from going to Maggie?

The tree line blurred behind my eyelids, and Maggie's voice filled my brain.

"Stealing's a sin," she whispered. We were in the back aisle of the Gulf station in Blessing, between the beef jerkies and the sour belts. Maggie's damp blonde curls clung to her red cheeks.

"I'm not stealing," I said, and smiled. "I'm just borrowing."

"I don't believe you."

"It's just a lollipop. It probably cost them two cents, and they're charging seventy-five. That's the crime, charging people crazy prices. They're practically robbing us."

Maggie shook her head. "Whatever. Jesus forgives you." She stopped walking and faced me. "You do believe in Jesus, right?"

I blew out a puff of air. Of course I believed in Jesus. That's why I wasn't afraid of going to hell for stealing a lollipop. Jesus wouldn't do that, not when he had bigger fish to fry.

"You have to believe." Maggie set her hands on my shoulders and gave them a shake. "You have to believe."

I blinked my eyes. The Jeep had slowed and was now surrounded by tall buildings of brick and glass and glimmering stone. Highways wider than rivers. Billboards asking if you got caught drunk driving – *Need a lawyer? Call the Sledgehammer to get out of the Slammer!* Busy people walked briskly across the intersections. I looked up at the building to my right, but I couldn't see the top floor. It was dizzying.

"Heads up, little tramp," Wes called back. "We're almost there. I think. I'm not exactly sure where it is. Do you recognize this area?"

"Not...really." I hadn't figured he'd ask me for directions. Didn't he know where the Neighborhood was? "Could we drive around a little? Maybe I'll see something familiar." I had no idea what I was looking for.

Wes sighed, and Hannah patted him on the arm. "It's fine," she murmured, "We won't be late. I've got plenty of time before class."

"You could just drop me off here and I'll find it."

"No way," Hannah said.

"Yeah, no offense," David said, stretching his arms out, "but you can't just drop girls off in the middle of a city, dude, we'd look like pimps or something." He laughed and poked Cash.

Wes glared at him. "David, shut the hell up." Wes was getting crabbier by the minute. I was outwearing my welcome.

Everyone fell silent as we navigated the city streets, hunting for a sign. The glass and marble buildings gave way to older ones. There were fewer people and more trash bags fluttering in the wind or caught in crevices.

Suddenly, Hannah sat up straight. "Wait! Is that it?"

She pointed to the left at a strange opening between two old buildings. I suppose I was looking for a shiny sign that said The Neighborhood, but this place only had a long piece of wood hanging from a tree near the curb.

"Neighborhood," Hannah said, squinting at it. "I think that's what the sign says."

"Looks like plain old hood to me," Cash said.

"Is that the place?" Hannah looked at me.

I hesitated. The whole block looked sketchier than I'd imagined. The Neighborhood had sounded like such a welcoming place. This area looked like a junkyard.

But I couldn't change my mind now. Besides, Jet might be in there somewhere. And if she was, I had to find her.

"I think this is it." I grabbed my backpack, zipped up Hannah's handgun inside, and climbed out.

"Are you sure about this? Want me to walk you in and help you find your dad?" Hannah asked, her forehead creased with worry lines.

"No, that's okay. This is definitely the place. Just a different side than we usually come in." I thanked Wes for the ride and Hannah for the gun, and then scrambled out. I stood on the sidewalk and waved as the green Jeep rolled away.

When they were gone, I turned to consider my new situation. The doorway to the Neighborhood was like a portal to a garden-city. The drab city walls ended a few feet from a driveway in the middle of the block, and on each side of the driveway, a shock of green took over. Flowering vines crawled up the brick walls and branched across the entry arch. Someone had attached enormous barns doors, along with a padlock, to secure the entrance. It looked so odd right in the middle of the city, but also like it belonged there. There was something eternal and protected about it.

One of the barn doors stood open, so I walked up to the entrance and peered inside. Music, dotted with static, floated out. An old-timey tune on a plinky piano. Someone was hammering on metal – a steady *chink, chink, chink*. And the smell of cooking meat hooked my nostrils like a finger.

An old black man in baggy pants and an older white lady stood by a table a few feet inside the doorway, and to the right was what looked like an outdoor garage sale. Wrinkled clothes hanging on a rack, cardboard boxes on the ground overfilled with pots and pans and plastic bowls. Another box filled with half-naked Barbie dolls, stuffed animals, and metal trucks. Sunlight filtered through the trees and across the pavement.

"Hello!" the old man said, spotting me. "Come on in."

I stepped inside and wavered. "Is this the Neighborhood?"

"It sure is." The woman smiled. She was missing a front tooth. "Welcome! Most everyone here is artists. We create, recycle, and reuse to create a sustainable community."

She pointed to a plaque on the wall that read "We create, recycle, and reuse to create a sustainable community".

She turned back to me. "Can I help you find something?"

"I'm looking for a friend of mine, actually," I said. "Have you seen a dark-haired girl? Spiky hair, leather jacket?"

The woman thought. "We have lots of people, in and out. I couldn't really say."

"Oh." I bit back a surge of disappointment. Everyone would notice Jet. She stood out – bright as a flash of lightning.

"Well, look all you want. We got the mercantile store here." She pointed to the cardboard boxes. It was only then that I noticed the rickety door behind the clothes and stacked boxes. "There's all kinds of stuff in Vera's store. Clothes…" She modeled her own flowered shirt and zebra-striped pants. "Bought these yesterday. And there's shoes and dishes and DVDs and albums and books and beads and jewelry, if you like that. All kinds of stuff, real affordable. Just follow the path around there to the left. Lots of vendors, inside and outside."

"Thanks." The entrance space was a kind of open courtyard. The cracked pavement underfoot was filled in with grass and dandelions and some other weeds that crawled across the pavement. Someone had put up walls of bamboo to divide the vendors here and there, and potted plants were scattered around the entire area. Some pots had tall bushes, some had colorful wildflowers, and others were dead sprigs, dried and carcassy.

I passed by the cardboard junk boxes and weaved my way inside Vera's Mercantile, looking for Jet around every corner and seeing only rows of junk. Vera had taken over part of the old hospital building, constructing rows and rows in a crisscross maze of bookshelves filled with thousands of trinkets and hundreds of cups and bowls and baseball caps. I examined a few of the dainty teacups and souvenir pencils and miniature dolls, but only half of them had price tags on them and I wasn't looking to buy anything anyway.

Vera herself stood at an old-timey cash register. She wore her gray-mare hair in matted pony tails and rocked her body to the folksy music that streamed in through the open door.

I nodded to the hippy cashier as I stepped back outside, where the light breeze instantly cooled me as I wandered through the courtyard square. People seemed to have put up their shops in random places, like pioneers staking their claims. The banging sound I'd heard earlier came from a blacksmith hammering hot iron. He'd set up his work-bench on a sawhorse and used tongs over a barrel of flames to heat up an iron rod, then beat the glowing tip into submission. Little sparks like embers danced onto a nearby carpet, where he'd set out his iron pot handles and gun racks and lucky horseshoes.

"That is a fire hazard if I ever saw one." I knew that voice.

I spun around.

Jet stood behind me, that slight smile curling up at me.

"You're here!" I cried, flinging my arms around her. It had only been a couple of days, but it felt longer. She smelled like campfire and leather and home.

"You mean *you* are here," Jet said, critically. "Calm down, puppy dog." She pulled away and gave me a once over, taking in my new clothes with a raised eyebrow. "I have been looking for you for two days. I thought you were dead or arrested."

"I thought I'd never see you again. I was afraid you'd forget about the Neighborhood."

"I was afraid you would forget you have my money." She shrugged. "And where else would I go?"

"I didn't spend your money, I promise. I spent a couple of dollars on a drink, but that was only my share." I pulled the folded money from my pocket, but Jet shielded her hand over mine and glanced past my shoulder at the blacksmith.

"Okay. Do not flash it around," she said quietly. "If you haven't spent any then we have enough, I think."

"For what?"

"Train tickets. There is a station a few blocks from here. I checked the schedule and the Silver Star train works. The train goes south to San Antonio, but continues on to El Paso on Thursdays and Mondays. I think we should leave on Thursday, eight forty in the morning. Unless you have other plans you care to share?"

I thought of Principal Huffman reaching for her phone. Did she make that call to the police? If so, they might assume I was headed into Austin. They'd look here sooner or later. I was so ashamed of letting my guard down, I couldn't bear to tell Jet about it. Besides, there would be plenty of time to tell her later.

"That's two days from now," I said, suddenly eager to be out of here. "Couldn't we go sooner? Wouldn't a bus be faster? We'd get to the border before that train even leaves."

"It is not safe," Jet said, decidedly. "And they will be looking for me on a bus."

"Who's looking for you?"

She gave me a level look. "No one."

"Does it have to do with that gang member you shot? Is it Mother?"

"Shhh – no. Blue, if you do not learn how to whisper, my fist will show you."

"Sorry," I whispered. "Who's looking for you?"

"Jesus, Blue. No one. Come on." She walked away quickly. I followed at her heels.

"Is it your family?" I guessed.

"I have no family." Her tone was flat.

"What about your uncle—?"

"I would rather die than go back to him."

Her anger was like Daw's heel on a beer can. End of conversation.

Somehow in the hours we'd been apart I'd forgotten how secretive she was. How firmly she shut down any questions about her life. It was infuriating.

We walked toward a collection of ragtag chairs and tables in front of a squatty little shack. You wouldn't really suspect it was a café except for the hand-painted sign that said CAFÉ. It looked more like a rodeo concession stand.

We pulled out a couple chairs, and Jet's mood lightened instantly. "You were right, by the way."

"About what?"

"This place. There are no cops here. They will not come through the front gate. That is the agreement, apparently. The

Neighborhood can stay as long as there is no trouble for the police. At least until the city tears it down."

"No Rangers?" I asked.

She shook her head and smiled. "And no electricity either, so no TVs. I mean, people have cell phones, but…" she shrugged. "Anyway, with our new looks, I think we can relax."

I melted into the chair and kicked my heels up on the table. She did the same.

"How did you even get here?" I asked, floating on the good news.

Jet held up her thumb. "I hitchhiked."

"Isn't that dangerous?"

"Everything is dangerous. I have my gun."

"Oh, I have a gun, too!" I unzipped my backpack and showed her Hannah's gun.

"Where did you get it?"

"Girl named Hannah. I sort of hitchhiked too."

She sat up and turned the gun over in her hands, and said absently, "You should not hitchhike. You are too young." She checked the ammunition and safety, and then aimed it at a rock with one eye closed. "This is a good gun. Better than mine."

"We can switch if you want. I probably won't ever use it."

She gave me another one of her looks and shook her head. "Put it in your holster. You do not want the police to stop you and ask where is your gun."

"They've never asked me before."

"Because, maybe, your father is a policeman?" That exasperated tone entered her voice again. "Blue, you are not in your safe little town anymore. Police will not know who your father is, only that they do not see your gun. Do not give anyone a reason to ask where is your gun."

"Okay. But I left my holster in Blessing."

"Maybe someone here can make you one," she said. "And it might be good to use the name Hannah. Just in case someone checks." She turned the butt of the gun up and revealed the serial ID engraved there.

So I wasn't Chris or Riley any longer. Goodbye Chris and Riley. I shrugged. "Okay. I'm Hannah. Is your code name still Cher?"

She frowned. "Mildred."

"Mildred? That's a grandma name." I laughed.

"Shut up. When I got here, someone asked me my name and I panicked. I was exhausted and this place reeked of mildew. All I could think of was Mildred, for some reason."

"Okay, Mildred." I grinned at her.

Her expression grew resigned. "I have many regrets, and this is near the top."

"Okay, Mildred. What now?" I looked across the little village. Watercolor paintings strung on clothespins, the sound of a harmonica echoing against the walls, a tattoo artist setting up a folding table – everything competed for my attention.

"I will show you around here, and the place where we sleep. The people are nice here. Nosy, but nice."

"Do you want to carry the train money now?"

She shook her head. "No. It is probably safer with a kid like you than with me."

I wanted to tell her I wasn't a kid, but the whole point of shaving my head was to make me look younger. As if she read my mind, Jet rubbed her hand over my fuzzy scalp.

"Come on." She handed Hannah's gun back to me and started walking. I checked the safety and tucked the gun behind my back.

"Mildred?" I called.

"Shut up."

"No, wait. Mildred!" I caught up with her, pulled her shoulder, and looked her in the eyes. I had something serious to say. "I'll be your family."

"What?"

"You said earlier that you didn't have family," I reminded her. "I'll be your family. We're cousins. Should I dye my hair black?"

She stared at me. For a second, I thought she was going to shrug my hand off. Instead, she said, "You are very strange."

"Thank you." The intensity of her gaze was hard to take. I turned away and changed the subject. "So. This whole area used to be a hospital, huh?"

There was a brief silence before she began walking again, motioning for me to follow. "Yes. This building here and that smaller building were part of St. Christopher's Hospital. And this square" – she pointed at a grassy area between the two buildings where people sat together eating or smoking or sleeping in the sun – "was some sort of courtyard. I think some of these people have been here for a long time. Everyone seems to know everyone, but still they are very…" She searched for a word. "…welcoming."

"The more the merrier. It's sort of cool here, the way they've set up everything." I nodded at the watercolor bats swaying on the clothesline. "Are they all artists?"

"Mostly."

"It's almost like they don't know that they'll be evicted in six months."

"I was thinking this too."

"Maybe they'll fight back. Maybe they'll band together and fight the city."

She made a dismissive sound. "Artists make beautiful things, but they do not make good soldiers."

I followed Jet around the square and back to the café again. A few artists had set up around the café, which sold sandwiches, canned soda, and coffee. Someone had turned a parking booth into a wheel repair shop. Bicycle and scooter wheels hung on hooks around the booth, and a rainbow-colored bike reared up like a unicorn against the corner. Here and there, a feral cat peeked out from under a bush. A brave tabby skittered up a tree. Tents and tarps dotted the space between the two taller buildings of St. Christopher's. In one, a woman was making bows and arrows from tree limbs and cord. In another, a bearded man polished and repaired guns.

"Hey." Jet approached the man. "Do you have holsters?"

He looked up. "Uhh..." He drew out the stammer. "I believe I do." He rustled through some items in a box and pulled out a leather-tooled holster, laying it out on a small table.

"I didn't tool it," he explained, although we hadn't asked. "Fairlee did. She got the leather shop, but that's shut until she comes back. I'm looking over her stock till then. She's real good."

He was right – she *was* good. I slid my fingers across the tooled vines and flowers. "How much?"

"Thirty."

"Thirty?" Too much. I stroked it once more, then pushed it back to him. "You know if anybody sells tape? Like duct tape?"

"You try Vera's? The mercantile at the front?"

"I'll look. Thanks."

He looked at me with interest. "You gonna make a holster out of duct tape?"

"Yeah."

"Tell you what," he said, straightening. "Bring it by when you're done. I'd like to see that. My name's Bryan."

"I'm Hannah. And that's Mildred," I added, trying to keep a straight face. Mildred was a ludicrous name for Jet. This was going to take some getting used to.

I wanted to see the rest of the Neighborhood before heading to Vera's for tape. St. Christopher's included two buildings, one three stories tall and the other five stories. The ground floors of both were claimed by painters and basket-makers and potters and glass blowers. But there were animals and livestock too. On the corner of the larger building, two cows and three goats pulled on tethered ropes, reeking of manure. A lanky couple shooed flies from their eyes and offered us samples of milk, warm and foamy. I wasn't sure I liked it as much as the cold kind.

"Those are the other tenants," Jet said, pointing up.

I gazed up at the higher stories. Several of the hospital windows were cracked or completely broken. Those that were still intact were propped open. Laundry hung on windowsills here and there, and one tenant had attached a line to a nearby tree where a bedsheet flapped on the breeze like a flag. A blonde girl sat in one of the windows, one of her legs dangling outside, like she was riding a horse. She leaned back against the wooden frame and looked out onto the square. In another window, a black man in a sleeveless undershirt smoked a cigarette and read a book. That must be where everyone lived, up there.

"So there's no electricity here, but do they have water?" I asked.

"There is water from spigots over there and there." As we walked, Jet pointed at two opposite two corners of the Neighborhood. "I have a jug that we will fill for water and for the toilet. I was approved for a room on the third floor, so we have our own space, at least." She showed me a ticket, which had a room number on it and a signature. "It is only for two nights. The roof is for the homeless who do not contribute to the Neighborhood."

The roof, four stories up, was dotted with makeshift tents. A few men leaned over the edge of the building and smoked cigarettes.

"It gets hot inside the building. We are lucky to get the third floor with a cross-breeze."

"How much does it cost?" I asked.

"Nothing. It is free here, as long as you are an artist of some kind."

"Are you an artist?" I asked.

"No. You are." She stopped walking. "You *are*, right?"

I felt caught off-guard. "Well…"

"You said you could draw my portrait," she reminded me. "I told them you would come."

I didn't know what to say. It was one thing calling yourself an artist. But having other people call you that is a whole other thing.

Intuiting my doubt, Jet said, "Blue," with an edge to her voice. "This is not a free place for just anyone to stay. There is a waitlist, and all the rooms are full. You have to get permission, which I did because I promised you were an artist." She gestured at my backpack. "You know, with your sketches."

"What would I draw, though?"

She waved her hand at the scene around us. "Anything. The vendors. Trees. People on the street passing by. The fleabag cats. People buy that shit."

"I don't have paper or pencils," I reminded her, trying not to sound as nervous as I felt. What if I got us thrown out of here?

"Do not worry about that," she said. "I will take care of it. You draw, and I will sell. Like an agent. Did you see the junk they sell at that so-called store?"

"It's not all junk. They have some nice things."

Her nose wrinkled. "It is literally junk. Donations and things from garbage cans. And visitors from the city come here and pay money for it. They will pay for your pictures." She seemed jumpy and over-excited, and her optimism struck me as strange, since she'd never even seen my drawings.

"Jet?"

"What?"

"We don't really have enough for the train tickets, do we?"

For a second I saw her consider lying. Then she said, "No. But we have two days. We can raise the money."

"How much?"

"We need one hundred and fifty."

"*Dollars*?" My voice rose. "What if we don't make that much?"

"Then I guess I will put you on a bus to El Paso and I will figure out something else. All I know is, I cannot take the bus."

At Vera's Mercantile, we found camouflage duct tape, which cost twenty-five cents. Turned out, everything was pretty cheap at the store, so we each bought a teacup for ten cents to take up to our room. Jet picked up a gallon jug from the stack by a spigot and filled it with fresh water, before we headed up a wide, worn staircase to the third floor.

Our room was small, with a bed pallet, an old armchair, and a bathroom. The door was solid and wide, but there was no lock. The walls were decorated with graffiti – spray painted names I couldn't read and animals with giant, sad eyes, and splotches of yellow and purple and green. It was beautiful, in a way.

"It's not bad," Jet said, as she poured herself a glass of water. "A little Spartan."

I pulled the duct tape roll out and ripped long strips and folded seams and sealed the edges and ripped more strips until I'd fashioned a green camouflage holster that wrapped around my thigh, just like Jet's. My gun fit the holster perfectly.

When I'd finished, I looked out the window. The glass was missing from the frame, and as I leaned out, a cool gust brushed my cheeks and gave me a prickle of goosebumps. I could see the courtyard with all the artists, and up a few blocks, the glass skyscrapers of Austin. A trolley car crossed an intersection two blocks away with a *ding-ding* of bells. And further down the street, a silver blue waterway gleamed in the sun.

"Is that a river?" I asked, glancing back at Jet.

"Yes."

"The Lady Bird River?" I'd read about it but never seen it.

"Maybe." Jet spread the bedsheet out over the thin mattress on the floor. "Should be called the bat river. Wait until the sun goes down."

"It used to be called the Colorado, but Lady Bird sounds so much prettier," I told her. "It goes right through Austin and all the way down to the Gulf of Mexico. Goes way up north, too. Almost to the border of New Mexico."

She yawned. "You are a river expert?"

"Not really," I said. "Hey, maybe we could borrow a boat and float all the way to New Mexico. They probably don't have border guards there."

Jet stretched out on the pallet, covered her eyes with her forearm, and muttered, "She is not a river expert."

"Why?"

"The river flows south and empties into the Gulf. You cannot float north. We would need a motorboat. And we would not exactly be inconspicuous. Besides," she peeked at me from under her arm, "do you know where to 'borrow' a boat?"

I snarled my nose up at her.

"That is what I thought." She closed her eyes again. "Stop hanging out the window. You will fall and break your neck. I have to rest for a few minutes. Take a nap."

She took a deep breath and sighed as she melted into the bed pallet. Her stomach pooched out above her belt, but I couldn't tell if it was her baby belly or her natural curves. I hitched up my shirt and examined my belly button. I took a big breath and watched my belly expand and then flatten out again.

"Jet?"

"Hmm." Her voice was sleepy.

"Are you feeling okay?"

"Mm-hmm. Just tired."

I dragged the chair closer to the window and stretched out in it, feeling the weight of the day on me. As I closed my eyes, I imagined rafting against the current of Lady Bird River, bluebirds and cardinals singing from the banks. The trees were trading their green for yellows and oranges. At the tip-top end of the river, in the map in my mind, the raft would bank itself, and I'd climb out. Marla would be there, waiting for me in a white dress that tied on the side. She'd shade her eyes as she watched me, and she'd know what to do. I'd call her Mom, and she'd call me Blue, and we'd turn around and hop onto a cloud that would float us to California, or somewhere else where everyone flung their arms tightly around that dangerous freedom to do and think whatever they wanted.

My heartbeat picked up. Once Jet and I got to the border, then what? Jet would go off and do her thing in New Mexico. I didn't want to hitchhike all the way to California. I needed Marla, standing there waiting for me on the other side of the border.

"Jet?" I said, but Jet's heavy breathing had petered out into a dozing "puh." I turned to my side and tried to get comfortable in the chair. Something hard poked me in the side.

I reached between the cushion and the side of the chair and pulled out a thin bag covering something flat and hard. I peeled down the plastic. It was a yellow sketchbook with a sturdy back and a little sticker on the front like the ones at Vera's Mercantile.

Two dollars. The cover was stained and several pages had been ripped out, but I flipped through it and counted. Thirty-one pages left. They were thick and smooth, much better than the printer pages of my artbook back home. At the bottom of the sack were five pencils with different hardness numbers and an eraser.

I wondered how Jet paid for them, since I had all the money. She'd done most of the talking and I hadn't thought to ask. I felt bad for not asking. I wondered how she ate and drank while I was gone, and what we'd do once we spent all the money in my pocket, and whether we'd sell enough drawings to buy the train tickets. The wondering tired me, so I closed my eyes. I hugged the sketchbook and leaned back in the chair and smiled.

"Thank you," I whispered.

THIRTEEN

I woke to the sound of locusts buzzing and people laughing far away. Jet's voice cut through the darkness, nudging me.

"Blue? Wake up."

I heard her feet shuffling, but couldn't see anything. I sat up, and something slipped off my lap and onto the floor. I took a few seconds to realize that I'd fallen asleep in a chair and we were in an old hospital room in the Neighborhood.

"Where are you? Why is it so dark?"

"No electricity." Her voice floated from somewhere. "There is light outside. Come."

"Do I take my backpack?"

"No. I hid it."

I stood up, muscles aching from the long day and the old chair, and stepped tentatively in the direction of her voice.

"Where are we going?"

"Food."

We groped our way out of the room and into the hallway, which was lit at the end with two tall candles in glass jars. On each one was a painting of a lady whose image flickered like a ghost.

Another candle had been left on the stairwell. It gave just enough light that we didn't stumble as we made our way down the stairs.

"Are those Catholic candles?" I asked Jet.

"They are called *veladoras*," she corrected me.

"Why are there women on them? Are they all Mary?"

"Not all. They are saints. You light a candle, and the guardian saints give an extra boost to your prayer. The *veladoras* stay lit for many days to remind you to be devout and recite a special prayer and believe."

"They must be very religious here."

"Hardly," she scoffed. "These candles are cheap, and they burn for a week. That is why they use them."

"Are you Catholic?"

"Yes. But not devout."

As we made our way to the ground floor, we could hear the sounds of voices and laughter rising to meet us. I was still thinking about the *veladoras*. "Do they work?"

"What?"

"The candle-prayers. The saints."

Jet stepped off the last stair into the courtyard, and in the glow of the full moon overhead and more candles on tables and windowsills I could see her face, squinting at me as she pointed to her belly.

"Look at me. You think I did not pray about *this*? Actually, I do not pray, but I did pray last month. A lot. And guess what? I am still pregnant. These candles." She threw a hand up and kept walking. "They are just a way to keep people calm while the world goes to crap all around them. But being calm is good. Calm people think. Calm people plan."

I knew that most prayers weren't answered. But I decided to pray to these saints because we needed help. We needed money and train tickets and food and good hiding places and saints for guardians.

BLUE RUNNING

In the courtyard, thirty or forty people had gathered around an enormous stone fire pit. Without the sun, the air had turned cool and damp again. October was right around the corner, when the days and nights would feel less like strangers. The firelight danced, casting its orange-yellow light across the square. Some people wandered from group to group, like politicians eager to put a word in. One man in a lopsided fedora played an accordion, which I'd never seen in real life.

It mesmerized me, the way he pumped his hands and pressed the accordion's button-eyes and didn't even look at it as he sang. Curly brown hair peeked out from under his hat, and his white teeth flashed when he smiled, which he did a lot. It was as if every verse, every phrase, was a reason to smile. When he finished playing, everyone stopped talking and clapped and called out for another song, and then went on with their private conversations.

The smell of grilling meat made my mouth water. Jet led me to a few barrels not far from the bonfire, where the community had a makeshift kitchen. One long-haired woman in an ankle-length dress two sizes too big for her held a pair of long tongs and tended to chicken legs and hamburgers roasting above a barrel with a red-ember glow. Over another open barrel, a few people were roasting hot dogs and sausages and anything cheap that could be skewered on a wire hanger. Over another barrel, a little kid in a sleeveless shirt and white underwear opened an aluminum foil bubble, releasing steam and the aroma of buttery popcorn, next to a man in a striped shirt who was roasting potatoes and corn on the cob.

My empty stomach clenched so hard I caught my breath.

"Jet." I tapped her arm. "Is the food free?"

She shook her head.

"How do we eat? Should we spend some train money?"

She shook her head and looked from group to group. "I do not see them."

"Who?"

"The couple who said they would share. They invited me this morning." She turned in a circle. "They are not here."

She looked anxious, and I realized there was a chance we might not get to eat tonight. But I'd had enough of being hungry.

"Follow me," I said. I tracked back to the hippy-woman flipping meat patties. There were about six left on the round grate.

"Hi," I said.

She glanced at me. Her silver hair was chopped short above her eyes, but hung straight and heavy past her shoulders. Her green eyes were startling.

"Has anyone ever told you that you have an interesting face?" I asked.

She looked at me with those emerald eyes and shrugged. "Well, I am an interesting person."

"I bet you are. Your eyes are so pretty."

Her expression grew suspicious. "You begging for food? 'Cause we got strict policies here. No begging in the Neighborhood."

"Oh, no ma'am," I assured her. "I was just wondering if you'd allow me to draw your portrait. Tomorrow, when it's light out."

"My portrait?" She laughed, clearly uncertain whether she should take me seriously.

"Yes. I'm an artist." My heart thudded at my own audacity but I made myself smile politely.

"She is the best sketch artist I have ever seen," Jet announced, figuring out what I was up to.

"Really. The best?" The hippy-woman flipped a meat patty, then put her hand on her hip. "Are you new here?"

I nodded. "I just got here a few hours ago."

"What's your name?"

"Hannah. And this –" I looked at Jet and smiled. "– is my cousin Mildred."

"My name's Vic." She sniffed and gave me and Jet a once-over. "Well, Hannah. I suppose I have to see for myself if you're really the best sketch artist in the Neighborhood. There's stiff competition here."

"I'm game." I nodded. "How about tomorrow morning?"

"Yep. I'll be over by Teak's candle shop. My husband and I make candles there."

"Deal." I held my hand out to shake hers.

She considered my hand a few seconds, then finally took it and shook. "How much do you charge for portraits?"

"Ten dollars," Jet said, lightning quick.

"But yours is free, Miss," I said.

"What?" Jet interrupted.

"It's free." I gave Jet a hard stare.

"That's real nice," Vic said, flipping a burger carefully, "but I can't let you give away your art for free. That's not how we do things here. You work, you create, you sell or trade. That's how you earn respect. That's how the Neighborhood does business."

She handed me a paper plate with three meat patties on it.

201

I took the meat patties and smiled. "Thank you."

"Go tell that little guy in the striped shirt to give you a potato," Vic said, pointing with her tongs. "Tell him I said so or he won't. See you tomorrow."

After retrieving the potato – the little guy had reluctantly handed one over after Vic shouted across to him – Jet and I divided the food between us while we listened to the accordion man. The others called him Darnell. His dark skin glistened in the firelight, and his warm, smiling eyes twinkled at me. He cradled the accordion on his lap against his flowered shirt. I couldn't take my gaze off him and made Jet stay and listen until she grew tired again and we filled another water jug and headed up.

Back in our room, Jet borrowed a saint candle from the hallway and checked under the ceiling tile for my backpack, which was safe and snug, and then she climbed back into bed and fell asleep again. She seemed so tired now – more tired than before. I felt wide awake. Too excited about being here with her again and safe at last, to sleep.

So I sat up watching the lights of the city through the open window. After the music stopped and the bonfire was extinguished, but the low voices of people still murmured in the courtyard below us, I went back to the stairwell and spoke to the veiled lady on the *veladora* candle.

"Dear Lady, this is Blue. Bluebonnet Andrews. Thank you for watching over me and Jet," I whispered. I held the photo of Marla in the candlelight. "This is my mom. I guess you know I stole the photo from my dad, so I'm sorry about that. But I'm wondering...if you know where my mom is...if…" I tried to think of a reasonable request from someone who hadn't prayed all her life. It seemed to me you can't just ask for a whopper of a miracle if you haven't earned it. "Well, I wonder if you could talk to her. Her name's Marla, if you forgot. And maybe you could help me find her. I think she's in California. Please, could you put some nice thoughts of me in her head? And help me find her phone number? That would be enough. Thank you."

In the flickering glow I looked at Marla's face, so easy and relaxed, as pretty as a movie star in an old magazine. The curve of her cheek, the slope of her shoulders, the wisps of hair – yes, I could draw her. Suddenly, I needed to draw her like I needed to know her. I looked down the black hallway, lit on the far end by another candle, and then picked up Mary and took her small light to the room, where Jet slept curled on her side. Tucking my feet into the seat cushions, I propped the sketchbook against my knees, and drew.

As I formed her mouth, I heard her laughing. And with each stroke of hair, I saw it shake as she caught her breath and shook her head. *No, no, don't make me laugh anymore*. The robe was the most difficult. How to make material appear soft without the jagged lines of electric jolts or animal fur? I erased the sleeve a few times before discovering that smudging the graphite with my pinky finger gave it the softness I was looking for.

"You're so happy," I whispered to my sketch when I was done. "What happened? Why'd you have to leave?"

"What?" Jet said, lifting her head a few inches off her pallet.

"Nothing." I turned over the photograph, as though there might suddenly be something written on the back, but as always, only one word was scrawled across the white: *Marla*.

At school a few times, I'd tried to track her down, but the internet was slow and the computers were old and the Republic's infamous firewall blocked me if I searched for California or any other state in America.

There had to be some way to find her. But I didn't know who her friends were or where she lived now. Suddenly, it seemed an impossible task. A needle in a haystack dream. And I'd bet everything on succeeding. If I couldn't find her, I'd be all alone.

"Jet?" I whispered.

"Hmm." She didn't lift her head this time.

"Do they have Wi-Fi in the Neighborhood?"

"No." Her voice were slurred from sleep.

I retraced the day. I'd seen a few artists using cell phones, but only a few. Without electricity, the Neighborhood was like an ancient city. People didn't walk around with their heads plugged into earpieces and bowed down to their phones. They talked to each other and did things. Their hands and eyes and mouths were always busy, always doing.

"Do you think someone has a phone with internet?"

"Yes. There are places with power nearby for charging. But I am asleep."

I carried the candle back to the stairwell. A man, sun-leathered or just dirty, stumbled up the stairwell as I set the candle on the top stair, but he didn't see me. He hummed to himself as he stumbled to a room a few doors down. Back in our dark room, I felt my way to the chair near the window and curled up. I hugged the sketchbook to my chest and lay my head on the armrest.

"Jet?" I listened for her breathing. "Jet?"

"Hmm."

"I want to find my mom tomorrow. Will you help me?"

There was such a long pause that I thought she'd fallen asleep again. Then she spoke. "That will be hard, since she is on the other side of the Wall."

"No, I mean, I need to find her-find her. Like, on the planet."

I heard Jet turn over.

"You mean, she is not at the border?"

"She doesn't know she's meeting me at the border yet."

She grew more awake. "So when you said the other day that you and your mother had a plan..."

"We didn't really have a plan," I said slowly, like dipping my toes in a pool, testing the waters. "I was being overly optimistic. As Daw used to say."

"Hmm. And you do not know where she is now, on the planet?"

"No, I do not."

"Jesus, Blue." Jet's voice held more wonder than frustration.

"Daw told me that she moved to California before the borders closed," I explained. "But that was ten years ago. I don't know if she's still there. She never wrote or called. Far as I know." Jet didn't say anything. I had to fill that silence. "Her name's Marla. Maybe somebody here knows how to get past the firewall and we could look her up in America. If there's internet here."

"Jesus," Jet said again. She did not sound like she thought my chances were great.

We were both quiet in the dark. Amid the panic of Maggie's death and all the chaos, I hadn't realized how impossible it might be to find my mother. She could even have remarried – changed her name. Then I'd never find her.

Jet's voice cut the silence. "You are up a creek called shit."

"Well," I said, but couldn't think of a suitable comeback, so I clamped my lips and squeezed my eyes shut.

"This is not a game, Blue," Jet grumbled. "You have to know things. You have to plan."

"How am I supposed to plan everything exactly right?" My voice grew heated. "I was running from bad people when we met. I didn't know where I was running, I just knew who I was running from. Excuse me for not having a perfect plan and excuse me for hoping that my mom will realize she made a mistake leaving me and she'll want me back. But then," I added with a viper strike of meanness, "that's not something you'd understand, is it? You don't even care about your own baby."

If I hurt her, she didn't say so, and I couldn't make out her features in the darkness. Silence stretched between us and I hugged the sketchbook tight until the spiral coils dug into my collarbones. The accordion started piping its music into the night again, and several drunk people below us sang a tune that was impossible to decipher, but I could imagine them, arms slung around each other's shoulders, swaying, fumbling up the words as they belted out the song. It helped somehow, listening to them. When they stopped singing, the locusts took over and filled the night with their echoing *cree-crees*.

Finally, I heard Jet move again, the gentle swishing of her body against a thin sheet. "When I was 12," she said quietly, "I did not have my mother, either. I lived with my *abue* – my grandmother – in Guadalajara. My mother was always gone.

206

Months at a time. Always had some excuse about a job she needed to go to. She was too young and mixed up in drugs, I think. Gangs. But I was happy living with Abue. Abue was strict, but she loved me. One day when I was nine, my mother showed up while Abue was at mass. She said "*Vámonos!*" Gave me a little plastic bag and told me to fill it. That was all I could take – what would fit in that sack with the stretched-out handles. I never saw Abue again."

She paused, and the black night spread like a universe between us.

"My mother said she was all cleaned up. Sober. Was going to save me from 'stinkin' poverty.' She was going to take me to America where her half-brother lived. Uncle Chago." There was venom in her voice when she said his name. "But she didn't take us to America. Uncle Chago was here. In this fucking Republic. It was worse than Mexico City. Took us two weeks to get here, smuggled past the border by terrible men, and when my clean, devoted mother finally came face to face with Uncle Chago, that was it. She was gone. She had a needle up her arm before I even put on my pajamas that first night. We lived with Uncle Chago and his wife, Beezie. I called her Beastly. She taught me English at home by sitting me in front of the television and beating me until I learned to speak enough to get by without raising suspicion."

Jet paused, and I untangled my imagination from Beastly's red hands and Jet's bruised back. "What about your mother? Why didn't she stop Beastly?"

"My mother was out working for Uncle Chago, but she was messed up most of the time. When I was twelve, she was arrested for prostitution and the Rangers sent her to the border cages to be deported. She died there. In a cage."

"Oh Jet." I imagined her mother, an older Jet with long hair and bony arms, curled up on the floor of a cage like a dog.

She kept talking as if I hadn't spoken. "After that, the beatings were worse. Beastly called me Dirty Scaler and Leech. Like I was not even human."

"Wasn't there anybody who could help you? There's always somebody."

"Always somebody? Blue, that is some white privilege bullshit."

"Daw says white privilege is an American lie."

I could almost hear her lip curl. "Daw sounds like a charmer."

"What I mean is... you helped *me* when I needed it."

"Of course. Because I am a decent human, even when I do not want to be. But who would I go to for help, Blue?" Her voice was brittle and wounded. "A very nice schoolteacher named Miss Sweetie-Pie?"

I didn't answer. I suspected she'd never been to a real school.

"Or the police?" she continued bitterly. "They are so helpful and compassionate to immigrants."

I swallowed down my own stupidity, but it just stuck in my throat, refusing to dissolve.

"There was no one to protect me. But you know what? One day I woke up taller than Beastly," Jet said, "and on that day, when she was in the bathtub, I pushed her head under the water and held it there. Just long enough to make her scared."

"Did she drown?"

"She might have choked. A little." In spite of the dark, I knew Jet was smiling. "But I pulled her up by her long black hair and held up a pair of scissors to her eyes and told her that if she ever touched me again, I would cut off all her hair and eyebrows and eyelashes while she was sleeping and say a curse that her hair would never grow back. And if she told anyone or tried to kill me, the curse would spread to her fingernails and toenails." She paused, and the silence was like a smile. "She never touched me again."

I stared in her direction. "You know spells?"

"No, Blue. I am like you – a good storyteller. Anyway, it was not Beastly I should have been afraid of. Uncle Chago gave me fake papers and made me work for him. I worked as a cashier at the Dairy Queen making deals with the cops and Rangers and anyone else passing through. Sometimes taking backpacks from bikers who knew a secret word and stashing it in my locker until the next biker came through with another secret word. I knew a lot of them."

"Secret words?"

"Bikers. You remember the man in the green bandana at the station? The shootout?"

"The guy you shot?"

She ignored that and said only, "I recognized him."

"That's why he smiled at you," I said, stitching it together. "But he was in Mother." I nearly choked on my tongue. "That means… Are you...part of Mother?"

"No. I was not in that gang. Uncle Chago was. He never said it out loud, but everyone knew. I knew." She drew a breath. "Anyway, last year, everything changed. At home, Uncle Chago stared at me too much. Kept saying things. You are asking for trouble with those legs, he would say. Sticking out your titties like that. You be asking for it. And he would not stop pushing his body against me when he walked past me. Even in front of Beastly."

My heart raced. I knew what she was going to say before she said it.

"One night, he woke me in my bed and took what he wanted. I was strong, but not strong enough. I fought, but not hard enough."

I could imagine her, all arms and legs and fists. Struggling with all her strength. Did she scream? Would it have mattered?

"And all I kept thinking was where would I get help if he cut me up? Where would I go for help? The friendly police? I would be sent to the cages like my mother. And die there. Nowhere is safe in the Republic for me. You cannot trust no one."

"You can trust," I said.

"What?" Suddenly she lashed out. "You correct my English *now*? Fuck you, Blue!"

"No! No!" I scrambled off the chair and found her curled up body on the mattress in the darkness. I wrapped my arms around her back and shoulders and held her tight. "No, I meant you can trust *me*. You can trust me, Jet. I won't tell, I promise, I promise. I promise. And your English is better than mine, I swear."

She didn't speak. Her body shook in small convulsions. It made my eyes sting, this silence. Still, I held her, attached like some barnacle on a boat. Anchored there, barely rocking.

It was a long time before she spoke. "Blue," she whispered, half-choked. "I cannot have this thing inside me. I want it out. I *need* it out."

"I'm so sorry," I said, softly. "I'm so sorry that happened to you."

She went absolutely still for a long moment. And then she reached back and squeezed my hand.

I tried to imagine how it would feel to be raped, to have your arms pinned and your throat closed and your lungs full of darts, but I couldn't. But I *could* imagine being sentenced for life for something you didn't do. I could imagine the feeling of losing yourself in a split second.

"I promise," I whispered again, and her hair stuck to my lips. "I promise."

FOURTEEN

"Sleep with your gun under your pillow," Jet whispered as I drifted off to sleep. I didn't have a pillow. I was back on the chair by the window, giving her space. So I tucked the gun between the seat cushion and the armrest, and left my hand wedged there, just in case.

I stared at the moon until my eyelids, like weights, fell closed. Sometime in the night, I woke to the sound of howling. At first, the howls made my hair bristle, and my fingers instinctively closed around the metal beneath me. But the howls were followed by bursts of laughter, and I realized it was just drunk people. Drunk artists weren't scary. They were both impressive and a little sad. The last heroes of festivals and parties, yes, but not without a price.

I heard other noises. Someone moaning here and there, whether from pain or pleasure, I couldn't tell. A small child crying. A woman and man arguing, their voices carrying across the open yard and open windows. *You were, I know it! I know it!* The woman's clear words interrupted by the static of her rage. It took me hours to get back to sleep, and when I woke up, it was one of those blink-eye mornings, where the whole night passes in the span of two seconds and you get the feeling that you've been handed a terrible injustice, robbed of the dreams you were due.

The aroma of coffee and bacon lured me down to the courtyard while Jet still slept, curled in a cocoon. The Neighborhood was waking up below us. I strapped my holstered gun to my thigh and headed downstairs with my sketchbook and pencils. The morning still had that dewy-wetness everywhere, and my shirt felt damp as I sat in an old wicker chair in the café and began to sketch the tall, bald man making coffee on the patio. His name was Steve. His apron had bright yellow flowers on it, and something about that made me instantly like him.

"Gonna be a hot one," he said, peering up at the cloudless sky and rubbing his belly. "September can't never make up its mind. But I like it hot. Brings in business."

I showed him his portrait halfway through, and he brought me a cup of coffee and a bowl of oatmeal so I could take my time finishing the sketch.

"That's pretty good," he said each time he took a break and checked on his portrait. The third time, he asked what else I could draw.

"Could you draw the whole store?" he suggested.

"Sure."

"And me in it, there, where the barista stand is. Only could you draw a little goatee here? I'm thinking about growing it out again. It's a good balance with the cue-ball." He patted his smooth head.

"No problem." I actually thought a goatee would suit him.

"And maybe, like, a bird on the shrub there, peeking out at me."

"You got it." I flipped to a new page in the sketchbook, turned it horizontal, and started arranging shapes on the page. He hadn't told me he'd pay for a sketch, but I needed the practice, and he'd already given me coffee and breakfast so I considered us even.

Later, as I was adding a little cardinal to the bush in my drawing, he brought over a scrap of cloth. "It's extra," he said as he folded it into a long strip. "Gonna be hot in this sun. You wear this on your neck to keep the sweat off or douse it in water to keep you cool."

He tied it gently around my neck and stepped back to admire his handiwork.

"Thank you." I touched the soft cloth lightly, surprised to find this thoughtful gesture had almost brought tears to my eyes.

A while later a lady stopped and watched me draw. I thought I recognized her from the day before. She was the one at the entrance, the welcome lady who'd told me to come inside. I finished Steve's drawing and then hesitated. I needed to sign it. Signing it was the most important part. How else would people know who drew it, and who to pay if they wanted their own portraits or storefronts done? But I couldn't sign it my real name, and I didn't want to sign it Hannah. I hovered my pencil over the bottom right corner and waited until it came to me. Then I drew my name in large letters: BB.

"Does that say BB?" the welcome lady asked over my shoulder.

"Yes." I carefully peeled the page away from the book.

"That your name?"

"I'm Hannah," I explained. "But my artist's name is BB."

"Oh." The welcome lady nodded. "Well, that's amazing. You're quite the artist, Hannah."

"Thank you. I'll be selling sketches today, in case you come across anyone interested."

The welcome lady smiled and she waved goodbye, and I couldn't tell if she was just being nice or if she was trying not to laugh at me or if she really meant what she said, but Steve beamed when I handed him the new sketch. He pinned it right then to his register stand.

I picked up the wicker chair to test the weight. "Do you mind if I borrow this chair to do some more sketches? I'll bring it back, I promise."

"No problem." He gave my coffee cup one more top-off. I turned around and nearly bumped into Jet, her charcoal eyes smudged and her hair sticking out all ways to Sunday, like she'd rolled out the window and onto the street.

"Where did you go?" she demanded. "I woke up and you were gone!"

"Coffee?" I held the steaming cup out to her. She took it, and her furrowed eyebrows softened.

"You were asleep," I explained, "so I thought I'd get a head start and practice some sketches."

"Yeah? Let me see."

I showed her the sketches of Marla and the coffee man. She pursed her lips and nodded. "Not bad."

"Gee, thanks. Last night you said I was the best sketch artist you'd ever seen."

"That was to impress Vic. I was building your credibility." She looked at the sketches again and shrugged. "I mean, you are no Michelangelo. But definitely not bad."

"Again. Thanks." I pointed to the sketch pinned to the coffee shop post. "He thinks I'm good."

"Did I not just say that?" Jet said, following me.

"No. That's not what you said. You said I wasn't bad."

"And you are not!"

I spun around, ready to thrust out my sketchbook and tell her if she's such an expert, why doesn't she just draw everyone herself. But then I saw the amused gleam in her eye.

"You're mean. After I gave you coffee and everything."

"Okay. You are a good artist," she exclaimed, almost laughing. "So good! I think you are the next da Vinci. Da Vinci should be very scared."

I cocked my head, trying to figure her out.

"You see?" she said. "Empty praise is..." She waved one hand in the air. "Honest praise keeps you from deceiving yourself and others. You seemed worried before if you were good enough to sell art. So I tell you that you are good enough to sell sketches. Does that not make you happy? Relieved?"

"I guess."

"Frankly, I was a little worried. You were talking about your art the way Beastly talked about her own cooking. A starving dog would not eat her food."

I picked up the wicker chair. "We need to find that lady who wanted me to sketch her. The one with the hamburgers."

Jet's smile faded. "Vic? Are you sure? That woman gives me the creeps."

"What? Why?" I was surprised by her reaction. Vic had seemed nice enough last night.

She just shrugged and cradled her coffee cup.

We found the candlemaker stand, but Vic was nowhere in sight. I pulled my chair up to the archer's booth and sketched him as he bent a bow into a half-moon and flexed his arms like a Roman soldier. Then I sketched the girl in the booth next to the archer, all in a trance staring at him. She was about Jet's age. Her wide eyes I made wider with long eyelashes. Her body leaned toward him, her chin jutting out. She had it bad, in real life and on the page.

"She's smitten," someone said behind me.

It was the accordionist, Darnell. Still wearing the flowered shirt from last night, but without the accordion. He smiled and tipped his hat at me. My heart raced.

"That's quite remarkable." He nodded at my work. "I'm Darnell. How do you do?"

I shook his hand, which was cool and steady.

"I'm – uh, Hannah," I stammered, hardly remembering myself. He must have been in his twenties, way too old for me to act silly over. But slapped silly I was.

"You're a sketch artist?" he asked.

The heat rose to my cheeks.

"Yes," Jet interrupted. "She is the best. Would you like a portrait? For you, ten dollars. As a favor."

"I'm tempted," he said, and studied my sketch of the girl. "Is this one sold?"

"No," I answered.

"It's Lizzie. I know her mother." He smiled. "She would not like the way Lizzie is staring at Otto."

"But he's not even in the picture."

He leaned over and said, "Let's hope it stays that way. Lizzie's a wild one. But Otto's even wilder."

"Oh."

"Are you new neighbors here?" he asked, glancing at Jet.

"Yes," I answered, before she could speak. "We saw you perform last night. You're really good."

"Thank you. And your friend is…?"

"Mildre—"

"Millie," Jet interrupted, and shook Darnell's hand.

His smile broadened. "You'll love this community. Everyone helps each other here. Not like the outsiders. Don't get me wrong. Outsiders are welcome – they keep us in business, after all – but they're not like the people here. The Neighbors are like family. Will you be here tonight… at dinner?"

I nodded.

"Bring your sketchbook," he said. "Could you sketch me playing by the bonfire?"

I nodded again.

"Good." He reached into his front pocket. "Here's ten dollars. Prepaid. I'll see you tonight, Hannah bandana."

When he left, I turned around and waved the ten-dollar bill at Jet. She high-fived me and put the money in her back pocket.

"I like him," I said.

"Really." Her tone was dry. "I would not have guessed."

I moved the wicker chair to Vera's Mercantile and started sketching people browsing the aisle, heads bent over. Then people smoking cigarettes under the stubby live oak tree in front of the store. Then a squirrel that had scampered down the tree and had approached me cautiously, freezing every few inches and flicking his bushy tail.

An old man, another Neighbor, gave me five dollars for the sketch of the squirrel. Jet had an idea to put the money on the bandana, so I untied it and she spread it on the dirt right in front of me. "To inspire people," she said as she played around with the five and ten-dollar bills, folding them this way and that until she was satisfied that it looked like grateful donation tossed at our feet. She guarded it, just in case someone had the idea of snatching it when they walked by.

It seemed to work. When the outsiders started coming in, a lady in a pink floppy hat and sunglasses set down her canvas shopping bag and asked me to draw her grandkid, who was running in circles chasing pigeons. I had to imagine the little twerp feeding the pigeons instead of stomping at their tail feathers with squeals of glee. The grandmother in the pink floppy hat handed Jet a ten, which she set on the neck cloth. A few outsiders stood behind me and watched me sketch, and that drew even more attention.

Some people dropped coins on the cloth, just because. The welcome lady came over to say hello with people in tow. First time visitors to the Neighborhood, she said.

"As you can see, everyone here is an artist or craftsperson of some sort," she announced. "Here at the Neighborhood, we only take cash. We encourage haggling, but please remember that we are all struggling artisans, and this is our living."

She held up a crown of white flowers.

"I make these," she said proudly. "Laurels with honeysuckle and chamomile."

I took my eyes off my current sketch of a Neighbor with tattoos from neck to elbow. The tattoos were more like smudges on my paper.

"This laurel is for our newest artist," the welcome lady said. "Umm, what's your umm…"

"Hannah," Jet said from the ground. She'd found herself a grassy spot to lie on nearby. She shaded her eyes. "And I'm Hannah's agent. Millie."

"Oh, yes! Mildred. I remember."

"Just Millie," Jet corrected her, firmly.

The welcome lady placed the white-flowered laurel on my head as I finished sketching the tattooed man. Everyone oohed and ahhed.

"I'm next," said a woman with a gravelly voice. It was Vic, standing behind two outsiders. She pushed past them. "You ladies will have to get in line to wait your turn. Sorry." She grinned, flashing silver molars. "There's some candles and handcrafted candlesticks round the back of the café. Everyone loves them. Great gifts. Best booth in the Neighborhood, swear to God. Big sale, too, better hurry."

The welcome lady scowled as the outsiders cooed about needing candles and shoved off toward the café. "Vic, you can't steal customers."

"I ain't stealing nothing," Vic said. "I'm just being a nice host, telling people what's available. Geez, Louise."

"I've told you not to call me that, neither."

"Fine. Louise. Goodbye. Louise." The lady walked back to the entrance gate and Vic sighed. She eyed the cloth with the small pile of money on it.

"Nice kitty, there," Vic nodded at the cloth.

"Yeah." I barely glanced up from my work.

"You want to come over to our booth? We got shade, and lots of folks hang out in our corner. Could earn you some more commissions."

It seemed like a good idea, and it was getting hot in the sun. So I said, "Okay."

But when I glanced at Jet I could see that she didn't love the idea of moving away from the entrance. All I could offer was a shrug as she folded our kitty up and threw the cloth bandana at me. I wondered why she was upset.

Vic chuckled and took my chair for me. "Reminds me of the summer I painted the Seen River in Paris in a wicker chair just like this one."

My jaw gaped. "You've been to Paris?"

"Yes, indeed. Before the borders closed, I painted them bridges and castles and all them boats coming down the Seen. You ever been to Paris?"

"No," I said. I was kind of doubtful that she had, either.

"You ought to if you can. It's a beautiful city. I had my beret and my wicker chair and my canvas and my easel." Her eyes looked out over the condemned buildings as though she was admiring the Eiffel Tower itself.

I stole a glance at Jet, who rolled her eyes. Vic kept rambling as we walked.

"You know how I got that beret? This one artist – François was his name – they're all called François over there – well, he challenged me to a paint-off after I wouldn't move my easel over for him. Put up his beret as a wager, and we painted a bridge in front of a whole slew of tourists."

"Which bridge?" Jet asked.

"What?"

"Are there not a lot of bridges on that river?"

Vic frowned and huffed. "Well, there are lots of bridges. It was Bridge Two or Three, I can't remember. Not important. What's important is I won. Every single tourist voted for my painting. Unanimous." She grinned, silver caps glinting.

"Where is that beret now, Vic?" Jet asked.

"Oh!" Vic turned back to Jet. "That reminds me. The Neighborhood manager's looking for you, cousin Mildred. He needs to talk to you real urgent."

"Why?" Jet looked taken aback.

"No idea. Better go find out. He seemed real angry about something."

Jet squinted at me, hesitant to leave.

"Don't worry," I said. "I'll be near the candles. Just come find me when you're through."

"Okay." When Vic turned away though, Jet tugged my shirt and whispered, "Be careful."

"I will," I promised.

I followed Vic around the bend in the L-shaped courtyard until she planted my chair a few feet in front of a small booth filled with tall candlesticks and stubby votives and candle holders made of glass and ceramic and wood.

"Teak? Teak!" she hollered at the unmanned counter. Up popped a white-bearded man with rabbit eyes and tanned skin. He seemed positively scared of the world, but when his eyes met mine, he smiled.

"That's Teak, my husband. Set yourself down," Vic said to me. Then she hollered at Teak again in a jolly way. "This is Hannah. She's gonna sketch my portrait. She traded me a portrait 'cause I served her dinner last night. What do you think of that?"

"Fine," Teak said. "Very nice. You like candles?"

I was about to answer, but Vic boomed, "'Course she likes candles! Who don't like candles? She ain't got time for chit chat, Teak. She's got to start sketching."

I flipped open my spiral and situated my pencils on the ground. Vic kept talking, to me or Teak, I wasn't sure. But I was glad because that meant she wasn't asking me to explain myself. I didn't feel in the lying mood.

"Yeah, I miss Paris, I surely do." Vic took Teak's chair and placed it in front of me. Then she settled herself into a pose, looking off into the distance in a thoughtful way, but talking the whole time. "I made some nice money over there. Commission work. You know what commissions are? When people pay you to create a piece of art. Kind of like you're doing now."

"What're you talking about going to Paris?" Teak called out.

"It was before we met, Teak! Jesus, hush." Vic added, just for me, "He don't know nothing about it. He's a little..." She looped her index finger in circles by her ear.

Vic talked about Paris the whole time I sketched her, and her adventures got grander and grander as I filled in cross-hatches of her shirt. By the time I'd smudged the gray-wisp ends of her long braids, several people had gathered around me. And before I finished, a few asked if I could draw them, too.

I wondered where Jet had gone to, but Vic took care of them. She wrote the customers' names down and told them a portrait was ten dollars.

"And I'll throw in a free half-priced candle from Teak's booth! Right here."

The customers with their shopping bags and coffees smelled Teak's candles while I sketched the first sitter.

"'Course, I'll have to deduct five dollars from your commission to cover the loss of the candle-discount," Vic told me privately. "But what we have here is a partnership, you and me. You get access to my candle customers, and we split the profits."

It was pretty obvious that Vic was trying to scam me. After all, I'd brought the customers to her. Or to Teak. I didn't mind helping Teak sell his candles. He seemed nice enough. But Vic's niceness was like a shiny wrapper around something sinister. I just wasn't sure how to get away from her.

"I'm sorry," I told Vic. "I've already got an agent."

"Oh yeah? Cousin Mildred?"

"Yes." I concentrated on drawing my sitter. She was one of those rich collectors who came to the Neighborhood to find antique treasures. Her shopping bag was loaded with brass lamps and dishes from the mercantile. She glanced at me every once in a while, but mostly she talked on her phone, so that's how I sketched her. It wasn't the most artistic pose, but she'd probably commissioned the sketch just so she could sit down and rest her high-heel feet.

Vic crouched over my shoulder and her low voice buzzed like a wasp in my ear. "How well do you know that Mildred? I know she ain't your real cousin."

"What do you mean?" My heart ricocheted, but I kept my eyes steady on the portrait.

"For starters, she ain't even look like you. In fact, I seen her before. On the news. You mighta hooked up on the road somewhere, but there's people looking for her. They even got a reward hotline. I should report her, but looks like she's not dangerous. And looks like she don't want to be found. Am I right?"

I finally gathered the courage to look Vic in the face, but I didn't know what to say. Maybe I looked frightened because Vic smiled and chuckled. "Well, if she don't want to be found, I'm not going to toss her to the wolves. That's not how we do things around here. We look out for each other."

This, I realized, was why Jet had warned me about her. She'd spotted the danger from the start.

Vic winked and stepped back. She ambled in a slow circle around me and the rich lady who was still talking on her phone. As she took a step past the rich lady, Vic dropped a set of keys. The lady glanced down, then turned her body and kept talking.

It took only two seconds for Vic to slip her hand in the lady's purse and pull out a wallet, and another second to palm a credit card and drop the wallet back into her purse. I was so surprised, I didn't realize I'd stopped drawing. My pencil and my breath stilled, waiting for someone to scream out "Thief!" But no one did.

Vic pivoted toward two other ladies at Teak's booth and called out, "Who's next? Was it Ashley?" She checked the list and bowed grandly to the woman named Ashley, who was holding two tall glass candle holders. Ashley seemed amused by Vic's humble bow and walked over to me.

I finished up the lady's portrait, scrawled my signature at the bottom – BB – and showed her the drawing.

"Hold on," she said, cupping her hand over the receiver. She grunted as she rose and gathered her shopping bags and open purse. She didn't even notice she'd been robbed. She frowned at my portrait. Maybe she hated my sketch. Maybe she'd tell everybody I was a fake. I studied the portrait again. It wasn't hideous, but it wasn't very complimentary of her nose either.

"That's good," the rich lady murmured. "How old are you?"

"Twelve!" Vic called out. I was getting younger and younger. Vic offered Ashley the folding chair, and she set her purse and glass candle holders on the ground behind it. While Ashley was distracted floofing her hair, Vic's fingers dipped into Ashley's purse and whipped out another credit card, quick as a snake tongue.

My heart stammered again, taking away my speech. I was sure the ladies would discover the trick and call the police, and we'd be sent to jail before Jet even came back from... where was Jet?

"Twelve," the rich lady marveled. "You are a prodigy." She reached into her purse for the same wallet that Vic had robbed. She pulled out a ten-dollar bill as I carefully peeled the paper from the notebook. "Keep drawing, and you'll be making a lot more than this someday."

A blend of pride and shame raced through my veins as I took the ten. As soon as the rich lady walked away, Vic was beside me again, plucking the bill from my shaking hand.

"I'll hold this for you. And that bandanner of money as well." She walked over to Teak's booth with all my earnings.

Jet was still gone, but I felt her presence, her eyebrows furrowed and her hands on my shoulders, shaking me to judgment. I cleared my throat and steeled my gut. "Ashley," I said. "I'll be right back."

I hurried over to Vic. Teak was busy talking up his candles to the customers.

"Did you just…?" I paused, trying not to draw attention from Teak's customers.

Vic shrugged. "Did I just what?"

"I saw you. I can't draw portraits while you're doing… that. That's wrong."

But she wasn't shamed. "Wrong? These people are rich. They got so many cards, they won't notice one missing. Besides, I don't even use most of them. I'm more of a collector."

"Still," I whispered. "I'm not going to distract people so you can steal."

"Well, you don't have a choice, now do you? You'll do exactly what I tell you, or you can say bye bye to your cousin Mildred – or whatever her name is." Her eyes slit into triumph as she pushed me along toward the wicker chair again. "Listen, I'm real friendly with a cop. He comes by here sometimes off duty, just to look around. Nobody even knows. I could have called him and said I seen that runaway girl. Right here in the Neighborhood. But I'm a sympathetic person. I know she don't want to be found. Must be something bad she's running from. If I know you, Hannah – and I think I know you – you wouldn't put your friend in a bad situation."

Right then, Jet rounded the corner, kicking up dust and glaring like she'd just been on a wild goose chase. Vic gripped my arm and hissed in my ear.

"You keep doing your little drawings, and I'll keep doing my thing, and everybody's happy."

I wrenched my arm free and rounded on her. "What about what you said last night? About artists and respect?"

She rolled her eyes. "You sound like Teak and everybody else here. Too good for their own good. Pie in the sky. Even if he sells a thousand candles, ten thousand candles, hell, it ain't ever going to be enough to put a roof over our heads once they close this place down. So you sit, zip your lips, and draw. Oh, and tell your friend I'm taking over the money now. I'll give you your fair share. Don't you worry. We're partners now. I'll take care of you."

"Who wanted to see me again?" Jet demanded as she approached us. "I found Mr. Jim, but he did not know what I was talking about. Everything is fine. No problem."

Vic shrugged amiably. "Guess I was wrong. Maybe he was talking about some other Mildred."

"That woman is trouble," Jet growled as Vic walked back to Teak's booth.

"Yeah," I said, watching Vic go. "Yes she is."

FIFTEEN

I waited until Vic was gone to tell Jet what had happened.

"Vic recognized you. From the TV pictures. She took the money from my first customer and says she's in charge of all the commissions from now on. And if I don't agree, she'll call the police on you." I kept sketching Ashley as I spoke, my voice low.

Jet stared at me.

"That's not all," I whispered. "She's robbing these ladies while I do their portraits. If she gets caught, she'll rope me into it."

Jet's face closed. "We need to get out of here. Now."

"Where will we sleep?"

"On the street."

"But the police—"

"It is better than here." Her tone was decisive, but I'd had time to think this through.

"I'm earning money here," I reminded her. "I think I can earn enough for those train tickets. If we leave now we can't get to the border."

"How can you earn if she's taking the commissions?" The strain in her voice was the first sign of fear she'd ever shown me.

"She promised she'd give me my share. I'll just do as many portraits as I can today and tonight. We'll have enough."

"What if she calls the police on me?" Jet hissed, her furious gaze fixed on the candle shop.

"She won't, as long as I'm making money. I'm afraid if we try to sneak off she'll call the police anyway, and we'll have to hitch out of Austin."

Jet leaned back and groaned at the sky. "Okay, we stay for now. But I am watching her. Be ready to run."

Vic sauntered over just as I finished up Ashley's portrait.

"Cash only, I suppose?" Ashley asked, and put a ten in Vic's outstretched palm. "Is this your granddaughter? She's really talented."

"Yep." Vic patted me on the shoulder.

Liar, I seethed shrugging off her touch.

When Ashley left, Vic unzipped her red bag and tucked the folded ten-dollar bill inside. I caught the flash of blue plastic before she zipped the fanny pack back up.

"Did y'all have a nice chat? You understand how things work here now?" Vic gave Jet a saccharine grin. Jet set her mouth hard and didn't answer. "Relax, Mildred. You're scaring the customers. How about you go sit in the booth with Teak, or go somewhere else, I don't care. I'm watching over Hannah now. We got work to do."

Jet wasn't going anywhere near that shop. Instead, she backed away a few feet, choosing a spot where I was fully in her view. She sat in the shade and watched me for the next three hours as I worked.

Vic had a strange, edgy charm she could turn on and fine-tune according to who she was talking to. Sometimes she acted like she was my poor widowed grandmother, and sometimes she was my agent who rescued me as a street urchin. It worked. The little crowds behind me created enough curiosity to keep the commissions coming nonstop for hours.

We took a break for lunch, and Vic insisted we order sandwiches from the Neighborhood Café. I hated to see Vic spend our money, but then I was given the best tuna salad sandwich I'd ever had and I changed my mind. Jet ate her meal with silent fury, and I suspected she was scheming. Just like me.

"How much did we make?" I asked Vic between bites.

"Well, you were Miss Popularity. You did seven altogether. Got a good thing going here."

"Seven? That's seventy dollars," I said, excitedly.

"Not...not quite. I been giving these people discounts on candles for having their portraits, so I got to recoup that five dollars. And then there's my small fee."

"What fee?" Jet demanded.

"My keeping-the-peace fee." Vic's thin lips curved up.

Jet stood up, towering over her, fists clenched at her sides. "That is bullshit. You're a thief."

Vic didn't look worried. "Hey – my fee is a pittance. But there are other people good at keeping the peace. The police for instance." She wiped mayonnaise from her bottom lip. "I know someone personal. I could call him if you want. He's a Ranger."

After that, Jet clammed up for the rest of the day. She sat on the curb fuming, never losing sight of me. All afternoon, Vic doted on me, especially in front of potential customers. The day had heated up and she brought me cold Dr. Peppers and attached an umbrella to my wicker chair when the sun beat down on me. I tried to remember how many people I drew, but I lost track.

Some hours it was crowded, with someone new ready to sit as soon as I signed BB on the page. Then I'd sit for a while without a commission. When it was slow like that, Vic would run off behind Teak's booth and smoke. She'd lean out every few minutes, looking me over, belching out a plume of smoke. When she came back, her voice was a bag of gravel. She wouldn't let me move to another part of the courtyard because Teak might lose customers. To fill the time, I drew Jet, sprawled on the curb, but still looking fierce and beautiful in her own unique way. Sometimes I drew Vic, with slit-eyes and snake-fingers. I was deep in the details of this when a voice spoke behind me.

"What's up, Buttercup?"

I looked up and there was Darnell. My heart kicked.

"I thought I was Hannah bandana," I said, trying to sound disinterested.

He smiled. "You're both. You contain multitudes."

I sort of melted.

"Walt Whitman," he said. "Read him and fall in love with yourself." He glanced at my sketch and his eyebrows drew together, but all he said was, "You're still drawing me tonight, right?"

I wanted to tell him about Vic but she was just a few feet away, glaring at me, so all I said was, "Yeah."

Darnell held up his hand and I slapped it. "Righteous. See you tonight."

He talked like no one I'd ever heard before. And I don't think I'd ever seen anyone so happy. He even walked happy.

"Hey!" Vic hollered to me from the candle booth. "Come here."

232

Reluctantly, I said goodbye to him and climbed to my feet.

"It's late," Vic said, when I reached her. "Let's call it a day. I got to stop by Vera's and do a little shopping before she closes. And I got to get the meat ready for the bonfire tonight." She unzipped her small leather bag and fanned through the cash. "Guess I'll pay you now. You earned a lot. Bravo, Hannah. 'Course, I had to deduct some for sandwiches and all those Dr. Peppers you drank."

"Okay. I don't need sodas tomorrow," I said. My hands itched for the money. I'd never earned so much cash, and it was making me light-headed.

She handed me four bills. Twenty dollars.

"That's all?" I asked. "But… that's not fair. I sketched twenty people."

"It's completely fair!" She erupted so violently, she broke into a cough before continuing. "You don't understand the hidden expenses of business. I'm talking investments, expenditures, tax shelters. You know what those are?"

When I just stared at her, unable to believe her audacity, she nodded. "I didn't think so. We have to set you up a permanent booth in a few days, just for portraits. I have to buy some plastic sleeves for the sketches. Make them look fancy."

I kept my mouth shut about that extra booth. I knew exactly where I'd be by tomorrow. On a train to El Paso. One way or another.

★

Jet and I spent the next hour in our room brainstorming ways to get the cash from Vic and get out of here. It was a shame, really. I loved the Neighborhood. The glass blower's delicate green orbs and the Welcome Lady's intricate patterns of shells and stones and beads. Darnell and his accordion and the cool breeze on my bare legs as I sat on the window ledge and looked out over the courtyard, already glowing with candles and lanterns and small fires in the dusk. Wild grapevines crawling up the buildings and birds swooping down across the square. It was beautiful and simple. For a while it had felt safe.

"I wish we could stay and keep doing portraits. Everyone else is so nice. And when the Neighborhood is torn down, we could just follow them to the next place."

"Are you forgetting something? What about me?" Jet shifted on the bed pallet and propped herself up on her elbows.

"I'm just dreaming. I know what you have to do. But in this dream, you stay with me and..." I hesitated before finishing the sentence. "You have a little baby."

She sighed and fell on her back again.

"I think you'd be a good mother someday," I told her earnestly. "You tell me to be careful hanging out the window and you worry about me even though you won't admit it, and you even told me to take a nap."

Jet balled her fists in her eyes as if my words physically hurt her. "*Why*? Why do I have to be a mother when I have not even been a child! I am only sixteen, Blue. My childhood was stolen from me. You think I do not feel bad? Yes, I feel bad. But do *not* make dreams for me. You have no right."

I shrank away from her wounded fury. "I'm sorry."

"It is too late for sorries."

"I'm sorry," I said again helplessly.

She stood up. "What about your promise? Was that nothing?"

"No, it wasn't nothing. I was just dreaming."

"Well stop dreaming about my life and what I want," she snapped. "I have enough people doing that for me!"

She stormed out of the room, and I could hear her pacing in the hall, breathing heavily.

Down in the courtyard in the gathering dinner crowd, I spotted Vic. Her long, gray braids swayed as she tended a fire-barrel. A man in a plaid shirt lingered a few feet away. I didn't recognize him. As she spoke to him, Vic's whole body seemed charged. She was laughing like a young woman and leaning toward him. Then she turned and looked straight up at me. She knew I was there all along. *This is my cop*, her laughing eyes seemed to say. *I could tell him.*

"I hate this place," Jet said from the doorway. "We should leave tonight. The more we stay here, the riskier it gets."

"Look." I nodded at the courtyard.

She didn't budge.

"Come here and look!"

I pointed to the man in plaid, who was chuckling with Vic and Teak.

"I'm a cop's daughter – I know a cop when I see one. I think he's a cop."

She stared down at the courtyard. "I knew it. We should go now."

A sudden cool gust whipped her bangs in front of her eyes, but she stood like a statue.

"What would happen if the police found you?" I asked.

"They would take me to Uncle Chago."

It puzzled me that the police would hand her over to Mother, but the lines were blurred in Texas. And I couldn't let that happen, not ever.

"What if you told the cops what he did? Maybe they would…" I tried to finish the sentence with something positive, but came up blank. Illegals didn't get foster parents. They didn't get adopted. They went to the cages. They died in the cages before they could get deported.

"The cops would do nothing. If Uncle Chago finds me, he will beat me. But not in the stomach. He will make me have the baby, not because he loves it, but because it will be another thing to own." Jet turned to look at me. "Everything ends with Uncle Chago. The police. The Rangers. Uncle Chago owns them. Because they all have their hands in the pot. You only have to dance with the devil once for him to own your soul. But he will not have my soul. Or my body."

I slid off the windowsill into the darkening room.

"You're right, Jet. You can't stay here."

"Good. Let's go now," she said with a wave of relief.

"Not us. You." I climbed up on the chair seat and pulled the cash from behind the loose ceiling tile. "Take the money and wait for me at the train station. That way, if Vic snitches to the cop tonight, you'll be gone before he gets here. Tomorrow morning, if she asks where you are, I'll tell her you're sick and staying up here."

She squeezed the bills tightly. "There is not enough for two tickets here."

"I'll figure something out," I said, although I had no idea how. "I'll get the money Vic stole from me. What time did you say the train leaves?"

"Eight forty in the morning."

"I have to get the money before then," I thought aloud.

She didn't move. "What if you cannot?"

"I will." My voice held a confidence I didn't feel. I wasn't ready to part with Jet again, not after we'd just found each other.

She held up the small stack of bills. "You trust me with all of our money?"

"You trusted me with it after the shootout."

"Not really." She gave a faint smile. "You took it before I could stop you."

I looked out the window, but the cop had disappeared. Vic was alone. "You'd better go."

"Blue." She stood there looking at me, breaking something in my heart. "What if we cannot find each other this time? We should stay together."

I took a breath and raised my chin. I couldn't help Maggie, not now. But I could help Jet. "I'll find you. Now, go."

Jet stuffed the money into her jeans and grabbed her bag. She put her hand on my shoulder. "Thank you."

I nodded and swallowed a quiver in my throat.

At the door, she looked back. "I will not leave the station without you," she promised. And then she was gone.

SIXTEEN

An hour later, the bonfire danced in the center of the courtyard. A handful of musicians had gathered to the side, with guitars and upturned buckets and harmonicas. Two women danced with each other, surrounded by small children who leaped and played. With the main gates to the Neighborhood locked for the night and the outsiders gone, the artisans had closed up shop and relaxed with their cigarettes and beer and wine.

A little kid with a smoke-smudged face handed a paper plate to me. Someone had passed it around like a Sunday-service offertory and had collected a pork rind and a chicken leg and some roasted nuts and a hot dog wiener and half an orange.

"Mama told me to give this to you," he said, and then ran away to join the others. Mama turned out to be a lady I drew earlier in the day. I waved my thanks and ate alone, keeping my distance from Vic.

I needn't have bothered. Vic was happy like Daw was happy. Payday-beer happy. Laughing and dancing, her face flushed and excited.

The evening was filled with drumming and strumming and dancing and lively chatter, and the air smelled of sweet, smoked meat and roasted hazelnuts. I ate one food at a time, starting with the pork rind, and worked my way clockwise around the paper plate, worrying the whole time that Jet might not get any supper. That she might be cold or in danger.

The music thrummed in my ears, and I chewed in rhythm, thinking about how to get my money back, how to get my money back. Daw would tell me *Just go on in there and git it*. My foot tapped to the music, but my head was wrapped around the money Vic owed me. Take Teak's money box? I wasn't comfortable stealing.

I just wanted what she'd taken from me.

Even if I figured out a way to do it, I couldn't disappear until morning, as late as possible, with just enough time to buy tickets to El Paso and hop on the train. Any sooner and Vic would be scouring the Neighborhood for me. I worried she'd already called the cops, hoping for reward money.

"Hello, Hannah bandana." Darnell sidled up beside me and tugged on the tail of my cloth bandana. His accordion was strapped across his chest. He smelled like licorice and mint, and the firelight danced in his eyes.

"Where's Millie tonight?" He fiddled with his accordion, the white keys clicking softly beneath his fingertips.

"Oh, she's not feeling good." I folded the empty paper plate into a tiny triangle. "She's sleeping in the room."

"Too bad. I hope she feels better. Tell her to drink lots of water."

"Okay."

"You ready to draw my portrait? I wouldn't want to rush you."

I looked around for Vic. She'd sure enough accuse me of stealing her commissions if she saw me drawing. But I didn't see her anymore.

"No, I'm ready." I pulled the sketchbook from where I'd placed it under my rump.

Darnell's fingers practiced as he spoke, the accordion keys clicking. "I was thinking that I could use your sketch for the front of my demo."

I squinted up at him. "What's a demo?"

"It's a song that you send to producers so they can hear what you've got. It's a hard gig for an accordionist. You heard any accordions on the radio?" He smiled, and shook his head. "I'm a hard sell."

"I think it sounds real pretty," I told him. "People don't hear that every day. That's what makes it special."

He tilted his head, watching me sketch. "You play an instrument?"

"No."

"My dad taught me how to play," he said. "I wanted to learn guitar, but he made me learn accordion and about three hundred million songs from his home back in Louisiana. Least that's what it felt like when I was a kid. You heard of zydeco? Like this."

He unfastened a strap, and stretched out the bellows. It breathed loudly as the fan opened up, and suddenly the keys hummed to life under his fingers. The music skipped and danced like the children by the fire. It was the kind of music that made your heart pound out the rhythm. I smiled so wide my cheeks hurt.

"That's nice," I said when he paused.

"And something called the *bal-musette*."

His fingers slowed and the music softened, like birds humming on a wire. I sketched the ghost of his arms and hands, but the accordion was so intricate, I got lost in all the details. He stopped playing in the middle of the song.

"Stuff like that. I'm hoping to catch the ear of a producer here in Austin."

"I think anyone would love it." My stomach quivered like leaves. "Your dad must be proud of you."

He played a few more notes on the keyboard, looking over at the flames. "Dad's passed on now, but every time I play the *balmusette*, I hear him singing along with it."

"You think he's singing from heaven?" I asked. "Or like maybe he's still around here when you play?"

He lifted his chin and thought. "That sounds about right. I always feel like he's with me when I play. Maybe heaven's all around us."

I thought of Maggie, still all around me, even when I wasn't thinking of her. "Maybe heaven's all tied up in music."

"Now that's an idea. You already done with that portrait?" He leaned over to look, but I hid the drawing.

"No, this is just practice. I'm still drawing. You're playing over there, right?" I nodded at a group of musicians gathering across the square.

"Yep." Darnell re-strapped the bellows and pulled out a cell phone. "But first, I have a proposition. Before you start drawing, would you record me and the brothers playing? Just for fun."

He set his cell phone in my palm, and I stared at it for a moment. It wasn't anything like mine or my friends' phones, which were all hand-me-downs that were Republic-approved. Darnell's looked brand new. It was like holding a slim block of gold. Sleek and weightless and the most expensive thing I'd ever held in my life.

"Just the first song. Here." Darnell hovered his hand, unlocked the screen, and opened the camera.

Still I didn't move. "This looks really expensive. I'm kind of afraid to hold it."

"Don't worry. It's easy. The passcode is all sevens. I'll go over there and play with the others, like I did last night. And you'll record us? Would you mind, Hannah?"

I didn't mind at all. "What do I do when the song's over?"

"Just keep the phone till I'm back."

He showed me how to work the camera, and then he walked over to join the other musicians, giving them high fives and hugs. I wasn't used to seeing grown men hug each other but it seemed natural. Watching him, it seemed to me that Darnell belonged in this place and didn't belong at the same time. He treated the Neighborhood people like family, but his eyes were a little brighter, his clothes a little finer than everything around him, and that phone a lot more expensive than anything for sale here.

I pressed Record and moved the camera from the musicians to the artists laughing and slapping each other's hands. It gave me a secret thrill that he'd watch it later and think about me. Maybe when I crossed over to America I'd be able to buy a fancy phone like this one.

When Darnell started his song, I zoomed in on his face whenever he smiled and zoomed in on his fingers when he closed his eyes and played like it was the last song leaving earth. After a while, I moved the camera to the drummer, whose hands blurred against the upturned plastic buckets, and then to the woman wheezing whole chords from her harmonica. Another man shook his head as he played guitar, his hand sliding down the neck as the notes rose higher and higher. It sounded like a love story. And then Darnell joined in again, and I focused on him. All smiles, and straighter teeth than I'd seen on anybody in my life.

All around Darnell and his friends, people stood and sat in clumps, eating and talking and swaying to the music. I swept the camera across all the happy people, and I meant to return back to Darnell, I really did. But then I saw Vic, not five feet away from Darnell, swaying like a vulture, looking hungry for something food can't satisfy. I looked up at her over the camera. Part of me expected her to look straight at me and realize I was recording her. My heart raced, but something told me to stay right there. Don't move. Don't turn off the camera.

Vic didn't look at me. I hugged the phone to my chest, just in case, and leaned back farther into the night shadows until I felt a tree trunk against my spine. I tried to keep my hands from shaking. I didn't want to ruin Darnell's video, though I guessed I already had.

Vic wagged a bottle of beer. Her other hand rested on her hip, where she carried that small red bag. She side-stepped until she'd danced her way over to a group who were huddled together, conversating. Vic stooped over and fiddled with her shoe. When she stood up, she lost her balance and fell against the bearded man sitting closest to her. They both laughed, and she said something, waving her beer and leaning on him to stand up again. But when she stood up, she had a wallet partly hidden in her free hand. In one swoop, she slipped it into her bag, then walked away swaying her hips.

I drew in a sharp breath. I'd seen Vic steal money from outsiders all day long. But how could she steal from her own friends?

I looked down at the phone screen, at the red circle and the ticking timer, and slowly moved the camera to Darnell again. There he was in the middle of the music, mouth open, grinning, nodding his head and singing a string of doo's and dah's.

I'd ruined Darnell's video, but I'd caught Vic stealing.

We got her, Jet, I thought.

When the song ended, I tucked the cell phone safely under my thigh. And with my fingers still shaking, I drew Darnell's portrait. I stayed glued to the base of the tree and hid my pencil behind my forearm as I drew. I sketched out the shape of him, and then filled in the details, crosshatching and shading and softening the edges with my pinky. After his portrait was finished, I stared at it a while, pleased with the way I'd captured the folds of his shirt and the firelight that danced across his face. I closed the sketchbook.

The music stopped, and Darnell looked over at me when everybody was clapping. He nodded and winked as if to say, "Hannah-girl, I didn't forget you." He started another song, something about Mama and money and high and dry.

I propped up my knees and cradled Darnell's phone in my palm. My thumb grazed the glass, and the screen lit up. I stared at the apps. None of them looked familiar. *Souterrain. Libertad. WhatsApp.* One was a fire icon with a hose spraying water on it. *Firewall.* I glanced at Darnell once more before I pressed the little firehose. A browser opened.

I typed in "Maggie Wisdom" and "death," and the first link took me to the announcement of her funeral. Her school picture filled the screen, and beside it, a small paragraph. "Our darling Maggie flew away to be with the Lord..." I took a sudden breath and pain shot through my heart. I swallowed a lump and blinked hard. I wanted to be back in Blessing, back with Maggie. I wanted to see her face again and to sit in the front row at the funeral and cry and be hugged by Mrs. Wisdom. But none of those things would ever happen.

I could hardly bear to know what her parents said about me. What they accused me of. But I skimmed to the end of the announcement, and there was no mention of the gun or a murder or me. They didn't say at all how Maggie died, just that she was in the arms of angels. Reading over the description of Maggie and her survivors, I got the feeling that I was already erased from memory.

Until I clicked on the other links in the search.

BLESSING POLICE HUNT FOR OFFICER'S DAUGHTER

WAS PORN MOTIVE FOR MURDER?

RANGERS JOIN HUNT FOR BLUEBONNET

All of the reports had that same stupid photo of me from eighth grade. I'd cut my own bangs because I'd fallen asleep with a wad of Big League Chew in my mouth and Daw wouldn't take me to the salon to cut the gum out.

I was sort of glad now that I looked so raggedy in the photo. It was a far cry from my current look. Still, all those stories made my stomach hurt. They'd all decided I was a murderer and a degenerate, too.

But I was just Blue. And Hannah and Riley and Chris and anybody else I needed to be until I could find my way to Marla again, and then Marla would say my name and set the world right. Marla had run once too. She'd escaped. In my heart, I knew she'd help me get to safety. I just had to find her.

I stared at the screen on Darnell's phone, a lump growing in my throat. All around me, everything was alive and laughing and happy. Even Vic, who was now sitting down with a bottle on her knee, half asleep as she rocked herself and nodded along with Darnell's band.

I opened another browser and typed out "how to find Marla Andrews." Darnell's internet was faster than any computer or cell phone I'd ever seen. The results made me gasp – websites from California and New York. They were American. I scrolled down through dozens of images, but nothing looked like my Marla. I pulled her old photo from my back pocket and unfolded it. Already, the crease from the fold had erased Marla's ear and part of her neck.

"Damn it," I whispered, and smoothed out the picture on my thigh. In the light of the phone screen, I studied Marla's face again. Her blonde hair. Were those freckles, or just marks on the paper?

I scrolled through the Marlas. Black Marlas and white Marlas and young Marlas and old Marlas. I knew my mother would look different than she had ten years ago, but I didn't know how different. I was terrible with guessing ages. And what if, as I'd feared, her last name wasn't Andrews anymore? What if she'd married again? What if she had more babies and she'd forgotten all about me? I sat there staring at a screenful of Marlas like I'd been knocked off a fence.

"What'cha reading?" Darnell's voice snagged me. He sat down beside me, and I immediately closed the browser.

"Is something wrong?" he asked.

I shook my head. My mind was still lost in all the faces. How would I find Marla if I didn't even know her last name?

"You sure?" He tilted his head.

But all I said was, "I finished your portrait." I flipped open the sketchbook and handed it to him. "Is it okay?"

He studied it with a lopsided smile. "It's freakin' great. I can't believe you drew this. Can I?" He motioned at the paper, and I nodded. He carefully peeled the paper away from the spiral, then leafed through the other pages – the musicians and tourists and other half-sketched pictures.

"You're really talented. Don't quit drawing, okay?"

"Okay." I tried to smile.

"This here?" he pointed at one of the sketches. An old woman who was looking at something in the distance without smiling. She didn't look particularly sad, but I felt like we were sharing a secret as I drew her. Like we'd shared years of feelings in the ten minutes it took to draw her.

"This is truth," Darnell said seriously. "I think your art is truth, Hannah."

"Really?" But I was hiding the truth from everyone around me.

"You forgot to sign your masterpiece." Darnell put his portrait on the sketchbook and set the thing on my lap. I signed it slowly – BB – making the ends of the B into curlicues. I stared at it, not sure if it was artistic or childish.

"Why don't you sign your real name? You don't like Hannah?"

I looked at his phone, which had lit up again. A blue glow, a silent message. He'd find out soon enough, and something inside me wanted him to know my real name. Wanted to trust him.

"My name's not Hannah," I said quietly.

Darnell tilted his head again and waited.

"It's Bluebonnet."

"Oh. I get it. BB for short."

"Yeah."

"Bluebonnet. That's an unusual name. But lovely."

"Thanks," I said shyly. "Darnell is unusual, too. But lovely."

"Not as pretty as the official flower of the Republic."

I looked down and hid my smile. Even with my nearly bald head and dirty clothes, he'd said pretty. Nobody had ever called me that.

Darnell fiddled with his phone. "Now, let's see that video."

"Oh that. I'm sorry. I think I ruined it."

"What? Looks fine." As he watched it, he held out the phone so I could see it too. The music streamed from the small speaker. "Ah! Good camera work. The firelight's good."

"It's just that... I caught something and lost track of you for a minute. You don't need to see the whole thing now, right?" I didn't want Vic to be caught too soon. Me and Jet both needed to get away first.

I glanced around to locate Vic, but she was slumped back in her chair, her head tipped to the sky and her mouth open, asleep. Her fingers still clutched that half-full bottle on her knee.

Maybe if she was drunk enough, I'd find a way to steal the money back tonight. But I could see her veiny hand grabbing mine like a handcuff. Caught in the act. She'd call her police friend, and they'd flood the train station with hounds, I was sure of it.

"What's this?" Darnell bowed his head down close to the screen and frowned as he watched Vic do her disappearing act.

I took a deep breath. "It's Vic," I whispered.

He watched Vic fall on the man, then stand up, curling his wallet into her wrist as she stood.

"What the...?" he whispered. "That's Hondo! Did she just steal his wallet?"

I nodded. "But you can't tell anyone. Promise. I'll get in trouble."

"Why? What's going on? Does she hurt you?"

I shook my head and tried to weave Jet out of the story as much as possible. "Vic's been stealing things from people all day and yesterday, too. Since I got here. She made me give all my commissions to her and she won't give it back."

"Chrissake," Darnell sighed. "I heard that there was a pickpocket, but we assumed it was someone passing through. It's her? Damn. Don't worry. I'll take care of this."

"No!" I grabbed his sleeve and scrambled for a reason. But I came up empty, so I told him the closest thing to truth. "If she finds out I told you, she'll do something bad. Really bad. She'll tell the police something terrible about my friend Millie. You know, she's not from here..."

But I could see in his face that none of this was a surprise to him. "I know she's probably illegal," he said.

It was a relief that he knew. I trusted him.

"It's not safe here for her. She's hiding now. Because of Vic."

We both stared at Vic. Teak limped over and tried to shake her awake, but she waved him drunkenly away with the bottle.

"The thing is, me and Millie were planning to catch a bus out of town. But it doesn't leave until tomorrow," I said. "I just need to earn enough money tomorrow for the ticket, and after we leave, you could use the video to prove she's a thief. She's got a bunch of credit cards in her bag, too. I'm pretty sure she bought stuff with the cards today. At the mercantile."

He raked his fingers across his head. "Christ. You know, a lot of Neighbors would be grateful to know that you caught her on camera."

"I don't want them to know it was me." I scuffed the ground with my shoe. "Please don't tell them, okay?"

"I get it. Where you headed? You got family somewhere?"

I considered how to reply. He would help. I knew it in my gut.

"I think so. My mother. She crossed the border when I was four, right before it closed. We got separated."

"Yeah, that's rough. Happened to a lot of people."

"You, too?" I asked.

He gave a thoughtful nod.

"Well, I've searched, but I've never been able to find her. The cell phones always run into firewalls and the computers at school aren't any better. *She's* where I'm headed, if I can just find her." I pulled absently at the camouflage tape on my holster. "That's what I was looking for on your phone. You have the *whole* internet outside the Wall. And then I started thinking maybe she changed her name." I drew a breath before adding the worst thought. "Maybe she's forgotten about me."

Darnell tilted his head and tapped his knee against mine. "That's doubtful. Who could forget you?" He opened his browser and typed as he talked. "Have you checked Beyond The Wall?"

I frowned. "What do you mean?"

"The website. It connects the Republic with the '*whole* internet.' I have hacker friends – some of them in high places, which is why I have the magic VPNs and all these apps." He tapped at things on his phone. "People put messages on an American app called Beyond The Wall, trying to find family and friends here. Sometimes the messages are coded so the people don't get tracked, or sent to the cages. Here. Take a look."

He held the device out to me. I saw an image of a brick wall with the word "SEEKING" at the top. Underneath were images like little sticky notes that people had left and a search bar on the side.

"Maybe she left you a message. What's her name?"

"Marla."

"Marla what?"

I hesitated. "Andrews."

"Looking for Bluebonnet," he typed. Then he looked up into the black space in front of us and paused. "Andrews," he whispered. He looked at me like a puzzle, then said, "Oh," like he'd finally found the missing piece.

He'd seen me on the news. We stared at each other and I held my breath, wondering if I'd made an awful mistake. Then he smiled and put his hand on my shoulder. It was warm and solid and nice.

We huddled over his phone.

He typed "blue bonnet" in the search bar and explained, "You probably should search for your name, not hers."

My heartbeat picked up as the hits filled the page. We scrolled down, scanning the posts. Darnell murmured them aloud as he skimmed through. "Last seen in a blue station wagon...We lived in Blue Mound...always wore his favorite blue cap...Blue Ridge...."

I noticed the odd space in my name and pointed at the search bar. "Bluebonnet's one word."

He deleted the space and tried again. I leaned close to see. I could feel the heat from his head against mine.

Photos came up of children in fields of blue. Photo after photo. It was tradition in Texas, getting your photo taken every spring, surrounded by the wildflowers. That happened to other kids, not me. Daw hadn't taken a photo in his life.

"Lots of bluebonnets," I said.

"But not the one we want," Darnell added, scrolling with his thumb. "Well, let's try Marla."

He typed in a few letters, M-a-r-l, and then added an asterisk. "That's called a wildcard search. It'll bring up anything that begins with those letters."

Like a miracle, there was Marla's name: *Marleen (Marla) Andrews.*

Searching for my daughter, Bluebonnet. If you have any information, please contact me.

It was an old note. Years old.

"She's there," I whispered. "She was always there. The whole time." I was stunned. Shaken to the core. She'd been there all along, looking for me. And I couldn't see. They didn't *let* me see. It was like the whole Republic was hiding my mother from me, putting up a wall of fire to keep us apart.

I couldn't seem to breathe. I touched the message with wonder. There she was. Right there on the smooth screen.

Darnell's voice lowered to a whisper. "I can also dial outside Texas."

I gaped at him. "How?"

"Just dial these numbers first. Best kept secret in the Capitol."

He dialed the digits into his phone. Six numbers and a star.

I couldn't understand how this was possible. All of America's phones were six secret numbers away?

I stared at Darnell. Who *was* he?

Before I could form words, he'd pressed a button, and a telephone started ringing. He thrust the phone at me.

"Take it. Talk to your mother."

The phone rang three times. I froze. And then a voice, clear and high. "Hello?"

It was a woman. A stranger's voice.

My whole body went clammy. Darnell shook the phone, his eyes wide. When I took it from him it shook in my hands.

"Hello?" the woman said again.

"Hello?" I said back. "Is this Marla Andrews?"

"Yes. Who is this?"

The receiver rattled against my ear, and my voice came out high and strange.

"Mama?" The word came out before I could judge whether it sounded babyish. I didn't care though.

"Who is this?"

"Mama, it's me. Blue."

There was a long silence.

"Is this a joke?" Her voice cracked.

"No. I'm your daughter."

"Blue?" A gasp. "My baby? Can it – is it really you?"

"Yes…it is," I said as I wiped my eyes.

"Blue? Are you okay? Where are you?"

"I'm okay." I smiled and tried to keep from crying, but there were already tears on my cheeks. "I'm in Texas. Are you in California?"

Darnell walked a few steps away, giving me space.

"No, honey," Marla said. Her voice was gentle and sad, but her questions tumbled out in a familiar desperation. "I'm in Arizona now. Where are you? Are you still in Blessing?"

"No." I sniffed and wiped my nose on my forearm. "I'm in Austin. I'm kind of in trouble. But I can't talk long. Can you meet me near the border? I'm going to El Paso. Can you come pick me up in two days?"

"Baby, the border's closed."

I lowered my voice to a whisper. "I'm gonna cross."

"Oh honey, no. No!" Her voice rose sharply. "That's suicide. You can't do that. Promise me!"

"I have to. I'm in trouble."

"What happened? We'll figure it out."

"My gun went off when my friend was cleaning it, and they think I shot her on purpose." I said it quickly with steady words, but my heart flopped like a reeled fish. I glanced at Darnell, who was still turned away from me.

"Oh God. Hang on." Then her voice became strained and distant, muffled, as she spoke to someone else. "They're saying she murdered her friend." Other words filtered through: "death penalty" and "nightmare" and "governor". Then her voice came back to me, clearer and steady. "Where's your father? Is he with you?"

Something turned on like clockwork inside me. Suddenly I felt an icy calm. Like all those times Daw came home drunk and I had to take his shoes off and hide his gun in the underwear drawer and throw the bedsheet over him. Make my own dinner. Put myself to bed.

I stopped crying.

"No. I'm with a friend. Daw's back home. I've gotta cross. Please pick me up. Please?"

"But Blue, you can't." Marla's voice cracked again. "I've missed you, baby."

"Me, too," I said, even though I hardly remembered her. I missed her like you miss a secret that was never shared with you. And I needed her to focus. "Will you pick me up? Can I stay with you for a while?"

My voice broke. It was pathetic, begging your mother for a safe place to stay. Not knowing if she'd say yes.

"Listen." Her tone grew firm. "Promise me you won't cross illegally. That's a death sentence. I'll make some calls and ask for an asylum application for a minor. Maybe they can fast-track it. I don't know if it will work, but we'll try. I've got some connections. People who can help."

I thought about Jet, alone at the train station, waiting for me. "There's someone with me. She needs to cross, too. She's in trouble."

"Oh. That's not…" Marla's tone changed. "Look, can we talk about that when I see you? I can make it to El Paso in about five hours, but we have to get the asylum paperwork underway first."

"You'll get the papers?"

"I have a good shot. I'm an attorney, and, well, my husband is, too. I got married again, Blue. To a wonderful man. Anyway, we'll figure it out. Just don't climb the wall. They'll shoot you. How are you traveling? By car?"

"Train," I said, as if it were a certainty. Because all of a sudden I felt like it was. "To El Paso. Should I call you back when we're there?"

"Yes. We'll have to meet at Sunland Park. That's where the West Gate is."

"Sunland Park," I repeated.

"If I can't get the papers, we'll figure out something. Just don't cross on your own. It's too dangerous."

We both fell silent. I didn't want to tell her I was crossing no matter what. But I also didn't want to hang up yet.

Very quietly she said, "I love you, Blue. I always have."

I'd never told anyone I loved them. Not even Daw. He wasn't the type to gush out feelings either. It caught me off guard, Marla saying that.

"Okay," I said. The phone went dead. Maybe there was a time limit. I didn't know. She was just gone.

I wrote the six-digit secret password and Marla's phone number on the back of my sketchbook, careful to make each number neat and clear. I couldn't lose her again.

I walked over to Darnell and handed him the phone. He'd slung his accordion over his shoulders again, and the air around him smelled like smoke and leather and oil. He flicked a cigarette on the ground.

"So that's settled?" He smiled and cocked his head again, like he didn't know all my secrets. Like everything was the same.

I smiled back. A true smile. "Thank you so much. I don't know how to…" I wanted to hug him, but I just kept shaking my head. He'd given me back my mother after ten lost years.

"Happy to help." He picked up my lost sentence. There was still a trace of concern in his brown eyes. "You're sleeping up there alone tonight?"

"Yeah."

"Thing is, I'm thinking it's not so safe for you here." Darnell rubbed his whiskered chin and looked around. "Well, you go up. I'll sit out here. Keep my eye on Vic."

We both looked across the square, but Vic was gone.

Darnell scanned the crowd. "I don't see Teak. They must have gone up to bed. You're in this other building?" He gestured at mine. "Good. I'll keep watch for a while anyway." He paused. "And Bluebonnet – sleep with your gun ready."

"Okay." It had always felt safe up there with Jet, but now the thought of sleeping in the room alone gave me shudders.

"We'll get your money back from Vic tomorrow. Count on it."

"All right." I believed him.

"I think this calls for some Neighborhood justice, if you know what I mean."

"Are you going to kill her?" I whispered, my eyes stretching wide.

"What? No!" He seemed to find this idea hilarious. "We have meetings and votes and shit. We can't have thieves living with us."

"What if she tells the police about Millie?"

"Tell you what – I'll tell them you're headed to Mexico." He paused. "You're not going to Mexico, are you?"

I shook my head.

"There you are then."

We both stood up, and I shook a cramp out of my leg. I wasn't ready to leave him, but I felt awkward, standing there. *He's a good one*, I thought. I half-twirled around and walked away.

"Bluebonnet!" he called.

I stopped and turned back to him. He closed the distance between us and put his face right up to mine. "If I don't see you tomorrow, promise me something."

"What?" I asked.

"Promise me you won't stop drawing. Keep making art."

"Okay." I felt lighter, hopeful.

"And don't listen to anyone who tells you to stop. They don't know nothing." He winked. "I mean it. You're a real artist. And real artists don't care about the Republic's sacrosanctity. Know what that word means?"

I shook my head.

"Good. Keep it that way."

He held an arm up, a gesture I didn't realize I'd been waiting for, and I accepted that invitation. I fell toward him and hugged him tightly.

"Thank you." I choked out the words against his chest. My heart was too full.

I stopped by the toilets downstairs before heading up, then felt the pressing need to rinse my face of the smoke and dirt and tears. It was quiet and empty in the far corner, with only a dim cone of light from the streetlamp. I checked my holster before I crouched over the spigot, turned the handle, and held my hands under the cool water. The clean water on my face and neck and head felt like a baptism.

On the way back to the room, I took the long route through the closed stalls and stands. I passed a few people who waved and smiled like they recognized me. Vera's Mercantile was closed, with a metal gate drawn down over front. But several rows of giant tubs labeled *"Everything 50¢"* were left out on the other side of the gate, like an honor system.

Next to those, in a plastic chair, snoring like a rattler, was Vic.

She must have wandered off the wrong way to go to bed, gave up, and passed out in front of the shop.

I glanced around. Music and voices still echoed from the square, but there was nobody nearby.

Vic's red leather bag hung loosely on her hip, dangling nearly to the floor, the zipper half open.

It was my chance.

I froze watching her. I thought of the candy I'd stolen from the shop that time, and Maggie's stern disapproval. *But this is different,* I told Maggie in my head. *This isn't stealing. This is taking back what's mine.*

One thing I knew for sure – Jet wouldn't have hesitated. And I couldn't either.

Setting down my water jug, I stepped lightly toward her, pausing to hear each breath rattle through her nose. She was a snake, all right. But I'd watched her all day filching money from other people, and I was a quick study when I wanted to be.

Crouching down next to her chair I pinched the zipper and slid it the rest of the way open. The bag bulged with stolen cash. Barely breathing, I scissored two fingers into it and pull out as much as I could in one go. Vic, completely hammered, never moved.

I counted out what she owed me – exactly $180 – and tucked it in my pocket. But I didn't put the rest back. I trailed the money and stolen credit cards up to the mercantile gate like breadcrumbs. Feeling bolder now, I borrowed an old pen from the 50¢ bin and scrawled VIC on a few bills, then I poked the rest of the stolen cash through the chinks in the gate.

When I was done, I ran up the dark stairs in the flickering light of the saint candles back to my room and climbed on a chair to retrieve my backpack from its ceiling hiding place. I made sure Hannah's gun was solidly in my holster, and then flew down the stairs at the opposite end of the building, close to the entrance. I glanced around for Darnell on my way out, but *no, he'd be on the other end*, I reminded myself, a little heartsunk. I didn't want to leave without saying goodbye, but I had little choice.

There was one more thing I needed to do, though. I dashed toward the entrance when I saw the bald man from the coffeeshop, locking up the front gate.

"There's a thief at the mercantile!" I announced, breathless.

His eyes flew open. "What the—"

"Someone's been stealing money," I continued. "They dropped credit cards on the floor. Darnell told me to get you."

He didn't wait to hear more. Pulling out his pistol he rushed off toward Vera's. I knew he wouldn't shoot Vic, but I kind of wished he would.

It was nearly midnight and my adrenaline was high when I hopped the chain link fence that separated the Neighborhood from the other buildings. The bright downtown lights seemed blinding after the darkness of the Neighborhood. I jogged along the sidewalks with my heart thumping because the devil wakes up at midnight, as Daw always said.

It surprised me to find the streets were still alive with cars and trucks. A lot of folks were awake, too. Drunk people singing arm in arm. Stray dogs, half-starving, half-mad, stopping to stare at me. When a few men came marching down the road with rifles on their shoulders, I ducked into the shadows between the streetlamps. On their black shirts, white reflective lettering announced what they were: "The Protectors".

Volunteer militia. I knew their type. More dangerous than a normal street thug.

When I had to dodge a few more on the next street, I began to worry anew about Jet. She wasn't the brand of human they were trying to protect. What if they'd found her?

I didn't have a map of Austin. I'd figured finding the station wouldn't be hard, but after twenty minutes of hopping from shadow to shadow I still hadn't found a single sign for the train station.

After a while I retraced my steps and took a few turns down other streets, looking for signs. The more I walked, the more sleeping bags and tents I saw lined up along the buildings, filled with people. Like clams, they'd sealed themselves out of sight of guards and police and drunkards. It was too crowded for me. I picked up my pace and stumbled, nearly landing on my knees. When I righted myself, I realized I'd tripped on a human arm, sticking out of a roll of blankets. I didn't wait to see if it had grabbed me or if it was a sleeping person or if it was even *attached* to a person. I ran.

I took a few more wrong turns before I found a street sign that pointed toward the old downtown train station. In my head, I'd imagined it would be as giant as a cathedral – like the ones I'd seen in books. But it was actually no bigger than the gas station owned by Miss Olsham back home. It sat all by itself at the end of the street. A single street lamp cast a circle of amber on the red-tile roof and the brick circle drive. It was eerily empty. No police, no homeless people.

I tip-toed up to it, all my senses on alert. I hadn't seen a human in two blocks. I felt for my gun as I walked into the shadows of the covered porch. Two empty benches. A trash can. A cold breeze cutting through. When I tried the handles, the doors didn't budge. Locked solid.

I mashed my face to the window, but the lights were all out.

Jet couldn't be in there. She had to be nearby though. She wouldn't have gone far. I kept to the walls and made my way around to the back of the building, saying a little prayer to the candle Mary.

Please let me find Jet.

The back of the station was deserted as well, but it was hard to tell by moonlight.

Panic threatened to unfold inside me, but I made myself think. The Jet I knew tucked herself in corners and hid beneath trees. She wouldn't be out in the open.

I drew the gun from my thigh holster and stepped gingerly toward the dark mass of overgrown bushes and trees beside the station. A coyote howled from somewhere. Much closer, something loud rustled in the undergrowth. A raccoon, maybe, or rats.

"Jet?" I whispered. Nothing.

Carefully, I made my way around the line of shrubs until I reached a small clearing. There was just enough light to see a few logs, an upturned grocery cart, and giant cardboard boxes of some sort.

And then, there she was, a dark figure curled on a plank of plywood. I knew it was her even before I saw her motorcycle boots.

There was no point in waking her now, so I sat in the small empty space where her knees bent and kept watch. But I was too sleepy to stay awake for long. I drifted off quick. When I woke up,

I was balanced at the edge of the plank beside Jet, my head on my backpack. I would have fallen off if her arms hadn't been wrapped around me.

SEVENTEEN

We waited as long as possible to leave the safety of the tree line and purchase the tickets, so the train was almost full when we raced down the platform to the cheapest coach cars. People were wrestling their baby strollers and suitcases into the storage areas, and once we elbowed our way past the clogged-up entries, we couldn't find any free seats. They weren't like bus seats, all facing forward, but a combination of forward ones and booth-like seats with narrow tables between them. All the folks had staked out their spot. Every couple of aisles, we'd get hopeful, but instead of an empty seat we'd find someone saving it.

"That's saved. My husband's gettin' a drink," a woman carrying a baby said. "Sorry."

"This whole table's taken," another woman explained when we saw an empty booth with a single gun on the table. She looked down the train car for somebody, and we kept moving.

Nobody argues about seats when there's a hundred guns to settle things.

The crowds made us nervous.

"There are too many people," Jet whispered in my ear as we moved into the second car. "Too many eyes to see us."

She was right, but there was nothing for it. We had to keep going and trust that we could blend in.

We kept our faces tilted down as we moved through three cars hunting for two empty seats before the train whistled and got us nervous. We settled on the first table in the third car, even though two men in business suits were already seated there. We took off our backpacks and slid into the booth.

The train crawled out of Austin like a living thing. Jet gave me the window seat, and as we click-clacked over a dark green lake, I leaned against the cool glass and watched two bats flapping against the buttery sunrise. Relief washed over me now that we were on the move and alone again. I gazed at the buildings behind us and felt the tug of gratefulness, even as each second took me farther and farther from Darnell. I'd probably never see him again, or ever understand who he was, but he'd stay with me forever. Tall buildings gave way to tall trees that gave way to houses and football fields and brown dirt and sand-colored fields with marooned haybales, one thing blurring after another.

Every now and then, a tinny woman's voice announced arrival times and station stops. Looking out the window, I'd never seen such pretty oranges and reds and yellows. In Blessing, the fall leaves turned from green to brown overnight, then dropped to the earth like dead moths. Here, the trees were like a storybook, too pretty to be real.

"I love trains," I whispered to my reflection. The big windows, the clacking wheels, the rocking motion, like a toy being tugged by a giant boy. The staticky voice of the engineer making announcements that were nearly impossible to understand. The smell of hot coffee and the crackling of plastic-wrapped sandwiches.

The bright sunlight of the outside world made me tired, so I leaned back against the headrest and glanced at the men opposite us. They both tipped their heads back and rested as we pulled out of Austin, only opening their eyes to drink from plastic cups. A bottle of Jack Daniels sat on the table between them. Both wore ties and had slicked back hair. Every once in a while, I caught a whiff of soap and pine trees, some cologne that itched my nostrils.

"God, I miss airplanes," the older man said out of nowhere.

"I know. I never thought I'd say it, but I miss the old days when we had to take off our shoes and belts. Remember that?" The younger man with a thick mustache laughed. "Hell, I'd trade in my gun for just one flight to El Paso."

"Naw, you wouldn't."

"Naw, I wouldn't," the Mustache agreed. "But I still miss it. It was – what – just an hour and a half in the air?" He laughed again like he'd bitten into something sour and shook his head. "Fuckin' airlines."

The older man caught me looking at him and nudged the Mustache. The Mustache gazed at me and Jet and raised his eyebrows. "Oh, pardon my manners. Can I offer you a drink?" He held out the bottle of Jack Daniels to me.

I looked at Jet, who rolled her eyes. I shook my head, and the Mustache burst out laughing.

"I'm just kidding!" he roared and slapped his knee, and then slapped the older man on the shoulder. The older man laughed unconvincingly. And in that moment, I understood that it wasn't the older man who was in charge, but the younger one.

"You ever been on an airplane?" Mustache Man asked me. "No."

"You?" he asked Jet, but she was looking down, fiddling with a cell phone in her lap. A *cell phone*. Where had she gotten a cell phone? And what happened to being off the radar and untraceable? I wanted to ask her, but Mustache Man wouldn't stop talking, and you couldn't fit in a private question edgewise here anyway.

"That's right," Mustache Man said. "You're too young to remember anything before. Airplanes were the bomb. You'd drop a couple hundred and catch a flight to New York, California, or—" He paused to burp. "Abu Dhabi. They packed you in like sardines in these itty-bitty seats, no room at all – knees all up in your fuckin' beard."

"We didn't know how good we had it," the older man agreed.

"That's for damn sure. Remember?" Mustache poked him. "'member, Dex? An hour and a half from Austin to El Paso." He snapped his fingers and snorted. "You were a crazy son-of-a-bitch if you took a train. Now look at us."

I knew I shouldn't engage with them, but I couldn't help myself. "What's it like up there? In the sky."

"Oooh." He looked out the window, squinting his thick eyebrows together. "You're way up there. So high, the clouds spread out beneath you like a cotton tablecloth."

Old Dex's eyes lit up. "Yeah. You ever had a snow globe? It's like you're inside one, skimming along the inside of a snow globe, the glass right above you."

"And your sinuses swell the hell up – 'member that?"

Dex nodded and smiled as Mustache drank and remembered and drank some more.

"Man, I'd get the worst sinus headaches. Your ears have to pop because of the change in air pressure." He slurred his s's a little. "But if they don't pop, you'll burst your eardrums. Happened once to me, swear to God. Blood oozing all down my neck when we landed."

The Mustache leaned over the table and spoke softly, his eyes as serious as a Sunday school teacher. "Listen up. Airlines never cared for but two things: greed and regulations. They didn't like the Secession, but they sure stuck around long as there was money to be made. Hiked their rates so high nobody could afford to fly and then blamed it on the Republic. And then those fake regulations about firearms. Unconstitutional! I mean, nobody's going to hijack a plane if everybody's armed."

"They were worried about misfires and oxygen and—" Dex started. But the Mustache snorted and kept talking.

"Naw, they all pulled out like cowards – I mean, they would because they're American. Now we've got one airline for the whole Republic." He emptied his cup again and refilled it. The more he drank, the more he emphasized his words. "I tell you, the Wall was the best thing we coulda done, but this no-fly zone crap is the highest form of patriotic sacrifice." He paused to toast. "To President Apato. And here we are. On a train for twenty hours for a three-hour meeting. That right, Dex?"

"At least we have our self-respect and no California pricks flying over the great state," the older man agreed.

"And libations for two days instead of two hours," the Mustache said, raising his glass.

A few minutes later, they were passed out, heads leaning against each other and mouths half-open in drunken snores. It wasn't yet ten o'clock in the morning.

As soon as they passed out, Jet got up and motioned for me to follow. We tiptoed out of the car and passed through three more before we found two empty seats, facing forward.

"We cannot sit with them," she told me. "They are the type to watch the news."

"Where'd you get the phone?" I asked.

"Found it," she said simply. She looked pale all of a sudden.

"Where?"

"Can we just not talk for a few minutes? I'm feeling…" She pressed her hand into her mouth, then stood up and bolted out of the car, back toward the toilets.

I was starting to learn that any sort of vehicle except a motorcycle made Jet throw up.

The train stopped for a while in San Antonio, so we got off and stretched our legs in the station. We had enough money to buy a slice of pizza and a lemonade for the both of us. Jet looked anxious the whole time. Worry etched all over her face. To cheer her up, I told her about Vic's demise, including as many details as possible about her snoring and the trail of stolen cards. Jet smiled, and for a few minutes, seemed to relax.

Packed with people, the San Antonio station was nothing like the one in Austin. This one had high ceilings and scores of benches, and birds living in the rafters.

We were getting used to blending into a crowd. The only drawback was the police who patrolled the station.

I hunkered down in my chair, watched a pair of uniformed officers stroll by, and chewed my pizza slowly, letting the dough turn soft in my cheeks. They tapped on a homeless person with a bully stick until he stirred awake.

"Where's your firearm?" the cop demanded.

The homeless person peeked out of his blanket cocoon and grumbled.

"Where's your firearm?" the cop said louder.

The other man rocked and wriggled in his cocoon until his hand appeared with a pistol in it. The cop checked the chamber, and then turned it upside down and inspected the serial number. He tapped on his little device, waited, and then read the screen with a blank face. Then he handed the pistol back to the homeless man and said, "Get on out of here. And keep that firearm locked. Play your part." He walked on.

Play your part. It was drilled into us at gun safety camp. We all had to play our part, pay attention, pledge our allegiance while the Republic lumbered its way into becoming a strong nation.

Jet stared at the table and chewed her food silently. She'd been quiet ever since we left Austin.

"You okay?" I asked.

She nodded and stared at the train departures sign.

"You're not sick?"

"No."

"You're not mad?"

"No."

But something was clearly wrong. It was like she'd crawled into herself and I wasn't invited. For a whole hour on our layover, she wouldn't look at me. With no one to talk to, under the soaring ceilings and canyon echoes of the train station, I sketched a crow as it pecked at a piece of crust.

After lunch, we climbed back onto the train, steering clear of the two businessmen who were drunk again and howling with laughter. The horn blared and the clacking revived and the buildings fell away to nature again. If I craned my neck, I could see the train cars behind us as we rounded a bend, the silver metal glinting like a thousand torchlights. I could see where we came from, but not where we were going. All I knew was my mother was waiting for me at the edge of El Paso, and that she wanted me. She'd said she loved me. She'd never stopped thinking of me, even when I'd stopped thinking of her.

The train passed a rock quarry that looked like piles of moon dust, and then into wide open fields, farms with pinstripe rows. It rolled past hours and hours of sand the color of bone, dotted with scrubby trees, across red earth that rose and rolled into hills and then into mountains. It was wide open space out there.

"How come people are always talking about not enough space for outsiders?" I asked Jet. "Looks like plenty of room to me."

Jet leaned over and looked out, breaking her silence. "It was never about room. It is about fear. About keeping things the same. People want to make the world better, but they have eyes in the backs of their heads. They look backwards, at the past, and think everything was better then."

"When? When was everything better?"

She shrugged her shoulders. "Never."

"Well, where we're going, we won't have to deal with people like that."

"Where are we going?"

"El Paso."

"I mean..." She leaned into me, and her leather-clad shoulder touched mine. "Where, after that? I have been thinking a while, and if you want to stay with me, I would not mind." She still smelled like trees and campfires, in a good way.

"Really?" This was a surprise. I let my head fall against hers. "I didn't tell you yet, but I found my mother."

"You did?" Jet sat up. "How?"

"On Darnell's phone. I talked to her and everything."

Her eyes searched mine. "That is great. Why did you not tell me?"

"I wanted to. But you seemed sad today and…" I paused, trying to sort out my own head and dig for the truth. Why hadn't I told her? "I think I just didn't want you to feel bad. 'Cause I have a mom now, and you don't. And it's not fair."

Jet was motionless, her expression impossible to read.

"Marla wants to meet me at the West Gate with papers and everything. We might not have to scale the Wall at all," I whispered. "It's a good thing you have a phone now. We can call her when we're close."

"It is good. You will be with your mother," Jet said, but her eyes were hooded.

I leaned back and tried to paint a picture in my head of Marla waving at me and hugging me at the West Gate, but I couldn't muster up the imagination or the warm feelings. I thought of American schools instead, with books and computers and art classes every day. I'd sleep in my own bedroom and paint it sea foam green. In this dream, Jet lived with me in my sea foam room, and we slept in bunk beds.

"Where are you meeting your aunt?" I asked. "She's in El Paso, right?"

Jet traced the edge of the phone with her index finger. The black polish on her nail was half chipped away. The screen lit up briefly and demanded a passcode, but she kept tracing the edges until the screen winked off again.

"Jet?"

"I texted her, but she has not answered."

"Did you call her?"

She nodded. "No answer." The morning's distant sadness settled on her face, but I wouldn't let her close off again.

"Did you leave a message?"

"Yes."

"Maybe her battery is dead. Maybe she lost her phone. Do you have another way to reach her?"

She shook her head. "The last time I talked to her was before I passed through Blessing. She texted me to tell me where to pick up the money she wired. I never signed for the money, but that guy probably did, and who knows what message he sent back to her. She might think I changed my mind. She might think I am not coming."

It seemed like such a long time ago, that man in the gas station who stole her money. I imagined the look on his face when he realized that we took his motorbike, and a wave of satisfaction settled over me. Soon your sins shall find you out. Maybe what Daw said was true. It's what gave me hope when people were mean. But it also struck me with fear, because who was never a little mean?

"So..." I turned over her problem like a puzzle piece. "You haven't heard from her since before you and me even met. And she's not answering your texts. You don't know where to meet her."

Jet shook her head.

"Do you know where the place is?" I asked, hesitantly.

"What place?"

"The place. For, you know." I glanced at Jet's stomach.

"The clinic?"

"Yeah, the clinic."

"No. I hear there are many near the border. I can find one. But I do not have the money. My aunt was going to help."

I put my hand on hers. "It'll be okay. We'll figure something out. I was thinking maybe you can stay with me. I think Marla won't mind."

"Maybe." She didn't appear convinced.

"No, really," I said. "I told her about you."

"You did?" Her eyes searched my face.

"Yeah, I think she'll get us both out. I'm sure of it. She's a lawyer, and she's going to get the papers. She'll help you."

We were sunk down low in our seats, heads together. I couldn't see out the window, but I guessed it was more of the same movie I'd watched for hours. Empty stretches of land interrupted by neat rows of plants and more land, a few houses, then dirt and sand.

"There is a deadline," Jet said, so softly I could hardly hear her. "Even in America. I do not know if... what if I missed the deadline? I want to have my life, Blue. What if Uncle Chago steals my life?"

"He won't." I squeezed her hand and spoke as if I knew things I didn't know. Can you steal a life, even a life as tiny as a seed, and still get to keep your own? I didn't understand why Jet had to suffer because of Uncle Chago's sin. Why did the sin come chasing after her instead of him? Nothing made sense.

With her boots on the seat back and her knees folded into her chest, she seemed smaller. Like she could have been younger than me. The train rocked us like a cradle until my eyelids were so heavy I stopped fighting sleep.

When I woke up, Jet was on her feet, looking down the aisle. It was dark. Middle of the desert dark. And the dim glow of light coming from the floor made her face hover like a ghost above me.

"That man was looking at you," she said softly as she sat down beside me.

"Which man?" I rubbed my eyes.

"The mustache man was looking at you. He was standing right here when I walked up, staring. And he rushed away when I got closer."

"You think he recognized me?" I said, triggered by fear.

"Maybe. But probably not. Your face is not all over the news."

"How do you know? Maybe it is."

She wagged her phone in the air. "I have checked the news. It is all about the President's affair and a truckload of deceased migrants in Texarkana now. Looks like the news has forgotten both of us."

I sighed. "Where'd you go, anyway?"

"To the toilet. The train makes everything worse." She rubbed her stomach tenderly like a bruise and sat beside me.

"How much longer to El Paso?"

Jet's thumb brushed across her phone and the clock flashed 4:28 AM. "Too many hours. If only we did not make so many stops."

I lifted up to look around the car. People were covered in blankets, sleeping in their homemade tents. A few people slept upright with their mouths gaping open and their ears plugged tight with earphones. I sat back down, wide awake. Ranger Kern crouched in the back of my mind, ready to spring, ready to pounce, no matter how much distance I put between us. No matter what Jet said about the news.

"We'll text Marla at six. I know how to do it. Still no answer from your aunt?" I asked.

Jet's lips tightened. "Forget it. I will be fine."

"But I bet—"

"Drop it. If we talk about it, it just makes things worse." She wiped her mouth, and a faint smell of vomit drifted past me. "Draw something. I like to watch you draw and it will keep me distracted."

"Okay." I pulled out my sketchbook and pencil. "What should I draw?"

"Something funny. Or cute." She sighed and rested her head on my shoulder as I flipped the book open to a clean page. I outlined a squirrel with cartoon proportions. A bushy tail, enormous eyes, and cheeks filled with so many acorns, the stems poked against its cheeks. I could feel Jet's smile against my collarbone.

"Put more acorns in his arms," she suggested. "Like he has too many. More."

I drew more acorns and more acorns until they were falling off the pyramid in his arms. Then I drew worry lines around his eyes and arched up his eyebrows like a little prayer. "Why you fall, little acorns?" I said in a squirrel voice.

"That is good," Jet breathed.

"When I grow up, I want to make movies," I told her. "Animated movies, but not cartoons. More realistic. All the animated movies are made on a computer now. But I like real cartoons, drawn by hand. There's something more alive about them. Something... warm, don't you think?"

"Yes."

"Maybe I'll work for Disney. You think there's a special school where they train you how to make animated films?"

"Probably."

"Then I'll get a job and save up money and go to one of those schools. Maybe Marla will help me. She lives in Arizona now, but she used to live in California. You think California's as bad as people say it is?"

"Every city has its good and its bad. Even in the Republic. There are good people everywhere. They are just harder to find sometimes."

I turned to look at her. "What do you want to do? In the future."

She considered this. "When I was little, I wanted to be a veterinarian. I loved animals. I wanted to work with large ones, cows especially. Cows are smart. People think they are stupid, but they can recognize each other and they will go *trade places* so they can eat beside their best friends. Funny, right?"

"Yeah," I marveled.

"I helped save a little calf when I was about nine. At my abuela's, in Guadalajara. The calf was born sick, and I slept with it in the shed for three nights until I was sure it was not going to die. I fed it from a bottle for weeks. Bonito, I called him." She smiled at the memory. "I made a collar and a leash, and he followed me around like a dog. I loved Bonito. But Abue had to sell him at auction. I cried for weeks. I did not eat meat for three years." She sighed a little laugh. "Now, I do not know. I will probably work at a factory. Wherever I can get a job."

"You can still be a veterinarian. I think you'd be a great cow doctor. You could specialize in rescuing all the sick baby cows. You can do anything, you know? I heard there's all kinds of money in the States for going to college. Even for people who aren't Americans."

"You have to graduate from high school first," she said. "I have never been to school."

"So go to high school then."

"Go to high school. Just like that?"

"Yes," I said. "We'll adopt you and you can go to high school."

"All right." She smiled. "It would be nice to sit in a classroom and yell at football games and watch food fights and graduate like other teenagers."

"There aren't a lot of food fights anymore."

"One would be enough."

The future seemed simple and clear. "You'll go to vet school and I'll go to art school and we can live together to save money. Then we can go to Disneyland together and ride all the rides. Want to?"

Her smile widened. "Sure, if you pay. Vet school is expensive."

"Deal."

She leaned back in her seat and closed her eyes. "That is a nice dream, Blue. Thank you."

At 6 AM sharp, I sent Marla a text on Jet's phone and we waited like birds hovering over an egg. She didn't answer.

"Maybe your phone's broke. Maybe the code didn't work."

"Where are you supposed to meet her?"

"Sunland Park. Sounds nice, doesn't it? Sunland. Like Disneyland."

We looked up Sunland Park on the map, but lost the Wi-Fi almost as soon as the image loaded.

"We have to get from the station to Sunland Park. It is a little north of El Paso," Jet said. "We will have to take a bus."

"That costs money. How much do we have left?"

Jet pulled out the remaining cash and we counted it twice. Seventeen dollars and forty-nine cents.

"That's not enough. We could hitchhike. Or borrow another motorcycle."

"Borrow?" Jet raised an eyebrow.

"We'll leave it at a gas station with an apology note, and we could put the seventeen dollars in the seat to pay back the gas we used. That makes it borrowing, not stealing."

"It is one plan, at least."

★

BLUE RUNNING

As the train pulled into El Paso, the sun rose over the red desert and sleeping mountains huddled in the blue haze. It was like a painting, so pretty in the window. On the platform we stood on spaghetti legs, shook our feet, pulled on our crushed backpacks, and stepped off into the cold station where the hope in my chest was punctured.

The station's grand windows had been built to impress the visitors passing through, but now El Paso was the end of the road. Here, all the trains turned around and carried passengers back into the belly of Texas. I studied the cracked mosaic under my feet – tiny tiles shaped into a ribboned bow – and the rows of wooden seats lined up like church pews in the main concourse.

Jet's hand found the crook of my arm as we stood there and looked out at dozens of heavily armed men. These weren't cops or the Rangers. Their uniforms didn't match, although most of them wore baseball caps and camouflage or T-shirts with Republic slogans. They were ragged and bearded. Some stood at attention with their hands folded on their AK-47s, legs planted like oaks, eyes like hawks on the passengers. But others were more relaxed, talking or laughing in small groups with their rifles slung over their shoulders. Someone in street clothes flashed a guard a hand sign in the shape of a gun, the way we used to play cops and robbers with our fingers, only this gun was pointed to the sky. The guard nodded without smiling and flashed the sign back. The more I watched, the more people traded signs with the guards. They seemed to be working together.

I felt instinctively for my own gun in the tape holster. It felt completely inadequate here.

One of the guards flicked the hat off a passing old man, who left his hat on the station floor and hurried away. I couldn't blame him. There was something about the guards that was unpredictable and menacing.

The air was laced with oil and smoke and fear. A train horn blared behind us. It was as if we'd stepped right into a military zone.

"Close your mouth," Jet said.

I closed my mouth.

She pulled me to a gift shop and quickly grabbed a Republic flag bandana and baseball cap. She laid a ten on the counter and said to me softly, "I owe you ten."

"It's okay." I hadn't seen her so focused and determined as when she tied the bandana around her neck, tucked her hair under the cap, and looked at herself in a mirror. The way she looked into her own eyes and said something secret and binding, I trusted her.

I took off my flower bandana and pulled the baseball cap she'd given me days earlier out of my bag and put it on.

"Ready?" she asked.

I nodded.

"Head up. Like you belong here."

We walked quickly toward the exit. Past a guard using the butt of his rifle to push a teenager down on his knees. Past three men closing in on a young woman, whistling and grinning like hyenas. And finally, to the glass exit door.

Once outside, we moved with a little more fire under our feet. We crossed the small parking lot, dodging the cars lined up to collect passengers, and headed for the streetlamps and low buildings closest to us. The whole time I felt watched. I wanted to fade, to disappear until we could catch our breath and figure out what kind of hell we'd landed in. A few times, Jet pulled on my hand to slow me down.

"Do not run," she warned. "It cannot look like running."

I risked a glance over my shoulder. The train station looked smaller from the outside, except for one thing. On one corner was a red-brick bell tower, pointing up like a finger gun to the sky.

A few blocks away, the streets were busy with cars, but the people on the sidewalks thinned out, so we slowed down and looked for a café or a restaurant among the old buildings. Someplace to slip into and let our hearts stop pounding. Maybe use the restroom, splash our faces with water. The buildings looked more familiar here, made of painted bricks and with handmade signs in the windows.

"Do you feel like we are being followed?" Jet asked.

I glanced over my shoulder. I could see no one paying attention to us. Most people kept their heads down, minding their own business.

"No," I said.

"Something tells me that borrowing a motorcycle in this town would be a mistake. We need to find a bus station and schedule. It has to be around here somewhere, near the train station. We will have to sneak on."

It wasn't a great plan, but it was a plan.

"First, though, I need to pee. So…" She opened the door of a little coffee shop. "After you."

I stood in line behind five other people, pretending I was going to order something so Jet could use the toilet without being harassed. I knew she would want a cup of coffee, and I had a craving for hot chocolate, but I couldn't see how we could do it with just a few dollars left.

The bells on the door tinkled as more people squeezed into the small coffee shop.

I edged forward and breathed in the sharp aroma of ground coffee beans. It suddenly struck me that we'd done it. We were in El Paso. We'd made it *so far*. With everything against us, we'd done it. The Wall was close. And beyond it? The future. Whatever it was, it had to be better than the past.

The fog in my brain lifted, and something stirred in my chest like a butterfly. Like hope. I took a step forward as the line shortened, and leaned over to see if Jet was coming.

A man leaning against the corner wall caught my eye. My shoulders tensed. He wore a green bandana around his head and a black T-shirt with a skull on it. He was the kind of person who dared you to look into his eyes. I scanned the other people in the coffee shop, but they didn't look worried. Maybe Mother didn't exist here. Maybe green bandanas were just green bandanas in El Paso.

Without warning, a hand slipped around my arm and yanked me backwards.

It happened so fast.

One minute I was in line. The next, I was under the shoulder of someone who'd whisked me away so fast, my feet hardly skimmed the floor. I looked up, and to my surprise, there was Daw, lifting me on my rag legs, dragging me out into the street.

Before I could cry out, he whispered, "Don't scream, don't scream, Blue. I'm saving you. Don't scream, or they'll hear."

EIGHTEEN

"Wait," I said, my voice clipped by terror. "Wait, wait!"

Daw's wrist was hooked under my armpit, hiking my shoulders up to my ears. I struggled to breathe.

"Shhh!" He hushed me and nodded hello at people on the sidewalk, then hushed me again through his grinning teeth. "Come on, darlin'," he said loudly in case anyone was listening. "Mornin'," he said to somebody we passed.

"Wait!" I dug my toes into the cement and we dragged to a stop near a trash bin a block away from the coffee shop. Jet could still see me here if she looked.

Something between relief and fear washed through me. My legs shook as I stood there gathering my senses. It was Daw, not a gang member, grabbing my collar, but damn if we weren't so close to being free. Here he was, dragging me back to my execution like he was saving me?

Daw looked frantically around the street and sidewalks like he was searching for someone he didn't want to see. He wasn't wearing his uniform, but a flannel shirt that smelled of old cigarettes and sweat. Something was spooking him.

"What's wrong? What are you looking around for?" I demanded and looked around, too.

"It's not safe. This way." He pulled me toward another restaurant across the street.

I looked over my shoulder at the coffee shop. Jet was still inside. She'd come out, and I'd be gone.

"Who were you with?" Daw's words came out in a fury. "What were you thinking?"

"Daw—"

"Who's that girl with you?"

"Nobody!" I said angrily. "Just a girl I met on the train." I couldn't trust him. I was so confused by his sudden appearance it was hard to think.

Daw slung open the restaurant door and, once inside, pulled me to the corner and peeked through the window.

He was agitated, twitching every time anyone moved. "Dammit, Blue. It was lucky I followed you. Did you see who was in there?"

"Who?" I asked, baffled.

He gave me a heavy look. "Never mind."

With his jaw set from nerves or anger, he pulled me to a window booth that overlooked the street.

"Coffee," he told the waitress who was pulling up the blinds at an empty red booth.

"Why are you here?" I asked, but it sounded like an accusation. Fear prickled across the back of my neck, not because of Daw, but because of Jet. I couldn't have her think I left her. "I'm not going back. I'm fine on my own."

Rubbing his agitated fingers, Daw stared out the window, his brow creased deep.

"Who are you looking for?" I asked.

He glared. "Rangers. Police. Whoever else is looking for you. There's a *BOLO* on you, but maybe the police haven't heard it here. They got their hands full in this dump."

"How'd you find me?"

He turned away from the window and searched my face, my shorn head. "God, you're alive. You look so different."

I watched him warily. Unable to sit still, his eyes darting to the window and the door.

"Why'd you run off like that?" he asked. "I was gonna help you."

"Everyone thinks I murdered Maggie. No one believes me."

"I believe you. I trust you."

"You trust the Republic," I told him. "It's not the same thing."

He gave me an exasperated look. "So? I believe in the system. The law, the judges, maybe not the politicians. The Republic ain't perfect, but yeah, it's the best we got."

"What if the system's wrong?" I was thinking as much of Jet as myself. I was worried that she was looking for me. That she'd take risks trying to find me. "What if innocent people suffer?"

"It'll work out if we trust the process," he said, stubbornly. "You can't run, Blue. That ain't helping."

This. This was why I ran. This twisted logic. And his obsession with the law as gospel.

"You want me to go back. Even if I get sent to jail?" I asked. "People get the death penalty for murder. I didn't kill anyone."

"I know."

"I would never hurt Maggie. But they won't believe me. And they won't forgive me for running. You know that."

He mashed his lips together, and I could see he didn't want to listen.

"I see." I leaned back. "I guess you can't be a Ranger if you have a dangerous daughter on the loose. It'd look real good on your resumé if you brought me home. Show how much you believe in the system."

He squeezed his mouth into a sour pucker. "That ain't why I'm here."

"Then tell me the damn truth," I demanded. "How did you know how to find me?"

He cleared his throat and kept his eyes on his hands, knotted together on the cheap table top. "Marla told me."

My heart lurched. "What?"

The waitress walked up with two coffees. Set them down in front of us and walked away without a word. Daw and I sat staring at each other until she was gone.

"She called me night before last," Daw said. "Told me you were headed for the border. Said I had to do something to stop you from getting killed."

Steam rose from the two untouched mugs of coffee on the table.

"She knew our number? How come she never…" I couldn't get my brain to process this. Couldn't find the words. "I thought she was lost to you. To *us*."

"Well, it's hard to explain now. We don't talk. But this is an emergency." He looked confused, like Marla was an unfamiliar language. He was out of practice.

I had a thousand questions, not the least was whether he knew how to call outside the Republic too. But betrayal has a way of gutting you into silence.

"What else did Marla tell you?" I sputtered.

"That you were on a train to El Paso. That you were trying to cross. That was about it. Said she'd help you get through but that I could not let you run the border for any reason." He leaned forward, shoving his coffee aside. "What are you thinking, Blue? You'll get yourself shot. I didn't raise you to be stupid."

"I'm not stupid."

"I can help," he insisted. "I'll fix things."

Daw was talking like a hero, but his words weren't going to save me. He was the town's drunk deputy who couldn't keep his kid in decent clothes or pay his water bill on time.

He thumped his fingers against the table. "They ain't got a confession. And the evidence is nothing. People shoot themselves all the time."

"But it was my gun." I lowered my voice. "My bullet. And my sketchbook."

He waved that away, like he had a law degree all of a sudden. "They ain't got shit. Just a book of doodles and a gun she was cleaning."

I frowned. "You believe a jury will say I'm innocent?"

"I believe in justice. You didn't shoot her. And you ain't twisted, neither. You're a normal girl." He took a sip of coffee.

A *normal* girl? I didn't want to be normal – not the Republic's normal.

"Anyway," he continued, "I got no choice. If I don't bring you back…"

"What, you'll get fired? Were you *sent* here, to get me in order to keep your job?"

"No. Well…" His eyes darted to the window again. I hadn't seen him this alert in years. "Sheriff said I should fetch you, and he's right. I drove all night. Look. If you get caught they'll take you to jail. El Paso jail's no joke. And you'll wait there until the Rangers take you into their custody, and then who knows where you'll be or how you'll be treated. Least in Blessing, you're under our jurisdiction. I can keep my eye on you."

In jail. That was the part he wasn't saying. They could keep me safe in jail.

"Why start now?" I asked, disgusted. "You never kept your eye on me. You never took care of me."

Daw's face went struck, like I'd cursed him. "That's not true."

"I've been taking care of you since I can remember." I stared at him hard, right in the eyes. "Washing your shirts and trashing your beer bottles before they fell out of your patrol car. Living every day scared that you'd lose your job and we wouldn't have money for electricity or food. Not that we ever had enough. You spent it all on beer."

"I ain't been drinking, Blue."

"Oh, you quit, did you?" I asked, disbelieving.

"Nearly. I only had one on the way here." He rubbed his eyes. "Eleven hours is a long drive."

"Sure, Daw," I said, not hiding my bitterness. He'd never quit. That was the only thing I could say for certain in this world.

"I'm sorry if I wasn't a good father. I guess I made mistakes, but I was trying my best." He looked wounded. "Anyway, I'm here now. Doesn't that count for something?"

I didn't want to do this. I wanted Jet. I turned to look out the window, but the street was empty.

I couldn't get the idea of Marla calling him out of my head. I hadn't been able to so much as hint about her to Daw for the past ten years. Now, she was so close, just over the border.

I looked Daw in the eye and said what I'd never dared to say at home. "Did Marla ever say anything about me? Did she say she wanted me?"

Daw sighed and raked his red fingers across the table. "Marla's got a whole 'nuther life now. She's remarried. She's got kids. She left us, and replaced us. We got to face that."

"Did she really leave us?" I asked in a softer voice.

"You know she left the Republic. She chose to."

"I mean at the airport. I have this memory of us." I pulled Marla's photo out of my pocket and set it on the table. Her blonde hair, her tilted head, her smile like a love song. "She looks like this in my memory, probably 'cause this is all I have left of her. We're in an airplane, all three of us, and she's sitting next to the window. I'm tiny in your arms. And then you snatch me away, and suddenly we're running out the airplane, and Marla's screaming and calling for me."

Daw stared at the photo, wordless.

"Did that happen?" I pressed. "Is it a dream or a memory?"

He didn't answer. But I wouldn't let go.

"Did she leave us? Or did we leave her?"

291

At last, he lifted his eyes to mine. "It was complicated. She wanted to leave, and I didn't. Anyway, what's done is done. She didn't get off that plane and follow me." He sniffed and blinked hard. "She made her choice. And it wasn't us."

Usually, when Daw's cheeks turned pink, it meant he was drunk and I needed to get out the way. But he wasn't drunk. His bloodshot eyes filled. I'd never seen Daw cry in my life.

He rubbed his nose with his sleeve. "Anyway. We need to git. This place is infested." He nodded at the people sitting in booths, the waitresses, a busboy. They all had Jet's shiny black hair and dark eyes.

Daw leaned over, but didn't lower his voice. "Bet half them are illegals. The other half are sheltering illegals. It's not a safe city."

"Just because they're illegals doesn't make them dangerous."

"No? You haven't seen what I seen. I seen kids overdosed on drugs. I seen Mother riding through, shooting out the church windows for the fun of it. I seen them stealing girls twelve-thirteen years old, to be sold off for sex, and Sheriff and me ain't saved but one. One girl. And she wasn't really saved. She was ruint by them. I know, you got lots of people saying no, some of 'em are good, they just want a better life and whatnot. But you can't ignore the facts, Blue." He punched his index finger onto the table. "The Mexicans are the ones recruiting gang members. The Mexicans are trafficking drugs and recruiting our kids and killing our kids."

"Mother's not a Mexican gang," I reminded him. "They're the real threat. They're filled with all kinds of people. White and black and—"

"Yeah, doing illegal things."

"But not all illegals are bad is all I'm saying."

He shook his head stubbornly. "It just takes one to hurt you."

"It also just takes one to save you."

He gave me an odd look. "What's that mean?"

Again I peered out the window searching for Jet, but she still hadn't left the coffee shop. I had two seconds to make up a story, but I was so tired of making up stories. The truth should have been good enough. The truth should have saved us.

"I've been traveling with this girl," I said. "She's the one who watched out for me this whole time. *She* stayed with me and listened to me and fed me and doesn't call my art doodles. She's *good*, Daw. And she's illegal. She doesn't deserve to rot in a cage for trying to save her life. We're not hurting anybody. We just want a normal life. But everything around us is just… broken."

His face was full of hurt, but it was nothing like the hurt in my chest.

"How about this," I said. "I'll go back to Blessing with you, and I won't try to run away again if you can do me one thing. My friend's in trouble. She's just trying to get past the border to New Mexico. Could you maybe give her a ride a few miles north so she can find a safe place to cross? I'll never ask for anything again."

Daw heaved a deep breath and puzzled over me. "Who's this friend?"

I pointed through the window at the coffee shop. "She's in there. Wait." I squinted at a couple moving in jerking steps across the sidewalk. It was Jet and someone else – a man in a leather jacket.

"She's *right* there." I stared.

Jet's hands were behind her back as the man pushed her to the curb, his blonde hair strung round with a green bandana. "Is that Mother?"

Daw looked out, too, and sighed out a long "Shiiiiit."

The man whisked her to the street and yanked her like a doll onto a motorcycle. "Jet!" I called, and pounded the window as though she could hear me. "Jet!"

She didn't look up. Then he was on the bike, too, doing something to her wrists, binding her. Another biker pulled up beside him and paused before they both revved their engines and took off.

"We have to go, Daw! Please!" I jumped up. "We have to follow them!"

"Goddammit," Daw said, but as I ran out of the café, I heard him behind me.

From the sidewalk, we saw the two bikers roar into the distance.

"You said you wanted to be a good father," I said to him, half-accusing, half-pleading. "Here's your chance to prove it."

For a split second he wavered, staring at the backs of the motorcycles.

Then, "The truck," Daw said, and dashed around the corner. I followed him to our old Chevy parked in the shade of an empty building. We jumped in and slammed the doors.

"Go, go!" I insisted as Daw turned the engine and peeled onto the main road.

"This is crazy," Daw muttered. "I ain't got no backup." But he didn't slow down as we hurtled after the two bikes. They were already so far ahead they looked like specks on the road.

NINETEEN

Twenty minutes later, we sat in the parking lot under the red neon of the El Coyote Motel. The buzzing sign gave me the crawls, like that capital C might crash down right on the white hood of Daw's truck. The El Coyote's clay roof tiles and stone walls reminded me of the motel back in Blessing, the one you had to hold your breath every time you drove past because a lady was murdered there and everyone knew she haunted it. I didn't believe in ghosts, but I always held my breath anyway. Now I stared at the two rows of motel windows that spread out like wings from the main office, holding my breath for other reasons. Jet was in there, somewhere.

It wasn't yet eight in the morning, and all the windows were curtained off. We were on the edge of the city, not quite in the scrub of desert, but almost. The lot was half full of cars, but there wasn't a moving thing in sight except for a squirrel taking halting steps across the lot.

As soon as we'd pulled into the parking lot I had one foot out the door, but Daw had grabbed my sleeve and yanked me back inside the truck.

"Wait! Just hold your horses." Quickly, he scanned the line of motel doors on the two balconies, the main office with the Vacancies sign, and the rusted blue picnic tables on a small patch of weeds.

"Why aren't we going in? There's the office. We've got to tell them she's in trouble."

"Tell them what?" he asked. "That a couple of Mothers are holed up here? That there's an illegal on the premises? Or maybe that I'm a cop without any jurisdiction in this city but I demand they let me in the room?"

"Sure, all three." I pulled away from him, but his fist stayed tight on my shirt.

"That ain't gonna work, Blue. Some jurisdictions actually work with Mother. Not Blessing. Not me. But sometimes the police have to look the other way for the greater peace. In El Paso, Mother has the whole force by the balls. They pay off the militia, too. They own this whole goddamn city. I'm not gonna risk your life and mine because some zit-faced manager calls 911." He rubbed his hand across his forehead and down across his scruffy cheek. He looked like he needed a beer. "Why do they got her, anyway?"

I thought of Uncle Chago and all the things Jet had told me in private. "Because... I don't know."

He sighed. "Come on now. We can't mess around here. They make one phone call and we're gonna be surrounded by thirty bikers so hyped up they'll shoot out all these windows and that baby squirrel for fun. If I'm gonna risk my life here, I got to know everything you know. So I'm asking you again: why do they got her?"

He squinted at me and waited.

"Okay." I leaned back into the seat and Daw let go of my sleeve. My heart wanted to trust him, but my head kept shouting Why? Why are you going to trust him now, when he's never been reliable enough to feed you properly or give you a safe gun or buy you decent clothes or even stay sober for two days?

But I didn't really have a choice. I took a deep breath and told myself Daw was a good man at heart most of the time. He was just broken in places that I couldn't fix.

"She's my friend..." I started, but stopped and squinted at a moving curtain.

"What's her name at least?"

The curtain stilled again but I kept my eyes on it as I replied. "Jet."

"Jet? That's not a name. What's her real name?"

"I don't know – I can't remember. She goes by Jet. She was raped by someone in Mother, and she's just trying to escape. Her uncle's somebody important in the gang."

"Who?"

I was still watching that curtain. "All I know is she calls him Uncle Chago."

"Jesus H. Christ. Chago." He put his head in his hands. "So, you're telling me I'm looking for a minor Scaler, property of Mother's most notorious commander? My God."

"Prisoner," I corrected him. "Not property. He trafficked her over when she was little. She doesn't have anybody. Her mother died in the cages." Panic gnawed at me. "Daw, that can't happen to her. She's not going to the cages."

"Well I'm not here to haul her off to the cages so just settle down a sec," he said. He was sweating now and his hand was up like he was slicing the air between us. "Hand me a beer. Back there." He pointed to the small space behind my seat.

I gave him a withering glare.

"It helps me think." He wiped his forehead. "Go on."

I felt around behind me, and sure enough, behind the rusted coffee can that functioned as a first aid kit was a nest of beers on the floorboard. I yanked up on a warm can and pulled it free of the plastic rings, a move I'd mastered before I was six.

He popped the tab and sipped the foam, his gaze on the motel. "There's two of them in there, but hell, there might be a whole gang in that building, for all we know. If I can manage to get her away from them, maybe... don't know... maybe we could take her back to Blessing with us."

"But you promised me you'd drive her to the Wall."

"I didn't promise nothing. She got herself kidnapped before I could talk." He glanced at me. "Look, I'm an officer of the law. I can't help her cross the border. That's crossin' a line."

He took another sip of beer and turned back to the quiet building in front of us.

The unfairness of it all washed over me and stung my eyes. I blinked, fury brewing in my head.

"Then...I'm not going back with you." I folded my arms tight across my chest, my jaw set.

Daw swung me a look. "Like I said, maybe she can stay with us in Blessing until this all calms down and they forget about her. Then she can figure out how to get back to where she came from on her own, so I'm not implicated."

"They're not going to forget about her," I snapped. "She's pregnant. Uncle Chago's not going to let her go. It's his baby."

Daw stared out the window, blinking at the row of motel doors. "This story keeps getting worse and worse."

"We don't have time to talk about this, Daw."

"I know."

"So what's the plan?"

"I'm working on it. You see that room at the end, ground floor?" His eyes squinted and his voice came alive.

"Yeah. The curtain moved a minute ago."

"Good eyes. That's our target. Someone inside is surveilling the lot."

He set his beer carefully in the cupholder, pulled his gun from his holster, and checked the clip.

"What are you gonna do?" I asked.

He looked from the gun to the building. "I'll have to rush 'em."

"Alone?"

"Element of surprise." He squinted and sucked his teeth.

"I'm comin' too," I said, pulling my gun from the holster. "You might need my help."

He considered this as I prepped my gun, but he didn't ask questions about where I'd gotten it. "Well, I suppose I'll be coming out in a hurry with the girl. I might need you to drive. Just a few blocks. You ever drove?"

"No."

"Well, it's not rocket science." He moved the gears. "This is park. This is drive. This is reverse, but you won't be using that." He pointed at his foot on the pedal. "This is your go pedal and that's your stop pedal. Right is go, left stop. You're gonna want to go as soon as I'm back in the truck. Just press your foot to the ground and pretend you're in a go-kart. And stay away from other cars. Do all that and aim for the road."

My heart knocked around hard, but I nodded. "Right is go, left is stop," I said.

He pointed at a sheltered spot beside the motel. "Soon as I pull around to that awning there, I'll get out and you crawl over to the driver's side. Don't turn off the truck – don't even touch the keys. Just wait."

I repeated the instructions quietly. "Don't touch the keys. Get in the driver's seat and wait. Wait for what?"

He rolled the truck slowly toward the awning, close to the building where the view was better. "When you see that motel door fly open, put the gear in drive and pull up to me. See how you've got a straight shot?"

Daw slowed to a stop and put the truck in park. "Remember, keep your foot on the brake at all times unless you're wanting to go. Left for stop, right for go. Soon as you see me, pull up to us so we can jump in."

I nodded, suddenly out of breath, and pressed my foot into the floorboard. "Left for stop, right for go." It was simple but nothing and no one in the world was simple anymore.

"Right then," Daw said. He paused a second and considered the gun that I'd strapped back on my thigh. "Might could use that one."

"Sure." I handed him Hannah's gun, which he glanced over before tucking in his holster. He opened his door, and my heart raced at the risk he was taking.

"Daw—" I touched his arm. "Be careful."

He nodded and then slid out the truck like he'd melted. I climbed over to his bucket seat, careful not to hit the gear shift with my knees. The fabric was still warm from his body. I settled in and watched Daw run from the main entrance down the wing of rooms toward the door with the missing number. Halfway there, he paused and pressed back against the wall. He looked both ways, then out to the main road. A few cars zoomed by, but the motel was quiet.

I glanced down at the pedals and stretched my toes out, but I was too short – my feet dangled. I slid down farther and farther until my shoe made contact with a pedal. But I was almost lying down, my rear was at the edge of the seat, and all I could see was the bottom half of the steering wheel and a speedometer. I pushed myself up again to see out the window, but my foot was on the pedal, and the truck groaned loudly. I shot up and saw Daw frozen, staring right at me, only a few steps from the room.

I waved my hands sorry, and Daw shook his head and took another step, slow as a cat. I was in a panic now. I felt beneath the seat and around the edge, fumbling for the lever that would spring me forward. I caught a metal bar, pulled up hard, and swung my rear forward. The bucket seat slid up to the steering wheel. My head was still low, but I could touch the pedals and see out enough, I figured, to drive.

I scanned the building for Daw and found him standing beside the numberless door, his back to the wall, and his gun gripped beside his right ear.

I blew out slowly and whispered, "Left for stop, right for go." I pressed the stop pedal to the floor and slid the gear into D for drive. Then I sat up and watched Daw.

He didn't knock. He didn't shout. He pivoted his entire body and kicked the motel door in. In a burst of chaos and gunfire, he flung himself inside and disappeared. Two seconds later, the window pane fractured into pieces and crashed onto the sidewalk, along with the curtain rod, half sticking out the window frame.

My foot slipped and punched the go pedal. The truck pitched forward, but then I braked hard and hit my forehead on the steering wheel. My rear launched off the seat and nearly sent me through the front window.

"Shit," I yelled, rubbing my forehead. I yanked the seatbelt and snapped it in shakily. I stared at the open door and the smashed-up window and watched for Daw. There hadn't been any sign of him for far too long.

"Come on, Daw. Come on," I whispered.

But the motel door gaped silently in the dead quiet of the lot. A couple of curtains flicked open and shut, but nobody stepped outside. It was silent, but the kind of silence that follows gunshots, haunted by echoes.

I looked behind me at the lobby just as someone was locking up the glass door and running into the shadowy interior.

"Come on, Daw," I said again, my hands gripping the wheel so tight my knuckles hurt.

He didn't come out.

I couldn't wait. I pressed my foot on the go pedal and staggered my way up to the open door. Inside, through a slant of sunlight, I saw a body on the floor.

Before I could make out who it was, Jet stumbled out of the room and squinted into the light.

Her arms were tucked behind her, and one of her eyes was swollen shut.

"Jet!" Yanking off the seatbelt I threw the truck door open and the truck lurched forward again. Swearing, I wrestled the gear into park. Then I leapt out and ran to her, pulling her ragdoll body to mine.

"Are you hurt?" I asked, although I could see that she was.

She stood there dazed, staring at me blearily with her good eye.

"Blue? How did you...?"

"We came to rescue you." I leaned around her and saw the plastic cable ties on her wrists. I'd have to cut the ties later. "Get in the truck," I told her, and turned back to the body, my heart in my throat.

But she didn't move. "Who was that man who came in?"

"Daw," I said. "I have to check on him." I couldn't wait to explain. Leaving her there, I stepped carefully into the room. Broken glass crunched under my feet.

Inside there was carnage.

A man with white blonde hair and a green bandana sat slumped on the floor against the bathroom cabinet, his white t-shirt blooming red under his leather jacket. Another man lay face down on a bed like he'd fallen asleep there in his boots. My heart seized up. But that body was too big to be Daw.

"Daw?" I called and kicked a cushion out of the way as I took another step into the dark room. "Daw?"

In the shadow, under the broken window, I heard a wheeze. "Blue."

Daw was sitting on the floor half-propped against the wall. He was alive.

"Daw!" I rushed to kneel beside him. "Are you hurt? Are you shot?" In the shadows, I could hardly see anything. I searched his shirt with my hand. "Are you hit? I can't see, Daw."

"I done fucked up," he said, and I noticed he was gripping his leg.

"No you didn't. You saved her. You saved Jet."

"I'm sorry," he said.

He looked dazed. I wondered if he'd hit his head.

I looked over at the dead men. The tattooed knuckles on Green Bandana. The snakeskin boots dangling from the man on the bed. His limp arm slung over the edge. A gold bracelet peeked out from his sleeve. A beige felt hat lay upturned on the floor beside him. His face a frozen mask, eyes and mouth open in surprise at his last mistake. It was Ranger Kern.

Seemed like we all underestimated the people we knew.

I spun around and searched the dim room for a phone. Daw was wheezing again, trying to speak. "Listen, Blue," he gasped. "Take the truck. Go on home."

"No. I'm calling 911."

"They're already coming. Trust me." He tried to pull himself up, but winced and slumped back down, his breath escaping him from even that simple move.

"I'm not going without you," I told him, wondering how the hell I was going to get him out of here if he couldn't walk. "I can't leave you."

"Sure you can," he said. "You done so last week."

That hit me like a slap and my eyes burned with shame.

"I'm sorry." I was sorry about leaving him and sorry he found me and sorry that the world was closing in and nothing made sense anymore. I touched his leg, and my hand came away wet. "You're bleeding."

"Yeah."

"We just need to get you to the car. I can sew you up."

He shook his head slowly. "It's too much for you to handle. Get out of here before the police come. Take your friend and go." He looked over my shoulder, and I saw that Jet was standing a few feet away, her hands still bound behind her.

"Daw—"

"They'll fix me up here, when the ambulance gets here," he insisted. His voice rose. "Now, get on home, Bluebonnet. I done told you. I'll be right behind you."

All at once it was too much. Him coming here like this. Taking on Mother and the Ranger for me and Jet. Acting, for once, like a real father. Showing me what things might have been like if everything – every single thing – had been different.

I buried my face in his shoulder and both of us choked on a sob. That was when I realized his shirt was soaked with blood, too. There was blood everywhere. He was drowning in it.

I bolted upright, staring at him.

He gave me a strange, longing smile. "Jesus, you look like your mother."

His warm blood on my cheek – and the growing pool around his thigh – made me dizzy. "Oh no. No, no." I turned to Jet, who looked down on us with the light behind her like the Virgin Mary on the candles at the Neighborhood. "Jet, what do we do?"

Daw ignored this. "Take my wallet," he said.

"No." I was crying in earnest now.

"Take my goddamn wallet, Blue!"

It was an order. Biting back sobs, I patted his pockets and fished out his wallet, both of us straining from the effort. "Good girl," he wheezed when I had it in my hand. "They ain't got nothin' on you. You'll see. Everything'll be back like it was." He fought to breathe and closed his eyes. His voice grew fainter. "Just like before. Go on now."

I squeezed his hand and tried to will my feet to move, but they wouldn't budge. "Daw?"

He breathed out a soft, empty sigh and his eyebrows unknitted. I stared at his chest and waited for it to rise again, for Daw to curse me and tell me to get on home. But he just lay there like he was passed out drunk. For the first time in my life I wished he was. I wanted to sew him up, to mend all the holes from the past. I stared at his chest and waited for it to rise.

"Blue?" Jet said softly.

Breathe, Daw. I put my hand on his chest and waited. In the distance, a siren floated in the air.

"Blue?" Jet said again, her voice a buzz in my ear. "We need to go."

I nodded, still waiting for him to breathe, to rise up, to tell me what I'd damn well better do. And knowing he would not.

TWENTY

We're running on dead feet. The snow-snipped wind burns my ears as I run behind Maggie along the railroad tracks and wonder if we'll make it to her house in time before I lose my toes to frostbite. Pennies rattle in my coat pocket. We'd gone to the tracks to lay pennies. But the train never showed, and now my socks are soaked through and cold, and there's a foot of snow.

We're running on stumps, past snow-banked metal fences that divide the rails from private land. Hours ago I was delirious at the sight of snow, the miracle of snow in Texas. Now it's a curse, and I wonder if Maggie understands that I'm minutes away from lung frost. At some point, the fence ends for no rhyme or reason, and we keep trudge-running along the wood's edge, our wet boots crunching down into the snow. Maggie slows, and I look over at her face. She's staring ahead with determined eyes, her lips tucked under a bright red scarf, tears like candle wax on her cheeks.

"Are we close?" I cough.

"Yes."

I squint at the white world. We aren't close. I can't see her house through the trees, and her mansion is at the highest point in Blessing. "Are you sure?"

"Yes."

"I'm not."

"Well, shut your eyes and look. That's your problem. You have to imagine what you want to see. Vision it." She stops, closes her eyes, and holds her palms up to the sky. "My hands are not freezing. My house is close. God's will is good." She opens her eyes and they crinkle. "See?"

I nod slowly. That is my problem. I don't see.

She walks ahead of me, and I chant under my icy breath, "My feet aren't cold. The house is close. His will is good. His will is good."

★

"How bad are you?"

I tried to keep my eyes on the road as I drove, and Daw's truck between the white lines, but I veered off every few seconds and jolted the truck back into the other lane. Jet held her hand to her right shoulder in the passenger seat. Before we left the motel, I'd cut the cables on her wrists with Daw's pliers from the glove box. Then I noticed her jacket was torn at the shoulder.

"Maybe I should drive," she said, her brow creasing as the truck swerved unsteadily.

"We got to fix your arm. Is it bad?"

"No. Just bleeding a little. I think a bullet brushed by or maybe some glass cut it. I do not think I am shot." She pulled her bloody palm away and examined her shoulder.

"We got a first aid kit behind the seat. We have to bandage it."

I veered to the side of the road, but Jet reached for the wheel.

"Not here. Someone might ask questions. Keep going. Find a parking lot."

A few blocks ahead, I parked between a Chicken Wingerz and AutoPlus and gathered some old napkins from the floorboard for Jet.

"Here, press these on your arm."

She did as I said, and leaned back on the headrest and closed her eyes. I moved the beers from behind her seat and pulled out the coffee can that lived there. I shook the rusted tin can to hear the rattle, then peeled open the plastic lid.

Jet opened her eyes and frowned at the can.

"We got a couple small band aids, tape, little sewing kit. No gauze. Let's see your arm." I moved Jet's napkinned hand and with a gentle finger tugged down on the skin that opened like a mouth. Fresh blood poured out.

"Does it hurt bad?"

"No. A little. It is sort of numb."

"Good. I need to sew it up, else it won't stop bleeding."

Her eyes flew open. "You want to sew it?"

I pulled the thread from the kit and cut it with the tiny scissors. My hands shook so hard it took several tries to get the fresh needle threaded.

"I am fine," she said, but she leaned her head back again. "But the world is spinning."

"Don't worry. I do this all the time for Daw." His name stuck in my throat. I opened a Lone Star and poured the beer over the bloodied napkin and then on the wound itself. Jet winced, and the blood bubbled.

"It's the only alcohol we got," I apologized. "It's more to wash the area."

In the distance, sirens echoed. I held up the needle. "Ready?"

"Give me the beer." She took the can and drank the rest of it down. "Okay. Ready."

She squeezed her eyes shut and crumpled the can in her fist as I squeezed the mouth-wound closed. When I pushed the needle through the two flaps she screamed.

Daw had never screamed.

"I'm sorry, I'm sorry," I said, but I kept going and pulled the thread taut. Her red blood soaked my fingers as I held the lips shut and counted two, three, four stitches. Jet screamed each time.

"I'm sorry, I'm sorry," I whispered over and over and pulled more stitches with the red thread.

"Stop apologizing until you are done torturing me," she said between gritted teeth.

Sirens whined in the distance but I kept working.

I knotted the thread after six stitches and hoped it would do. "Done."

Jet opened her eyes and looked at her shoulder. She dabbed the wet napkin around the edges and nodded. "That looks good. No more bleeding. I will drive now." Her face was pale from the pain.

"What? You can't. You just got stitched up."

"I can drive with one hand. You cannot even drive with two. We are lucky to be alive after..." She waved her good hand at the steering wheel. "Let us not test God anymore."

Jet slid her arm gingerly into her leather jacket, and then opened the door and limped around the front of the truck. I got out, too.

"You're limping," I said in front of the grille. "What happened to your left foot?"

"They tried to break it," she said. "They failed."

"Is it sprained?"

She didn't answer, but held her good hand up, and I tapped it for luck. As soon as we traded places, I noticed the empty holster on her thigh. My holster was empty, too. I hadn't thought to search for my gun when I found Daw. A panic crept into my throat.

"Where's your gun?"

She looked confused at first, searching her memory. "They took it from me."

"Damn." Neither of us was armed. And though I'd grown to despise guns, I worried that we wouldn't survive without them.

Jet's cell phone rang. We stared at each other for a second before she fumbled with her pocket and pulled the phone out between us. My heart ricocheted as she answered it.

"Hello?"

"Hello? Blue? Is that you?" Marla's voice was clear and sharp even across the cab. Jet handed the phone to me, her face a mask of hope and fear.

"Marla?" I asked. "I'm here. In El Paso."

"Thank God. I'm almost to the border. I'm so close I can see the mountains."

"You are?" I couldn't hide my relief. "I wasn't sure you were coming anymore."

"I told you I was. But I'm afraid it's not the best news. I have the paperwork, but your father's supposed to sign it. And if I know Mark, he'll never sign. But I do have an email from the governor that grants asylum. So I'm driving on a hope and prayer the border guards accept the forms I have."

There was a long pause before I found my voice.

"Look. Daw's dead." I kept my eyes steady on Jet so I wouldn't cry.

"What?"

"Daw died. Here. In El Paso. He came to get me, and we had to help Jet, and there was a shootout… and he got shot. It just happened."

"Oh my God." Her voice grew unsteady. "I'm sorry. I'm so sorry. Poor Mark." She fell silent, and I could almost see her gripping the steering wheel and staring at the mountains ahead of her. "This actually changes everything. I think… I think it'll be easier. There's nothing to keep you there now."

Easier? I flinched. Nothing about this was easy. It was awful and bloody and terrifying.

As she talked, I felt like a balloon rising away from the earth.

"I need to call Will and have him call the West Gate," she said, thinking aloud. "He'll know who to call. He's looking forward to meeting you. He's a really nice man."

I didn't want to hear about Will right now. "What about Jet?"

"What about what?"

"Jet," I said firmly. "My friend, she's with me. I need to get her out. She got hurt in the shooting, too."

"Oh, honey." The phone went silent for too long. "I can't take her. I can only take you."

Jet unlocked her eyes from mine and turned to look out the front window.

"But she's with me," I said, "and she needs to cross worse than I do."

"I understand and I'm sorry, Blue. But you're family, you're my blood. I can claim you at the gate. I can't claim her."

My lower lip trembled. "You said you'd try."

Marla sighed. "Blue, I don't have any paperwork for her – I'd need signatures and legal documents. There's no time."

"But her parents are dead. She doesn't have anybody!" Something violent and desperate erupted in me. "I can't leave her."

"There must be someone in the Republic who can help her."

"No, there isn't. She's not Texan. She's...she's..." I fought for breath, but couldn't find the right words. It didn't matter that she was illegal. "She's my best friend."

Jet's gaze was lost somewhere far from me.

"Blue, honey. There's nothing I can do right now. We can try to help her later, once you're safe."

I turned my body toward the door, ashamed to even look at Jet.

"Look," Marla finally said. "I'll talk to Will, and maybe there's some special status we could apply for. She's an immigrant?"

"Yes."

"Well, that's a real complication. It could take months or years to work it legally. But we'll try, okay? First, we have to get you out. Get over to the West Gate in Sunland Park, and I'll meet you there." Her voice lifted. "Oh sweetie, you've got a whole family waiting to meet you. I've got to hang up and call Will right now. Okay?"

I nodded, unable to find my voice.

"Okay?" she asked again.

"Okay," I whispered.

I hung up. I could hear Jet breathing beside me. I couldn't look, couldn't move. My chest burned.

Jet clicked her seatbelt into place. I turned to her and she looked me hard in my eyes. "It is okay. Thank you, Blue."

"For what? I didn't do anything." My eyes welled. "I failed."

"You did do something. You listened. You believed me. You rescued me like a hero. After I rescued you, of course. You did everything right." She nodded, then looked out at the road and started the engine. "Seatbelt."

I buckled up with numb hands, and she pulled the truck back onto the highway.

"But what will you do?"

"Blue, I do not need a savior. I will save myself. We all have to save ourselves." She kept her eyes on the road. "Open the map app. I will take you to the West Gate."

We drove in silence up the highway, following the blue line up Highway 10 toward Sunland Park. Jet holed up in the corners of her mind, and I replayed Marla's words. *You've got a whole family waiting to meet you.*

Somehow, I had a mother again. I had a new dad who did important things and knew important people.

I pulled Daw's old wallet from my pocket and studied it. The leather was worn down to a muddy shine. I tightened my grip on it. I still had blood on my hands, either Daw's or Jet's, I couldn't tell. I rubbed my fingers against the rough seat fabric.

Jet steadied one hand on the steering wheel and cradled the other around her waist. Her right eye and cheek were red and swollen, but her gaze was fearless and straight ahead. I set the wallet on the tray between us.

"You can keep Daw's wallet. And the truck."

"Thanks." Her voice was calm, in spite of everything.

"Are you going to try to cross somewhere?"

"I have to."

"What about your ankle?"

"I will manage. I have no choice." She glanced at me. "If I stay I will always be hiding."

"From Uncle Chago?"

"Uncle Chago is dead," she said. "He was in the room, with the bleached hair. He was the one who stomped on my ankle."

I saw the man again in my mind – green bandana, dead, staring eyes.

"Did Daw kill him?"

"Yes."

The pieces fell into place. "That Ranger who died in the motel. I thought he was looking for me. But he was looking for you, wasn't he?"

"He was looking for a lot of people. He was a bad one. There are lots of bad ones."

"But some of them are good," I said, more like a wish than a contradiction. "Isn't that what you said, that there's good and bad?"

"Yes, I said that. Today, your Daw – he was a good one."

You didn't know him, I thought.

She tried to reach across the open space between us, but winced in pain. I reached over and took her hand. She squeezed it, then let me go.

In my head, Sunland Park was full of palm trees and breezy sunshine and happy people skateboarding down the sidewalks. But when we got there, all we saw was scrub brush and longhorns and sand the color of dry, dimpled skin. The road itself struggled to keep from being swallowed up by the desert. Half the buildings were boarded up and spray-painted. Hardly any cars on the road, empty sidewalks that disappeared under blankets of sand. It was nothing like I'd imagined. But we were still on the Republic side of the street. Maybe on the other side of the border, on the American side, things would be different.

Jet stopped at an intersection where a lone traffic light swung from a line. A few blocks ahead of us, the West Gate rose up like two church towers. A giant Lone Star Republic flag stretched across the high brick gateway, and two more flags hung limp from flagpoles flanking the checkpoint. A brick wall stretched from either side of the West Gate across the horizon as far as I could see. Attached to the small checkpoint building was a flashing red light. Warning and Danger signs were mounted on the sides of the road.

If we didn't get the message, a billboard to the right of the road made it clear: *Danger: Those attempting to cross the border illegally will be shot.*

But the Wall. I sized it up. The Wall was barely a hedge.

"All this time I was thinking the Wall was like the walls I'd seen on TV, with those spiral barbed wires, or like the iron ones that stand up like giant toothpicks all in a row. But that Wall's hardly even a wall at all."

"Blue, look over there," Jet said, pointing. "See down there, way down on the right? See those people dressed in beige camo?"

I followed her finger to the barely-there people, blending in with the barely-there Wall that blended in with the desert sand. They moved like mirages. Three of them leaned against the Wall. Slung across their shoulders or cradled in their arms were guns.

"Automatics. Probably M14s." Jet leaned in close. "Blue, those people are not regular Border Patrol or Rangers or off-duty cops. Those are volunteer militia. This is sport for them. The danger has never been the Wall. The danger is the people."

I scanned the Wall more closely. This time, I saw the movements. People in sandy camouflage clustered together on the ground like they were having a picnic. And farther down in both directions, almost out of sight, a few trucks.

"Are they guarding the Wall like that all the way around Texas?"

"They are always moving. They patrol, and you never know where they will be. It is even more dangerous at night."

The image of Jet's body flat on the desert sand flashed across my eyes. Jet pulling herself toward the Wall, a man in beige camo training the crosshairs on her, his finger on the trigger.

The light turned green and we moved another block toward the West Gate, where we hit a traffic jam. Ahead of us, a line of cars waited their turn for the checkpoint, their brake lights a steady, patient red. The world was quiet and fearful here. No music, no pulsing bass from other trucks, no horns. No birds or planes. Just the hum of the engine.

"I should let you out here, I guess," Jet said. "Before we get too close."

I nodded and reached for my backpack, though I didn't know why I would bring it. I didn't need anything in it.

"Can you see her?" Jet asked.

Behind the iron columns of the West Gate people huddled on the other side, peering into the Republic like visitors at a zoo. I couldn't see anyone clearly from this far back.

And then I saw a white dress, like a flag of surrender, not far from a soldier at the checkpoint. The woman's face was a blur in the distance, but with that blonde hair, her head leaning right and left like she was searching for someone... It had to be her.

She was standing, like she had my whole life, just out of focus. And in a few moments, she'd unlock a dream I couldn't even muster. I'd finally have a home without holes and a family who'd take care of me.

Jet searched the West Gate, too, as though she might recognize an older me on the other side. She frowned over the cars in front of us. "She will be there, right? She will take care of you?"

She gripped the steering wheel hard. Then her chin dipped to her chest, and she said, "Be careful at the checkpoint. Walk slowly and do not make sudden movements. Take off your baseball cap. Keep your hands away from your waist. Do not give them a reason to pull their guns on you."

I reached over and set my hand on her forearm, but she wouldn't look at me.

Behind the iron gate, Marla took a few steps left, then right, vying for a better place to catch a glimpse of me wherever I was. She'd forgotten to ask what I looked like. She was probably searching for a little girl with mousy hair, or maybe a miniature version of herself. The Bluebonnet she knew was thigh-high and wore dresses and spun around in circles to make parachutes as she billowed her way across the floor. Something in my heart told me that Marla would love me, no matter that Bluebonnet was now fourteen, practically bald, caked in dirt and blood, and wouldn't be caught dead in a frilly dress. She'd love me because we'd both been stolen from each other. She'd love me because she loved the idea of me as much as I loved the idea of her.

I took a deep breath and followed Marla's dress with my eyes as it swayed in the breeze behind the black bars. For me, Marla had been wrapped up in a white dream for years. She was perfect, frozen in that single photograph, like time suspended, a beautiful idea, a loving mother stolen away. I swallowed and a thought hitched there. What is a mother and what is perfection if I have never known either?

My hand was still on Jet's forearm. She hadn't pulled away. An ocean swelled in my ears. What is a mother, and what is a sister? What was this tearing of my heart?

I looked back at the Marla who searched for a little girl to rescue. And then at Jet, who was looking at me now, her eyes full of pain. What was tearing me inside was confusion and love. Not for Marla. I didn't know her. She was a stranger.

But I knew Jet. Jet had saved my life. She would never abandon me. I'd rather run the dangerous mile with Jet than walk across a safe bridge alone to Marla.

"Turn around."

Jet's fine, dark eyebrows drew together. "What?"

"Turn around," I told her. "Make a U-turn."

She didn't move. "Why?"

I didn't want to explain. All of a sudden I just wanted to get out of there. "Just do it. Hurry."

After a brief hesitation, she backed up the truck a few feet, turned the vehicle around and began driving away. I looked behind us, craning my neck to see the white dress.

But it had already disappeared.

"What is wrong?" Jet asked, as we retraced our path past the line of cars.

"I'm not going."

She shot me a sideways look. "What about your mom, your family? You cannot leave them."

"Exactly," I said. "You're my family."

"I don't understand." The truck slowed as she stared at me.

"You're my family," I told her, firmly. "I'm not leaving you. We're sisters. Anyway, I made a promise, remember?"

Jet's hand tightened on the steering wheel. Her eyes brimmed as she looked over the dashboard, shaking her head. "You are stupid."

"Maybe." I stared out the window. The low, dirty buildings beside the road blurred.

I was like two ends of a ribbon, a bow untied. Frayed at the ends. I could never tie it back for Marla, never pretend to be a perfect daughter. This time, I'd abandoned her and all her dreams, and that was terrible. But I'd tied the other end of the ribbon to Jet, and I would sacrifice everything to not let go of her.

I wiped my eyes and sniffed back the tears.

"Hey," Jet said, and she smiled at me. "*Hermana.* Thank you."

★

We drove up the road that ran along the border. The Wall winked in and out of sight, disappearing behind storage buildings or when the curving road weaved away and then near again. Every time we thought the guards were far enough away that we could stop and cross, another truck rumbled into view, then parked against the Wall with a fresh set of guards who sat on the truck's roof or paced on the Wall itself.

When the phone rang again, I turned it off and zipped it into my backpack. No more distractions or temptations. We passed through a bleak area where the road was lined with orange barrels and construction barriers. After that, the city was far behind, the blue sky was all around us and a red mountain slept in the distance. We drove past a single oil derrick tilting its arm like a metronome, and a metallic smell filled the air. We passed cows that grazed on the pastures between the guard posts and the road, but no people. At some point, Jet slowed near a couple of small buildings, and then parked in between them.

"Here," she said, definitively.

I looked around trying to see what she saw. A field stretched out toward the distant Wall. America, mysterious and vast and free, was right beyond it. So close. The strip of land was isolated and empty, aside from a few head of cattle lazing under the shade of a lone, pitiful tree. A cow bellowed, and the sound and smell of manure traveled to us at the same time.

"Here?" I looked down the Wall as far as I could see and spotted a truck in the distance, driving away, kicking up a cloud of dust.

"They have moved on from here a few minutes ago, I think," Jet said. "We should go now, while we have time."

It was a lot of open land to cross. "The Border Patrol don't shoot people once they've crossed over, right? We just have to get over before they see us?"

"Yes," she said. "But the volunteers, who knows? They do not care so much about rules. They collect dissolutions like badges."

I glanced at her. "Let's not be some man's badge today."

She nodded. "Or ever."

"See there?" I pointed to a line of scrub brush that zigzagged in sparse clumps toward the Wall. The tallest was no higher than my waist. "Those bushes will give us cover, and we can hide if the guards pass by."

"Okay." She scanned the area once more, her brow creased with thought. "That might work."

I left the backpack in the truck. The only thing I took was Daw's wallet, which I shoved into the pocket of my jeans. I hurried into the field and then realized Jet wasn't behind me. She was still standing beside the open door of the truck.

When I ran back I found her hopping on her right foot.

"Shit, shit," she swore, grabbing the door with her good hand to catch her balance.

"What's wrong?"

"I cannot do it." She leaned back against the truck. "My ankle is bad. It may be broken. Fucking Uncle Chago. There is nothing he won't ruin."

"I'll help you. Lean on me. Here." I lifted her good arm and draped it over my shoulder so I could act like a crutch.

"I cannot," she moaned, her face reddening from the pain.

"Yes you can. You just have to imagine it. Like a vision. Imagine what will happen once we cross over. Close your eyes."

She glared. "Are you joking?"

"No." I clamped my eyes shut and saw us limping our way through the low shrubs, Jet stepping onto my cupped hands and springing on top of the wall. "You can walk. The guards won't see us. The guns can't reach us. We're there already, and we're safe. We're safe." I opened my eyes. "Just imagine it."

"I imagine you have a hole in your head," Jet said, but some of the panic was leaving her face.

"That's your problem. You don't really see it."

"This is what I see." She closed her eyes and held her hands to her sides, palms up. "I am falling down. We are getting shot. We are begging them mercy. Now we are dead."

"You're not being positive," I chided.

"I am positive we are dead." Jet opened her eyes. Her empty gaze fixed on the horizon. "You should go back to the West Gate."

"We're not going back. We're doing this. Sisters, right?"

Jet clenched her jaw. "Right."

A cow wandered along the fence edge and stopped to gnaw on a tuft of weeds.

I tightened my grip on Jet's hand and pulled her weight onto me. "Let's just get to the fence where that cow is. Baby steps."

She blew out a long breath. "Okay. Baby steps."

We limped between the two buildings, heading for the pasture. Jet leaned heavily on me, and breathed out small, tight groans each time her left foot brushed the ground. By the time we reached the barbed wire fence, we were both out of breath, and she leaned on a wooden post to rest. She peeled off her leather jacket and dropped it at the base of the fence post.

"Black leather is not exactly camouflage in the desert." Her tank top was sweat-stained and gray. "Do you see anyone in those buildings?"

Leaving her there, I moseyed closer to the metal farm buildings and searched for movement. They seemed to be some kind of sheds or storage buildings. The windows were shuttered, so I hurried back to Jet. The sun was already sinking like on the horizon. In a few hours, it would slip below the Wall and leave us in darkness. A cool breeze pulled at my muscles, chilling my skin and making me jumpy.

When I came back to Jet, she was stroking the cow on its forehead. It was scrawny, with huge brown eyes, and Jet kept stroking it like she was under a spell. I'd never seen anyone pet a cow before. But then I remembered Bonita, her pet calf.

"Come on," I urged. "There's a little gate over there that should let us into the fields. I don't think you should crawl between the barbed wire."

I became her crutch again, and we hobbled our way to the gate. To my surprise, the cow lumbered along beside us.

"He's following us."

"She," Jet said. "I think she is in calf. Her udders are swollen."

As we traveled along the barbed wire fence toward the building, I scanned the road for cars, but it was quiet in both directions, except for a distant cow bellowing. By the time we reached the small wooden gate into the main pasture, my face was damp with sweat. Jet was heavy, and I was all but carrying her. But we were moving.

I opened the gate, and our cow stood on the other side blinking at us with its long brown lashes. Waiting. I paused.

"Shoo. Shoo!" I scolded, waving one hand.

"She won't hurt you," Jet chided me, gently. "Leave her alone."

She reached out and the cow stomped, then took a step forward and lowered its pink muzzle until its forehead landed under Jet's hand. Jet brushed her fingers up its forehead and cooed. *"Ah, Bonita. Sí, Bonita."*

My heart pounded against my shirt. I scanned the horizon for cars, for guards, for any sign of human life. Please don't let anybody be looking at us, I chanted in my head. Nobody's coming. Nobody's coming. I was suddenly exhausted, looking out across the pasture. It was so far and the Wall was so small, and I already needed to sit down.

"Let's go," I said. "We have to move fast."

She leaned on me, and we hobbled forward into the uneven field, pockmarked with hoofprints that had dried into sunbaked hollows. I stumbled a few times, and Jet moaned softly when her bad foot hit the ground.

After that, I kept my eyes peeled so I wouldn't stumble again. Our progress was slow but steady. Every few minutes, I looked up and saw that the cow was still walking alongside us. Jet's hand rested on her withers, so the cow lumbered alongside us like a brace and a shield. She seemed determined not to leave us. As if Jet were an old friend.

It seemed to take us an hour to get halfway across the field, and we traveled at a crawl, but the cow did not abandon us. Every once in a while, I looked back, out past the storage buildings and beyond to the red mountains that rose like ancient gods. *Nobody's looking,* I told myself. *No one can see us.*

Finally, though, the small, angry voice of an engine hummed in the air. Holding on to Jet, I looked around, but I couldn't see anything.

The humming turned and shaped into the twang of music. I shot a glance at Jet.

"Guards," she whispered, and we both hunched down behind the cow. But we were right out in the open now. The sun was a golden spotlight on us. When the truck passed us, we'd be in full view.

Jet hopped toward the cow's front legs and stroked the bridge of her nose from her forehead to her muzzle. "Shhh," she whispered near Bonita's ear. The cow stood still like we were her own two calves. Slowly, slowly, like a clock's second hand, the cow traveled in an arc under Jet's hand, both of us turning with her, behind her protection as the truck zoomed along the Wall and past us.

Jet kept stroking Bonita's forehead and scratching her jowls as we huddled low and waited for the engine to die away.

When only the dull roar of the wind filled our ears again, we peeked over Bonita. The Wall was clear. No trucks. No guards.

We headed west again. Bonita plodded beside us like a patient nurse.

We didn't talk now. My back ached from Jet's weight on my shoulder, and my shirt was soaked through with sweat. Twice I heard something skitter across the scrub around us, and it gave me a start, even though the cow didn't flinch. I thought about scorpions and snakes and other dangers once the sun set. They'd be waiting for us too, on the other side of the Wall. But I couldn't stop to think about that. I pushed the thought out of my head the way I pushed the thought of Daw and Marla away.

I don't know how long we'd walked when, "Look," Jet said, pointing.

With effort, I lifted my head. The sandy brick Wall was not even twenty feet away.

We both broke into grins of relief. Jet gripped me tightly.

Another low hum came across the wind, this time from my side. I knew before I looked that they were coming. The militia that had passed earlier must have turned around and now there was nothing to hide us. We were right in their path.

"Run!" I said.

We ran as best we could. Limping fast across the sand. Even Bonita picked up speed and jolted along beside us. My eardrums pulsed a watery drumbeat, and we seemed to move in slow motion, but then the Wall was right in front of us. It must have been no more than 8 feet high, and made of rough stone.

We could get over it. We just needed a little help.

"The cow!" I said. We were of one mind, Jet and me and that cow. Bonita followed Jet's hand and stood beside the bricks.

"Hop up!" I cupped my hands for Jet.

"No, you first," she insisted.

"Hurry! She likes you," I said, hoping the cow wouldn't bolt as soon as Jet's boot touched her back. The engine grew louder and higher. They had to be close enough to shoot. I didn't dare look behind me.

Jet put her weight on the cow, then stepped in my hand-stirrup with her good foot, and I launched her up onto the cow's back. The first shot rang out as Jet's gray tank top shimmered under the blazing pink sky. She screamed and scrambled from the cow's back to the top of the wall. Time paused, and I stared at her thin shoulders corded with muscles, willing her to fall over to the other side. But she didn't roll over or disappear. She lay there on top of the wall, looking down at me. She reached down to me with one arm, her fingers spread wide.

Another gunshot echoed.

"No!" Jet called, her face crumpling as Bonita stumbled against the wall, her legs folding beneath her.

Jet called out, "Blue!" and stretched her hand down to me.

Another sputter of shots rang out. The stone chipped and sent sprays of sand into my face. I scrabbled up onto Bonita's back. She'd fallen to her stomach and her sides heaved in great gusts.

When I looked up at Jet, the setting sunlight skimmed over her like fire, like gold.

I reached for her hand. She jerked me to her, and I glimpsed the whole pink horizon and rippled sun on the other side as I flew like a bird, like gravity forgave me for three seconds so I could clear the Wall. I half-cartwheeled, half-backflipped over the Wall, squeezing Jet's wrist as I came down on the other side.

We both fell into America together.

My heartbeat hammered my ears with the dull sputtering of gunfire. And there we were, in a heap on the ground like we were meeting all over again. I flung my arms around Jet and we huddled there gasping and waited for our hearts to come back to us.

Men cursed on the other side of the wall. A horn blared angrily, and the gunshots kept popping. I fought to breathe. Jet pushed me back and looked me over.

"Are you okay?" she asked.

I nodded, afraid to break the spell of safety. "Did you get hit?"

She shook her head. "Just a little bruised."

"The cow..." I couldn't say more. To my own surprise, I burst into tears.

Jet clutched me in her arms and rocked me. "I know." She wept, too.

"She saved us."

Jet wiped her cheeks and nodded. "We saved us."

We looked out into the sunset. In the distance, a shimmery line of buildings and cars glinted like a dream. I stood and took Jet's hand. She pulled up and steadied herself against me.

"Ready?" she asked.

"For what?"

"Another life."

I smiled.

We walked and looked over our shoulders every few minutes, tracking our distance, until we were so far from the Wall it was like an endless salute, petrified in the sunset. Ahead of us was a highway with speeding cars, the winking lights of restaurants and houses and churches and – somewhere – a place that would save Jet just as surely as she had saved me. It had to happen. I could see it.

Each step was like waking from a dream, each breath like sipping from a cup of hope.

EPILOGUE

I turned away at the West Gate, but I wasn't turning away from you.

I was turning toward me.

You'd already carved your new life into existence, and I knew the space you made for me wasn't big enough for Jet. Besides, Jet and I had gotten used to moving. We didn't stop at the border. We leaned in to the unknown and kindness caught us. A woman named Maryam caught us. And Diana. And Katherine and Meg. And dozens of other women who fed us and clothed us and taught us and housed us one day at a time until we arrived in California. Who could have imagined the intricate network for refugees that America had spread out like a latticework, so beautiful and sturdy?

They took us to a Women's Center, where I held Jet's hand. Where I learned how to abandon dreams that are naïve and hopeful, and create new ones that are etched in experience and compassion. Where she had the abortion, and where she taught me that there was no shame in saving yourself.

I thought of you often. When I saw the Pacific Ocean for the first time, bottomless blue and impossibly cold. I imagined you dipping your toes into the surf and running back laughing to the warm sand, the rocks, the grass. But I still wasn't ready to be rooted to you, or to disturb the roots you'd already nurtured.

BLUE RUNNING

We lived at a settlement house for girls, which was full of life and new dreams. I finished high school. Jet went to community college. Like twins, we graduated at the same time.

Now, I'm going to a university to study art.

I've thought of you so many times, but your face wasn't the one in the photograph that Daw kept in his sock drawer. The one of you laughing, unaware that chaos was crouching a few years or a few days away. Your image became the woman at the West Gate, shading her eyes, searching for the daughter who no longer needed to be found.

Blessing is like fable to me now, a town with a warning that you don't hear until you're far enough away to catch the echo. It was like that for you, wasn't it? That's why you stayed on the plane. I don't blame you. We do what we must to survive. We leave homes and friends and languages and histories. We leave babies.

But we also stay. We crawl through barbs and sand and manure. We wander together, half-clothed, fumbling for words, wiping the crust from our eyes. We stay to help our sisters stand up, to find our balance and to claim our lives.

I think you understand. When I see you, I hope you recognize the thread that made us both strong. And even if you glance past me, eagerly still looking for that little girl when I step off the plane, in your marrow you'll know me.

ACKNOWLEDGEMENTS

Texas made this book possible – friendly, proud, foolhardy, welcoming, beautiful, maddening Texas. A lot of people made this book possible, too. The talented and wickedly creative Amy Plum read the early chapters and saw me through to the end of the first draft, and then another draft. I can't express how grateful I am for her feedback, her shared Southern experience, and her faith in my stories. Katherine Boswell and Meghan Wadle, my writing group gals: our deadlines kept me writing through the most stressful periods of my life. Thanks for poring over the manuscript and giving me invaluable advice. Ditto to Andrea Witzke-Slot, whose long-distance feedback was so important. This book would not have been published, literally, but for the dynamic and brilliant duo Christi Daugherty and Jack Jewers: massive thanks for championing Blue and shepherding her into the world. I offer my gratitude to the experts behind the scenes: Helen Grant, Jasmine Aurora, Tory Lyne-Pirkis, Ashley Kaplan, and Martin Palmer. Readers often underestimate how important they themselves are to the writing process. They are every novel's *raison d'être*. I have the most supportive friends a writer could imagine, who somehow read whatever I publish and thus fuel my creative spirit when I'm afflicted by doubt—Brent Sawyer (can I give you a #1 Fan ribbon?), Jim Lindsay and David Kuhns, Samantha Mabry, Amy Jahnel, Karla Dickinson, and my dearest own mother, Bobbie Stephens. Immense thanks, all the rest of you lovely friends and readers who remind me why writing matters. And finally, *merci beaucoup* to my dearest ones for putting up with me and my imagination: Hervé, Julien, Trevor, and Carmina.